**WE THREE**

By Lucy R. Fisher

Author of Witch Way Now? And Witch Way To....?

CHAPTER ONE

"One more thing – could you send me my Tarot cards? They're in the cupboard with my old exercise books and stuff from school."

"OK, roger that. But I thought you were studying the past, not the future."

"I used to tell fortunes on the train to school – it stopped them being beastly to me."

"Are the students beastly?"

"No, but -" I didn't want to say too much, there were people in the office. "It would be something to do in the evening apart from playing darts in the pub."

"Playing darts, you?"

"I can't even hit the board. But the others do. Or billiards. The cards are wrapped in a bit of black velvet. You won't look at all the other stuff, will you?"

"No, of course not. How's everything otherwise?"

"Oh, fine, apart from the howling at night!"

"Well, you are rather near the moor! Perhaps it's the wolves who escaped from the zoo that time. I told you we never rounded them all up."

"I'd better go – they're ringing the bell for dinner."

The other girls write up the day in books bound in Laura Ashley remnants, but they just put stuff about finds and ground plans. I've got an exercise book labelled "DIG NOTES 1973", but I think I'll write my diary in it.

After we said goodbye, I went into the kitchen to join the others. It's a big room that used to be a dairy or laundry, with a bumpy brick floor. There's a big table down the middle with a check plastic tablecloth and a lot of mismatched chairs. "Go placidly amid the noise and haste" is stuck up on the wall, and a wooden spice rack with some dried-up herbs tasting of nothing. When it's your turn to cook you boil huge quantities of pasta or rice and make some sauce with red beans and tinned tomatoes and onions. Donna was stirring the sauce, and Nadine was grating cheese. Colin was setting out melamine boards with brown bread and butter, and plastic jugs of water. I sat down at the end of the table next to Gail. I hoped Mike wouldn't read my old diaries – he might get a shock!

Anyway, I'd better explain who we all are and what we're doing here. My name's Anna Savage and I'm 22. I've done a year of archaeology at Regent College, and this is my first dig. Mike and I got married when I was 18 – I met him when I was working in a boutique and he was looking for a missing person, who I found in the end. I'd got expelled from school and never did A levels, and kept dithering about whether I should do some after all. Eventually I did, and started a degree, and here I am on a dig in Cornwall, too far to go home to London for the weekend.

Mike is the regulation height for policemen, or maybe taller, but slight. He has light brown hair in a widow's peak, and blue eyes and a serious expression. I am small – four foot eleven – and have long straight black hair and what people call "elfin" features. That was how I got away being a child model for so long.

I suppose this story begins when we gave a dinner party in the spring term. We don't do that often, or go to them either. While I was doing A levels at the same college, my friends were Ginevra, from a hostel I'd lived in for a bit, and Christine who I'd met when I was modelling children's clothes, and some friends of theirs. But they've all finished their degrees now, and Christine dropped out to be an actress. Those days were fun, but they've all got jobs now, and I haven't really chummed up with anybody on my new course. Everyone's a bit serious, and goes home at night.

So I made coq au vin in a casserole and lit lots of candles. Our flat is above a launderette in Kentish Town and you can see trees in people's gardens from the back. The whole place sways in a high wind and the rain drums on the roof, but it's cosy.

We were going to buy a house with some money my parents put in the bank for me to have when I was 21. It was up near Waterlow Park, but it turned out to have subsidence and damp and a huge crack down the front. No wonder it smelt mouldy and was so cheap. The estate agents said we could have the furniture if we wanted, though, so we took a kitchen cabinet and a couple of paintings of the Bay of Naples and gave up on the idea of buying anywhere for the moment. We've put some of the money to my degree instead, since I'm only working part-time.

# 4

Quite a lot of my old friends came: Ginevra and Dave, and Christine and Benny, and Lawrence and Alan. I met Alan when I worked at the boutique which Lawrence ran, and we hung out with a lot of stoned hippies. Then later I met him working as a security guard when I was an audio typist at a firm that turned out to be rather weird. People kept leaving suddenly, and we could never work out what the company actually did.

We ate the casserole and had some "What are you doing now?" conversations. Then we had a Viennetta for pudding and cleared the tables away and I made some coffee in a jug and people lit cigarettes. We talked about what we did for fun. Mike and I go ballroom dancing at a club in Soho. Ginevra and Dave go to French films at a cinema in New Oxford Street. They like Buster Keaton as well and we went with them once. Benny told us where the best restaurants were in China Town – his family runs one – and we said we'd meet him and Christine there one day. Mike said he hoped Lawrence was keeping out of trouble.

"Certainly, officer!" said Lawrence. "I've had enough of being a guest of Her Majesty."

It was through Mike and me that Lawrence ended up in prison: the boutique was a front for the drug trade, and I told Mike about it because the guys at the top had kidnapped a girl called Ursula. She was the missing person. Actually I tried to get her to leave, but she wouldn't. And I was afraid that they wanted to sacrifice her to the devil or something, because some of them were into Black Magic. It didn't matter me telling the police that because they didn't believe me. In the end Ursula and I got away from the hippies and wizards but it meant the police rounded up a lot of people who'd been my friends, sort of.

"We're doing a petite clothing line," said Lawrence. "Why don't you come and model for us again, love? And you, Christine?"

"I've got a part in a play at the King's Head," said Christine. "But if I've got time I'd love to!"

"Tell us when it's on and we'll come and see it!" said Lawrence. "What's it about?"

"I don't understand the half of it, so I just look up at the ceiling and declaim! It's about feminism or something. What's happened to the rest of our gang?"

"Rowena and Harvey are engaged!" said Ginevra.

"And your little boy must be quite big now?"

"He's going to school!"

# 5

"I don't expect you earn much acting in pubs," Mike said to Christine.

"I waitress a lot of the time. It's still acting of a kind! I miss hanging out in the canteen with you lot. How are you getting on at SOAS, Alan?"

"I'm really into Buddhism now."

"Don't you have to shave your head?" asked Dave.

"Cutting your hair is anti-life!" said Alan. His hair is almost as long as mine, which reaches past my waist, though it doesn't have so far to go.

"It's odd to think of you with a different bunch," Ginevra said to me. "What are they like?"

"Not as friendly as you lot," I said. "It's a small group, and they're quite sweet, but a bit drab. They're not interested in clothes. I daren't mention I was once a model."

"Yes, the archaeology students always looked like that!" she said. "Dressed for a dig in the middle of London."

"I'm going on a real dig. I just got an offer of a summer in Cornwall."

"The whole summer! Where will you live?"

"Oh, they find us somewhere."

"Are you going with your mates?" asked Alan.

"We're quite a small department and we've all been sent to join other digs. The others will be from different universities. But it's with Roland Blair."

"Didn't he write a paperback on the Druids?" asked Alan.

"Did he? I'd better read it!"

Mike got out some small green glasses we'd bought in the corner shop and opened the Kahlua and Tia Maria Ginevra and Christine had brought. They went well with the Clarnico mint creams which were Lawrence's contribution.

"So where exactly in Cornwall will you be?" asked Dave.

"Bodmin Moor."

"Look out for the Beast! Or is it a Hound?"

# 6

When they all left Lawrence kissed me goodbye and said there'd definitely be some modelling gigs for us. "Any news of our old friends?" he asked quietly.

"Gilles and Dorinda and the girls from the boutique? They're all at liberty now – or still."

"So they never rounded up the Big Cheese again?"

I shook my head. They'd been involved in the trouble that put Lawrence behind bars, and at the nefarious firm where Alan and I worked.

"Well, here's hoping we never bump into them!"

Everybody went home, and I started washing up, but Mike said to leave it till the morning.

"The whole summer, though?" he said. "I'll miss you. Can't you excavate Canvey Island?"

"I'll miss you, too. I expect we'll get some time off."

"Commit a crime – then I could be sent down to investigate. And how will you manage the digging?"

"There's no regulation height for archaeologists. But I'd better get Roland Blair's book."

I couldn't imagine being without Mike and on my own again, like I was when I was kicked out of school and lived in a hostel and then a bedsit. It wasn't so bad when my parents were still around, but then they went missing – Mike pretends to think they're on the run from the law. They are on the run in a way. They had secrets.

CHAPTER TWO

The house idea came about because we didn't think we could have a baby in a flat. Ginevra and Dave live in a flat and have Richard, but they've got a garden. I ended up telling Fern all about it when we went to a barbecue at her and Stan's last summer. Stan's a colleague of Mike's, and Fern is about 40 and tanned from holidays in Marbella. She was wearing white bell-bottoms and Stan was dishing out sausages. She showed me round their garden, and we sat in a little bower she'd made. She drank Asti Spumante and said "This is the life!", and I had a diet Coke. They've got a couple of children who were running around with their friends playing with the garden hose.

"So when are you going to have some?" asked Fern. "You don't mind me being blunt, do you?"

I said, "Not at all."

"Though you still don't look grown up."

I knew she meant to be kind.

"It's because I'm so short," I said. "But I look a bit more grown-up than I used, don't I?"

"Perhaps it's your hair – that makes you look younger, I mean."

"I used to put it up when I was a temp. And I tie it back when I'm at Junk and Disorderly – the antique shop where I work sometimes."

"Yes, you don't want to knock stuff over! Is that fun?"

"It is – really. Anyway, I'm going to do a degree starting this autumn, so now wouldn't be a good time to have a baby. I went back to the doctors. They said they'd thought I'd develop more but I hadn't. They even said I might have had miscarriages."

"Ooh, how horrid!"

"So anyway, we got in touch with the adoption people. And they say they always need foster parents."

"I hope it goes well." She patted my hand. "What's your degree on?"

"Archaeology."

"Digging up the past?"

"That's right."

"I hope you enjoy it!"

I got stuck looking 14 for ages because my parents fed me a potion that prolongs life. I think they'd been planning to wait until I was older, but they were worried that people might notice that they never aged. Mum left her recipe book behind for me, and I looked through it for a way of reversing the spell. I think I found the formula, and I performed the ritual at midnight in front of an Egyptian goddess in the British Museum (I made sure I got locked in). So I hope I am not going to live for hundreds of years but will get old just like everybody else. Mike says I look more intelligent these days, so I hope for the best. If it hasn't worked, there are some wizards I can consult – if I can find them.

"I hope you didn't mind me asking you all these questions," said Fern. I said I didn't.

"I expect it's a relief to talk about it," she said, and actually she was right. Also I know she'll tell the others so I only have to explain it once. She got up to stop her kids soaking the guests, and I went over to where Shirley – she's married to Fred – was sitting at a picnic table telling fortunes with a pack of cards as usual.

"Shall I do yours again?" she asked.

Mike said: "Anna does it with Tarot cards."

"I could never puzzle those out," she said. "Do you want to have a go with these?"

"I can't remember how!" I said. "And anyway, you can't tell your own fortune."

"Right, you could do mine for a change!"

"I'd have to look up how to use ordinary cards," I said. "You do mine." I've still got that fortune-telling book I sent off for from Prediction magazine when I was at school. I didn't want to try telling Fern's fortune – I might have seen something she didn't want me to know. I do sometimes. It must be hereditary.

Shirley laid out the cards and told me I'd have good luck, and I'd travel and meet a dark man. Meeting Mike was a bit of luck, and his friends and colleagues have always been kind to me, especially when rescuing me from peril, like when I was drifting down the Thames alone at night on a houseboat. Well, alone apart from a ghost.

\*\*\*\*

In early spring, after the dinner party, Christine and I modelled for Lawrence again. We scampered up and down the catwalk in A-line skirts and long skinny jerseys for an audience of buyers.

Lawrence had hired a mistress of ceremonies who said things like: "Heather and russet are shades for autumn. Note the self belt and the 30s-inspired buckle!"

He said we could keep some of the clothes and I picked out a mauve ensemble and a tweed butcher boy cap. Then we mingled with the buyers, and Benny came to fetch Christine. Mike was working that evening, so Benny took us to a place in Chinatown and explained the menu to us and showed us how to use chopsticks.

I'd been studying archaeology for a term and a bit. The college was keen for me to do it. I'd done classical civ, art history and botany A Levels, and I think they needed more students. But I just can't get interested in metallurgy and stratigraphy. Perhaps it'll get more exciting when we actually dig stuff up.

I bought Roland Blair's paperback on the Druids, and another one by him on the Lost Gods of England. He's the famous archaeologist who's leading the dig in Cornwall I'm going on. They were more fun than the books on the course reading list.

I lit some candles for Imbolc, which is part of the witches' Wheel of the Year, and made a protective flower arrangement with dried lavender and rosemary and rowan twigs. I put in some hawthorn berries for colour - it's sacred to the Druids, according to Professor Blair. It also protects against lightning, and evil ghosts. All the ghosts I've met have been charming, but I suppose there might be some nasty ones. Coltsfoot brings peace, according to Mum's recipe book, but there isn't any around at this time of year. I just want mediums and covens and demons to leave me alone.

In the summer term, we got our instructions about what to take on the dig, and where to go, etc. We're leaving half-way through the term. I read the list out to Mike as he was trying to make sole Veronique and not burn the white sauce and I was cutting up the grapes. "We have to bring cagoules and wellies."

"What's a cagoule?"

"A nylon parka with a hood. I'll get some kids' wellies in Woolworths. They supply the trowels, but we have to help with the cooking."

"And the trowels will come in useful for serving slices of pizza. I think these soles are done."

So we poured the sauce over the soles, and scattered on the grapes, and had mashed potatoes and a green salad, and ate it while listening to a stack of records Mike had put on the record-player: Albinoni's Adagio, Rodrigo's Guitar Concerto, Pictures from an Exhibition by the Electric Light Orchestra, and Clockwork Orange by Wendy Carlos.

"I like this restaurant," I said.

"I've been coming here for years. Cheers!" And we clinked our glasses of 7Up.

"I'm not looking forward to the summer, much," said Mike. "Will you get time off for good behaviour? We might even go abroad, like we always say we will."

"They have nice beaches in France."

"We've left it too late again. Just don't get into any trouble."

"It's just a dig, what could happen?"

"Keep away from the criminal classes."

"I'm more likely to meet villains in the antique trade."

"Yes, looting, smuggling and faking."

"Looting – I suppose archaeologists might do that."

"You've got away with it so far. Don't push your luck!" he said, referring to my criminal past. Not crimes done by me, I hasten to add.

\*\*\*

When the time came, I bought a red cagoule from John Lewis's children's department, and some red wellies in Woolworths. I packed a rucksack with shorts and jeans and T shirts and a camouflage bucket hat, notebooks and pens, some paperbacks, and a tiny transistor radio.

"You'll have to keep coming home to get something to read!" said Mike.

"I promise I'll ring you and write to you often. I'm not sure if you can ring me, except in an emergency."

He wrote down the phone number from the sheets of info, and the address – Malison Grove, Malreward. The next morning we went to the station together, as he was working the late shift. I got some sandwiches and biscuits for lunch. I leaned out of the train window like they do in films and we kissed goodbye.

I sat in my corner looking out at the view, and sometimes reading. I wondered if there were other students on the train but I reckoned I'd meet them soon enough. I could just see us all getting off at Eldritch station and standing about awkwardly. People got into my carriage and out again. I ate my lunch. Just before Teignmouth the railway goes right by the sea – that was fun. Then a man said: "We're about to cross the Tamar", and we went over a bridge and were in Cornwall.

At last we stopped at Eldritch and I heaved my rucksack down the corridor towards the door. A student type on the platform lifted it down for me and said: "Any more for the Skylark? Are you joining our small select group?"

Just as I'd imagined, there was a bunch of youths clustered together, not smiling very much. "I'm one of the archaeology students, if that's what you mean," I said, and we joined the others.

"Apparently there'll be a minibus imminently," said one of the blokes. They nearly all had longish hair and beards, apart from the one who'd carried my rucksack for me. There wasn't time to even say "Hello!", because then the minibus turned up on the forecourt and we trooped out through the station and got into it and drove off.

"Before them lie the bright future of a new term – will they accept the challenge?" said the one who'd carried my rucksack.

"Try not to be so futile," said one of the other boys. They did some guffawing and pushing each other off seats, but otherwise nobody said anything much. We drove through the town, fields, woods, a little village, and then an imposing gateway came into view. We drove through, and up a drive with trees on either side, and towards a largish stone Tudor house. We didn't stop at it, but veered off to the right and stopped in a cobbled courtyard surrounded by stables. There were some people waiting for us, and our driver got out and joined them.

CHAPTER THREE

We piled out and a short woman with an untidy bun and a red face said, "Hello, everybody! Pick up your stuff and then we'll give you the introductory talk! And food!"

We found our rucksacks, which had been put in the boot. I slung mine over one shoulder and we gathered in a knot in front of the tutors. As well as the woman, there was a big man with a shaven head, and the tall thin man with short grey hair who'd driven the minivan. They were wearing jeans and fishermen's jerseys, and the female tutor had a big cardigan and a gathered skirt and a scarf wound round her neck.

"I'm Bridget, and these are Jonathan and Pete!" she said, smiling keenly. "Welcome to Malison Grove! We'll show you the dorms and let you get settled in, and then we'll meet in the kitchen for supper. That's it over there." She pointed to a door in the corner of the yard, and then led me and the other girls – there were three of them – to some more converted outbuildings.

"Here we are!" she said, ushering us into a big room with beds in a row. "This used to be the bakehouse. First come, first served!" We fanned out and put our rucksacks down on the beds, which had lockers beside them and reading lights. "Your showers and loos are next door. The US Army was here during the war, so the showers are really powerful, and the water's hot! The laundry's next to the kitchen and there's an airing cupboard where you can dry clothes. There's a phone you can use – it's in the lobby next to the office. You'll find it, it's got "office" on the door! I've got all your names of course, but you'll have to tell me which is which!"

We introduced ourselves. The others were Gail (pale blue jumper), Nadine (long dark hair) and Donna (large).

"Now I'll leave you to settle in – come to the kitchen in about half an hour." And she bustled out.

I picked a bed next to Gail and opposite Nadine. There were several other beds in the room but it felt rude not to cluster together, or bag the bed under the window. I wondered who would speak first.

"Well, here we are in the home from home!" said Nadine.

"It's not as bad as that youth hostel we stayed in for drystone walling," said Gail.

"What was that like?" I asked, thinking I ought to say something.

"Bunks, grey blankets, and no sheets," said Donna, who had thick shoulder-length light brown hair and a tanned face with blunt features. "What have we got here?" She pulled back the candlewick bedspread to reveal a flowery eiderdown. "Could be thicker!" she said, pinching it.

"And at least it's not a tent!" said Nadine.

"If I remember, you wimped out and slept in the youth hostel the last night!"

"And that was the lap of luxury, I don't think!"

Gail was unpacking her rucksack and putting her spongebag into the locker. I unzipped mine and began taking stuff out of it.

"We all go to Blackhampton university," she said. "Where do you go?"

"Regent College in London. We all got sent to different places."

"Most of the boys are from Blackhampton too," said Donna, who'd dumped her things on the bed opposite Gail. "We know each other from the course, and lots of us are in Drystone Soc, and Canal Soc, and Caving Soc, and Diving Soc, and Rambling Soc."

"Shut up! She'll believe you!" said Nadine.

"I don't think Regent has 'socs'! Anyway, I haven't really looked into them."

"Well, in London you couldn't really go caving. Perhaps there's indoor ski-ing or something you could do," said Gail. "We really do those things, except caving and diving. Donna's just joking."

"It might come in useful," said Donna. "I hear there's a cave somewhere on the site."

"Pot-holing would be claustrophobic, and I don't think I'd be any good at ski-ing," I said. "Though I used to go riding in Hyde Park. And sometimes I swim in the Ladies Pond in Hampstead Heath. And we play tennis at Parliament Hill even though I'm terrible at it. Are you all first years too?"

"No, we're second years," said Gail. "We went to Scotland last year. It was freezing."

"Oh good, you've got lots of paperbacks," said Donna. "I wonder if there's a telly here?"

"I hope there's a library in Eldritch," I said.

## 14

"Oh, bound to be. They have all the amenities. I expect they'll take us round the town. Apparently there are buildings with reused Roman columns."

"I can barely contain my excitement!" said Nadine, faking a yawn.

"So where do you live in London?" asked Gail.

"In Kentish Town."

"Where's that?"

"Kind of north, but not too far out."

"In a hostel, or residences? Or do you share a flat?"

"We've got a flat above a launderette. I did live in a hostel, and then a bedsit, before we got married."

"Married!" said Donna.

"I did notice you were wearing an engagement ring," said Gail. "Can I look at it?"

I took it off and handed it to her.

"Wow, it's so tiny!"

"It's a decent-sized diamond," I said, pretending to be miffed.

"I mean the ring – it's weeny!" She scrutinized it and gave it back to me.

Nadine was brushing her hair and looking at herself in a handbag mirror.

"You look beautiful, darling!" said Donna. "We'd better get along to the kitchen."

"It's nice to meet you, Anna," said Gail, smiling at me without blinking.

"Don't mind her," said Nadine. "She's a Christian. She's been born again."

As we we went towards the kitchen I told Gail: "I used to be a Catholic but I stopped going to church ages ago."

"She doesn't think Catholics count!" said Nadine from behind us. "She'll try and convert you all over again."

I didn't say that these days if I worshipped anybody it was the Ancient Greek gods, and their Egyptian avatars. They probably have Celtic and Viking equivalents as well.

# 15

"Ah, here come the ladies," said Pete, the big bald man, as we we came into the kitchen. Everybody else was sitting down, but Jonathan and Pete got to their feet. "Find somewhere to sit," said Pete, and we did. There were sandwiches piled on dishes in the middle of the table, which was several pushed together. We each had a pale yellow plastic plate and a Duralex plastic glass. I noticed Pete had a gold earring in one ear. He looked like a wrestler or a bouncer, but Jonathan seemed harmless.

"Welcome again, everybody," said Pete. "Some of us are new, including me, so let's introduce ourselves. I'm Pete and this is -" he pointed to Jonathan, who said "Jonathan" and Bridget, who said her name, and all round the table. "Let's go round again the other way!" said Pete, and we did the same again, saying our names as he pointed at us, only faster this time, and people began to giggle.

The boys were:

Colin (in the college scarf)

Malcolm (black hair)

Derek (red hair)

Gavin (blond)

They all had beards, apart from Colin, Pete and Jonathan. I was sitting next to Malcolm, who had a Scottish accent, with Gail on my other side, and Nadine was sitting next to Gavin.

"Now can we have two volunteers to dole out the soup – Gavin and Derek, you're nearest the stove," said Pete, and the two of them got up and started sloshing soup into primrose yellow plastic soup bowls, which we passed down the table to each other.

"Help yourselves to sandwiches," said Pete, and we passed them round and put them on our side plates.

"So what's Blackhampton like?" I asked Malcolm.

"Red brick," he said between slurps of Heinz tomato.

"It's more concrete," said Donna.

"Are you on a campus?" Gail asked me.

"No – Regent's in the middle of town, next to the BBC and Oxford Street, and C&A, and the Kardomah."

"Lucky old you!" said Malcolm. "You must have a choice of pubs."

"I suppose so, I don't go to them much, only sometimes to hear blues bands or go to the folk club."

"Apparently there's one here - it was in the handout," said Gail.

"It's in the pub in Malreward, where we'll go after dinner. You won't mind walking?" said Bridget.

"Before we get too drunk, I'd like to point out that breakfast is at eight in here," said Pete, standing up again. "And Bridget will sort out the cooking and washing-up rota. Can I have two more volunteers to wash up tonight?" He pointed to two more boys. "You and you. And then we get going at 9am. There's a lot to do! Roland will tell you all about it in the morning."

"Do the tutors live here too?" I asked.

"Roland and Fabia are staying at a B&B in Malreward - it's the nearest village, but quite big. The rest of us are staying here in the officer's quarters. Gareth's been home to see his family - you'll meet him tomorrow. Oh, and another thing - the telly's in a converted loose box, so you don't have to miss It's a Knockout."

I'd noticed the stable blocks had an upstairs - the tutors must live up there in what used to be hay lofts and tack rooms. The boys started cracking rude jokes and Colin, the short-haired one, smiled rather desperately. I made a mental note to be more detached but then Gavin said "Anna's looking disapproving!" and they all laughed some more.

We cleared away and fetched our handbags, and Donna put on some pink frosted lipstick that didn't suit her and Nadine brushed her hair again. We came out again into the stable yard and hung about waiting for the tutors. Most of the doors had OFFICE or STORES or AMMUNITION stencilled on them, but some still had stable doors, with the tops open. I looked in one and a pony came and stuck its head out.

"There's the telly room, everybody!" said Bridget, pointing to a door. "But that one is a real loose box and still has a horse in it and Mrs Collingwood told us to leave him strictly alone as he's a bit nervous. She's the housekeeper from next door and she runs the letting business."

I could see a big white horse moving about inside and stamping its feet. Of course horses are never called white but "grey", apart from the ones made out of chalk and carved into hillsides.

"Come on, chaps!" said Pete, and we formed a bunch and set off down the avenue.

"Who do the ponies belong to?" I asked Bridget. "The people in the big house?"

"Yes," she said, falling in beside me. "It's one of those Longleaty-type places where you can see round it, but there are things to do in the grounds, like pony-cart rides. There's quite a nice café and you're welcome to go there, but it's rather expensive. Do you like ponies? I miss my dogs! They don't have any here, apparently the owner doesn't like them. The gardens are worth a look, too."

I looked back at the house, which was grey and had lots of gables and turrets. It was set against a dark wood, and the moor loomed over it at the back.

"You can't see the stone circle from here," said Bridget. "It's behind the house beyond the wood."

"I meant to say," said Pete, turning round and walking backwards. "You're welcome to go round the big house for free in return for digging up its archaeology – just don't make a nuisance of yourselves or track in mud."

"There are some old pictures and armour," said Bridget. "You can't go over it all, I think somebody still lives there. But most of it's open to the public."

We passed through the gates and walked towards the village.

CHAPTER FOUR

The village, which we came to quite soon, had some houses arranged loosely around a little green with an oak tree in the middle. The pub was pseudo-Victorian, with plates on a shelf round the tops of the walls, and china jugs above the bar. The walls were papered in a dark William Morris type pattern, hung with sepia photos.

There were quite a few people sitting around, and leaning on the bar. Pete said "I'll get them in!" and asked us all what we wanted. Everybody seemed to like beer, apart from Bridget who said she'd have a white wine, but I said I'd have a coke. We sat down at tables.

Pete got Malcolm to help him bring the drinks over. "So you don't indulge!" said Malcolm, passing me my coke.

"She'll be drinking pints with the best of us by the end of the dig!" said Donna. I said nothing, and they began to tell stories of previous field trips they'd been on, which featured a lot of middens and cess pits and mud and "trenches full of nothing".

"Haven't you been on any field trips?" Gail asked me.

"Just to the Tower of London, and down on the Thames foreshore," I said. "We found oyster shells and pipe stems."

"They might have taken you somewhere in the holidays," she said.

"I suppose they might have."

"You can find a lot on the foreshore," said Pete. "Slipware, Samian ware, coins. Keep at it!"

"In the holidays I mainly worked," I said.

"Oh, where?" asked Gail. "What did you do?"

"Watch out – she's waiting for you to say you saw a strange light above the clock at Victoria station and suddenly you realised you'd been saved!" said Gavin.

Gail went rather red.

"I work in an antique shop a few hours a week, and in the holidays I'm there most of the time."

"It's all good experience!" said Pete.

"I just polish furniture," I said. "And stop people stealing things." I thought it best not to mention the modelling.

"Look, we can grab the dart board," said Malcolm, and he went to get the darts from a beer mug on the bar.

"Come on girls, let's show them what we're made of!" said Donna. "We can have a tournament."

So we all got up and stood about in a cluster.

"Everybody have a go!" said Pete. When it was my turn my dart just fell to the floor.

"I'm not having you on my team!" said Donna. I made a mental plan to stay behind and watch telly another time. The others started playing seriously and I wandered away and looked at the sepia photos. There were old agricultural scenes, and football groups, but I'd seen them in other pubs. They must come as a set. Then I got rather a shock – there was a photo of me in a camisole, surrounded by potted palms and round tables. I remembered that shoot – it was when modelling began to get a bit peculiar. In the picture I looked about nine. I hoped nobody would notice it.

Gail had sat down again so I joined her and she told me all about how she got "saved". "I was walking along in Nottingham one day feeling miserable and I saw this lorry go past with the words REST ASSURED on it. It's a kind of bed, but I knew it was a message."

"That's not a bad message," I said.

"Has anything like that ever happened to you?" she asked.

"Sort of - not quite like that." I see things in a crystal ball sometimes, but I wasn't going to tell her that.

"Anyway then God guided me to the right church. You live in London – have you ever been to All Souls next to the BBC?"

"It's practically opposite the college," I said. "But I've never been inside."

"I hope you don't mind me talking like this," she said. "There's a lot of prejudice."

"I don't mind in the slightest," I said. I was just grateful somebody was talking to me.

"You see, the Roman Catholics are more churchianity than Christianity," she said, emphasising the words in a particular way. I wondered if she'd been taught what to say, like the pub buying Victorian décor off the shelf.

"That's a nice pendant," I said. It was a fish made out of silver wire.

"It's the Ichthus fish," she said. "The early Christians used it as a secret symbol - it stands for '"Jesus Christ Son of God Saviour'."

"I see. Well, it's very pretty."

## 20

"Yours is nice too."

It's a plain silver crescent moon on a chain, the symbol of the goddess Diana, but I thought I'd better not mention that. The boys got more drinks and got a bit rowdy and came and sat down with us again. Malcolm pushed a chair in next to me.

"You'll meet Roly Poly tomorrow," he said.

"Roly Poly?"

"And Fabulous Fabia. And Gareth – as sooch!" said blond Gavin, who was sitting opposite with Derek.

"What are they like to work with?" I asked.

"Oh, they're all right."

"Don't you drink at all then?" asked Gavin. He was sitting next to Nadine and she put her hand on his knee.

"Not much," I said.

"Are you a Christian, too?"

"No."

"Not a veggie like Gail?"

"No."

"Hey, Gail, don't you know plants scream when you pick them? Salad is cruel to plants!"

"I hear you're married! You must be a child bride," said Gavin.

"I'm a mature student. I was 18 when we got married."

"It's an outmoded institution. And who wants to join an institution?"

I wondered how old they all were – probably 19 or 20. They started talking among themselves again, and Donna complained about bar staff who wouldn't serve her because she was a woman, and after a while it was closing time at last and we walked back in the dark with a lot of shouting and laughing. There was a faint light in the sky above the moor, but Pete put on a headtorch and Bridget took a pencil torch out of her handbag.

"Good thing you brought that, Pete," said Gavin.

"It came with the hard hats."

"They'll come in useful if a megalith falls on us." More laughter, then we were home. We said goodnight to the tutors and Bridget said "There's a bell to wake you up in the morning!"

In the dorm, we turned on our reading lights. "The bells! The bells! It's a bit an orphanage, isn't it?" said Donna. "All these beds in rows."

"I though you were used to youth hostels?"

"Oh, yes. I just felt a bit homesick for a moment, I suppose!"

We took our sponge bags to the bathroom, and I had a quick shower in case there wasn't time in the morning. I wondered when I'd have time to write to Mike. We got into bed and I read until the others turned off their lights.

"Goodnight, everybody," said Donna.

"Goodnight," we chorused. Everybody lay there in silence, then just as I was falling asleep a strange moaning sound came from from outside.

"What was that?!" said Donna, sitting up in stripy pyjamas.

"The hound, of course!" said Nadine sleepily.

"I thought it was supposed to be a Beast," said Donna. "The Hound was on Dartmoor."

"We can ask Pete tomorrow."

We lay down again, and the sound came again, more of a howl this time. It grew fainter and tailed away.

CHAPTER FIVE

We were wakened by a clanging bell – there was probably a rota for that too. The sun was shining and it was already quite hot, so I put on shorts and plimsolls and a pale green sleeveless shirt and fixed my hair back with a slide. The other girls were wearing jeans, though Nadine's were cut-offs to the knee, and scoop-necked T shirts. Nadine had put her hair in plaits, and Donna tied a red spotted bandana over her head, knotting it at the back of her neck. It seemed odd not to take a handbag everywhere. The others put theirs in their lockers and I did the same. I put a lipsil and a tissue in my shorts pocket. The others picked up notebooks and pens.

"Are you all taking notebooks?" I asked.

"Yes, there's an introductory lecture after breakfast," said Nadine. "It's in the instructions."

"Thanks," I said, getting out an exercise book and a pencil.

In the kitchen there was a buffet with instant coffee, Celestial Seasonings tea, ordinary tea, cornflakes, muesli and plastic jugs of milk. Also a lot of sliced bread so you could make toast. It was just us – the tutors must have a kitchenette in their flat.

"I'll just talk you through the rota," said Bridget, coming in followed by Pete. "It's fairly simple." She pointed to a blackboard on the wall. "I've got the master rota in this notebook, and I'll chalk it up every week."

"Shouldn't it be a 'roster'?" asked Colin, and the others giggled.

"We won't be going far most days, so you can come in here at lunch time and make sandwiches. Just leave the place as you would wish to find it! If you're still hungry you can nip to the village shop, or the café at the big house is nearer – they do Crunchies and KitKats, and oat and date bars, and homemade cake!"

"I hope everybody slept well!" said Pete.

"Apart from the howls!" said Donna. "Is it the Beast?"

The boys began making howling noises and saying, "I used to be a werewolf but I'm all right now-oooo!!!"

"Did you hear anything?" I asked Colin, who was sitting next to me.

"We did," he said. "But I expect it's only farm dogs or something. Are there any dogs here?"

"Bridget said not – the owner doesn't like them."

"A place like this ought to have dogs, somehow."

"Some say it's the bog settling," said Pete. "And others that it's the booming of the bittern."

Before I could impress him by recognizing a quote from The Hound of the Baskervilles, a car drove up in the yard outside and he said: "Here are our beloved leaders. We now move into the lecture hall – or converted billiard room. But finish your breakfast first."

We slurped our coffee, and chucked plates in the dishwasher, and in about ten minutes Pete led us to another a big room with wooden benches and a cinema screen on a stand, and a projector at the back.

"Find somewhere to sit," said Pete, "And I'll hand you over to Fabia and Roland. And Gareth and Jonathan."

"Thanks, Pete," said a man with dark hair and a beard and heavy glasses, who I recognised as the great Roland Blair from his picture on the back of his books. "I'm sure you've done a fantastic job as usual."

We sat down on the benches – the American army must have used the room for briefings, or something. I was between Derek and Colin. Professor Blair waited for us to settle before he got going.

"Welcome, everybody, to another summer season. Most of you I recognise, but for the new boys – and girls –" He gave me a piercing stare. "I'm Professor Roland Blair, and this is Fabia Thompson, and these two reprobates are Gareth Borthwick and Jonathan Leaf. Pete Beckerlegge you know, and Bridget Porter completes the set. Fabia, Jonathan and I are the "Blackhampton Team". The others are from nameless red-brick excrescences elsewhere in these islands. Anyway, I'm sure you've all introduced yourselves, if you're not already old friends. And by the way, it's all first names here. I'm Roland, this is Fabia and so on."

The other tutors looked a bit sheepish as he pointed them out, and he carried on: "We'll be having a look at the stone circle in the grounds here. Aerial photographs suggest that it's part of a much larger complex, that may have been utilised at several different periods, so we'll put some trenches in and see what we come up with. There may be a medieval great hall underneath the manor house, and there's a Victorian midden we had a go at in the days of Sir Finamore Whitelock. We've got some schoolkids working on that. And there's even what may be a bone cave in the woods – which is possibly the relic of a sacred grove."

"Everything but the kitchen sink," muttered Colin in my ear. "You know, I think cathedrals were modelled on caves. I'll tell you all about my theory some time."

"We aim to get a better picture of what's been going on here over the centuries," said Roland. Jonathan went to the back of the room and turned on the projector.

"Lights, please," said Roland. "Would somebody fix the blinds?"

Somebody did, the lights went out, and slides appeared on the screen. Roland pointed out features with a thing like a billiard cue: aerial views, plans and maps, and black and white photos of a stone circle.

In the dark, I could stare at the other tutors, who were sitting near the screen, apart from Jonathan, who was working the projector. There was another one with dark hair, a beard and glasses who looked like an older version of Malcolm and a shorter version of Roland – he must be Gareth. Fabia was thin, with shoulder-length dark hair shoved behind her ears.

Most of the others were taking notes. I jotted down "stone circle, crop marks, possible cursus or votive causeway", then I scribbled a quick description of the tutors with their names in case I forgot who was who. I also wrote "Gail Christian, Nadine glamorous, Donna mannish. Colin short hair, Derek ginger, Gavin blond, Malcolm black hair, Scottish. Gavin 4 Nadine, Donna 4...?"

"And now for the exciting part," said Roland. "Time for the film show. You're probably all too young to remember Sir Finamore Whitelock and his TV series, but he was a big star in the 50s – when there was nothing else to watch but What's My Line?"

The Blackhampton students all laughed dutifully.

"He was a flamboyant character," went on Roland. "Larger than life, a bit of an eccentric. And I should know. We're about to watch some highlights from the series filmed here. I am of course the real star – you'll see me looking weedy in baggy shorts and pointing at megaliths. There are a couple of other alumni here in your presence: Fabia was on the team, and Jonathan. Run it, Jonathan."

A black and white image appeared on the screen, very out of focus, and the boys yelled. Jonathan tinkered with the projector and Sir Finamore Whitelock appeared. He really did have a white forelock, but perhaps it was dyed. His hair was quite long for the 50s, but greased back, and he had an airforce moustache and a goatee beard. He was always in the foreground, waving his arms. He showed us round the stone circle and pointed out carvings on the megaliths.

"Of course there are folk tales about the stones," boomed Sir Finamore from the screen. "They can never be counted. They move about when nobody's looking. But my students are making a record and taking measurements." The boys, with very short hair and long baggy shorts, were clambering about with a tape measure. There were two girls holding clipboards, one who must be Fabia in an old-fashioned hairdo, and another one with long dark hair.

"I think that idiot is me," said Roland, indicating one of the boys, who grinned at the camera. "We can repeat that exercise. We weren't so thorough back then, and we were interrupted. As you'll see. You can just spot Jonathan and Fabia before Sir Finamore hogs the camera again."

Sure enough he came back into shot, declaiming. "And some say there is a hoard of gold and treasure beyond price under one of the stones!"

"Probably put it there himself!" muttered Colin.

"Local legend says that no good will come to anyone who interferes with the stones! We interviewed a villager from Malreward," explained Sir Finamore.

The film cut to an old man saying: "One of they stones fell and crushed a bloke once! And they have their guardians – you don't want to wake they!"

"What do you think of this tale that the stones go down to the river to drink once a year?"

"Not a river – the bottomless pool!"

"Very interesting! And yet some say the entire circle was erected by a 17th century antiquarian! We aim to find out the truth, thanks to funding by Blackhampton University, the Archaeological Society and the Pearman Foundation!"

The picture jumped, and Sir F was leading us through a wood of low trees with twisted branches covered in lichen.

"The oak wood," said Roland. "It's on our agenda."

"And now here we found something really remarkable!" enthused Sir Finamore. "When we were surveying what may be a grove sacred to the Druids, we came across – this!" He pointed dramatically, and the camera zoomed in on a dark hole, surrounded by ferns and the students, looking gauche.

"What lurks in its unexplored depths?" queried Sir F. "Unfortunately we don't have the resources to investigate this trip."

"Druidic!" muttered Colin. "That was all made up in the 18th century."

"Shush! I'm trying to listen!" said Nadine.

"Can't you stop muttering for one minute, Colin?" said Malcolm.

Now Sir F and the students were in a more open landscape, with the moor in the background. "A possible cursus, and probably a huge temple complex!" he was saying, windmilling his arms.

"That's what we want to get our teeth into," said Roland. "And now I think we'll break for coffee before the next thrilling episode."

The picture faded, and we went via the sunlit stableyard into the dark kitchen, where we had some instant coffee and biscuits, and some of us lit cigarettes.

Colin handed me a mug of coffee. "Do you want a suggestive biscuit? Or maybe it was the 17th century."

"What was? No, thanks."

"The so-called druids. I'm sure Sir Finamore planted half the stuff he found, like Schliemann at Troy, and he totally mucked up the stratigraphy."

"I'm enjoying it," I said. "I've never seen those programmes before. Were the Druids really all made up? I read Roland Blair's book, and they hung out on Anglesey, didn't they, before they were massacred by the Romans? Gruesome!"

"Oh, yes, there were some real Druids, but we know very little about them, and modern Druids are all based on 18th century research which is now quite discredited. Revival is an interesting study in itself, a bit like the witchcraft movement – you know they've turned it into a religion that probably never existed in that particular form?"

"Oh, did they really?"

It was time to go back to the lecture room. The projector started up again and we were back in the stone circle. The two male students were pulling on planks and poles that had been stuck in around the base of one of the megaliths, while Fabia lurked in the background. There was a rope round the stone, attached to a tractor.

Sir F came into view. "Legend has it," he told the camera, "that under one of these megaliths is a treasure beyond price. What might it be? A hoard of priceless Saxon metalwork like Sutton Hoo? Roman coins? Celtic torques? Viking silver? We are live from Malison Grove and soon we shall find out! All together now – heave!"

The tractor started up and the rope tightened, and the students put all their weight on the wooden battens. One of them splintered, but the stone wobbled in its socket and its earthy base could be seen.

"Stop! Stop this at once!" A man dressed entirely in tweed, including plus-fours and hat, marched into shot.

"Ah! We have incurred the wrath of the Archaeological Society!" said Sir F to the camera. "Good morning, Professor Burford! You can't stop us now! The stone is about to go!"

"Stop that! Stop that tractor!" commanded Prof Burford, striding forward. The tractor braked and backed. "If you carry on with this act of rank vandalism, sir, you and your students will lose all credibility in the world of archaeology, and will never receive funding or approval again. Or find a job anywhere," he added to the students.

"Touch not the stones!" cried another voice, and several men in long white robes and white headdresses came into shot. "The sacred stones must not be moved!"

"Ah, the modern Druidic contingent! Once again the forces of reaction have stepped in to halt the progress of science!" said Sir F, stepping in front of Prof Burford. "What a tragic missed opportunity! Don't forget to tune in next week!" The Druids and Professor Burford closed in on the students and the credits rolled again.

"Lights, please!" said Roland, and the projector stopped whirring and someone raised the blinds again. "I'm afraid there was no next episode. The dig was closed down – the Archaeological Society had its way. And the Druids. Of course, nobody would do such a thing today – uproot a megalith, I mean. But as you can see, this is a fascinating site, and so many questions were left unanswered. Now, let's have some lunch, and then we'll dig some holes. After all, that's what you're here for!"

We trooped into the kitchen to make ourselves sandwiches with sliced bread and ham and cheese and limp lettuce and tomatoes, and cups of packet soup.

"Thank heavens for salad cream," said Nadine, sloshing some on a slice of bread.

"Ooh, arrr!" said Gavin. "What price that villager? And those Druids! What a bunch of hams!"

"And Sir Finamore was the worst," said Colin to me. "But I believe he really planned to uproot the stones one by one, in the name of research! Poor chap, he died soon after that, I think. Sudden heart attack."

"Are you at Blackhampton too?" I asked him as we washed down our sandwiches with apple juice.

"No, neither is Derek, the red-haired bloke," he said. "I'm at Keele."

"Where's your Keele scarf?" asked Malcolm nastily. "I thought you slept in it."

"A friend of mine went to Keele," I said hastily. "But he dropped out. He said there was nowhere to go but Nottingham or a motorway service station."

"It's a bit like that! But there are bars on campus, and lot of clubs."

"Do you go cave diving and stuff like the girls?"

"I sing in the choir. How about you?"

"I go to a folk club sometimes, and ballroom dancing with my husband, and to the pub with his colleagues."

"Your husband!" He looked at my left hand. "You'd better take those rings off – you might lose a diamond while you're trowelling."

"That's an idea."

"Who are your husband's colleagues?"

"They're policemen. He's a detective sergeant."

"'Ello, 'ello what's goin' on 'ere, eh? We'll have to be on our best behaviour. But perhaps he's miles away?"

"Yes, in London. Too far to go for the weekend."

"I expect we'll have to work at the weekends."

# 29

"And now children," said Fabia, looking in when we'd finished our sandwiches and were drinking instant coffee. "It's bucket and spade time!"

CHAPTER SIX

Fabia and Pete led us through the yard and then we turned left and walked up the side of a field and ended up at a flat area which already had flags on beanpoles stuck in the ground. There were a few tents and plastic benders scattered about, and the moor began a few feet away, behind a wire fence.

"Gather round," said Fabia. "Roland has explained to you what we'll be digging and why. The plans and maps are up in the lecture room and I advise you to study them. This is where the crop marks indicate a cursus and a possible temple complex. But we won't know anything until we start digging, and that's your job!"

"They just called us in to do the heavy lifting," muttered Malcolm. Pete came out of one of the benders carrying a spade in either hand.

"And now I'll leave you to Pete's tender mercies," said Fabia. "Don't be too hard on them, mate."

"I'll leave that to you, dear!" he replied.

She turned back to the path, heading straight for the knot of students. Colin stumbled out of her way and tripped over a tussock.

"What was that supposed to be?" asked Fabia, and Malcolm said "Shall we dance?"

"Save it for the disco," said Fabia, walking away.

"Now, fellow sufferers!" said Pete. "Now we've got all this equality we can all fetch a spade or a pickaxe."

Gavin, Malcolm and Donna went into the bender and brought out the tools and put them in a pile at Pete's feet. He handed out spades to the others, then stood there holding the pickaxe.

"Now, what are we going to do with you?" he asked, looking at me, and the others snickered.

"Why don't you just give me the pickaxe and let me make a fool of myself?" I said, glaring at him from under my hat brim. Perhaps I'm getting the hang of sarcasm.

"I think I'll hang on to it myself. We'll let you loose on a trowel once we've dug down a few feet."

"I'm sure even you can manage that, darling," said Gavin, picking up a spade.

"Anyway, Anna, stand to the side for now, while I show the others what to do," said Pete. "You can always learn something." He pointed out some taped lines on the ground. "Divide it into squares, make cuts with the spade, and then remove the turf. We can pile it up – how about here?"

"Be sure to leave the trench as you would wish to find it," said Malcolm in an affected mincing voice.

Once they'd started marking out the area with more tape, and shoving their spades in the ground, Pete beckoned me over. "I've got plans for you," he said. "Don't think you're going to get off lightly. We'll leave the others to dig and delve for a bit."

Gavin muttered "It's all right for some," and Malcolm said, "Her or him?"

Pete led me to a tent near the edge of the field where there was a tap and a drinking trough for cows, or perhaps the horses and ponies. As we approached I could hear high-pitched voices and giggling. We went under the flap and were immediately in amongst a load of schoolchildren washing stuff in plastic basins on trestle tables, with a couple of teachers.

"Hullo Eileen!" he said to one of them. "They sent us a batch of students, but they aren't all the right size, and we can't send them back. This is Anna. Can she join your team?"

"Of course! I'll find her a toothbrush, and there's a spare basin over here."

"I hope you don't mind being stuck with the kids," Pete said to me. "But I don't think you'd be much use with a spade, and this is probably a better use of your time. You can keep up with what we're doing, and once we get to the trowelling stage you'll be properly involved. And you can tell us what's happening here. See you later!"

"Yes. Thanks!" I said. Eileen gave me a toothbrush and a sponge and set me in front of a basin of water and a tray full of little objects covered in mud.

"We're setting them out on this table over here when they're clean," she said. "I'm just here to supervise. We've been roughly sorting them by colour!"

"Where did they come from?" I asked, picking up a sherd. "We haven't started digging yet."

"From the dig 20 years ago. They found a rubbish heap behind the house and dug out sackfuls of this stuff all mixed up together.

There are a lot of animal bones - we're putting them in this pile here."

"OK," I said, and dipped my sherd in the water and scrubbed it - it was blue and white.

"Sometimes they have pictures on!" said a little boy on my right. "I found a house and some people and a camel! Where do you go to school?"

"Regent College in London."

"What are you doing in Cornwall?"

"I came with the other students. We arrived yesterday."

"You mean you're grown-up?"

"Yes, I'm 22. I can see my hands are going to get filthy - I'd better take my rings off."

I undid the chain of my pendant, took off my rings and put them on it. I washed a lot of sherds, and chucked animal bones on the pile. There were sacks of rubbish leaning against the tent poles, so I supposed we wouldn't run out of things to do, and when they found stuff in the trenches we could wash that.

We each had a plastic basket to put the clean stuff in, and when mine was full I took it over to the finds table and sorted it out a bit. After a while we had a break with lemonade and orange squash and biscuits, sitting in the sun outside. "The kids don't work all day, do they?" I asked Eileen.

"Oh no - it would probably be against the law! Just for an hour or so."

"It's instead of history," said the boy who'd talked to me. "It's much more fun! Better than a nature walk."

"What about you?" asked Eileen. "Do you get let off the end of term?"

"Yes - this is part of our course. This time next year the others will be doing finals. They're mostly second years."

We went back into the tent and carried on. The children sang Old Macdonald had a Farm, and Row, Row Your Boat and I joined in. Eventually Eileen told them to down tools and they crocodiled back down the field. I thought I might as well stay where I was so I carried on sorting the sherds and making a blue-and-white mosaic and then Pete came in and looked over my shoulder.

"It's almost in periods," he said. "Did you do that?"

"I've seen quite a lot of this Victorian and Georgian stuff – not in bits."

"Oh yes, you're in the antique trade, aren't you? What about this?" he said, holding up a fragment of cream and brown slipware between finger and thumb.

"That's quite rare," I said. "I suppose not much survived whole. 17th century?"

"I see we've got some medieval floor tile here."

"And there's some Tudor green glaze."

"Nice work. I'm by way of being the pottery expert. I know – look like it, don't I? It can be handy sometimes, looking like a thug. Perhaps you find the same? I mean, you look so harmless! Nobody could be frightened of you! And they could be wrong?"

"They'd be right, I'm a complete wimp."

"I don't believe it! Anyway, I see I'll have to give you a reference book."

"Thanks. We've got one in the shop and I leaf through it sometimes."

"How did you end up in the shop?"

"I went there as a temp, typing labels, before I decided to do A levels and a degree."

"Well, there's no harm in doing things back to front. I see you've taken your wedding ring off."

"Yes, everything's so dirty, and I was afraid the diamond might fall out."

"And you can type as well! We need labels and reports typed. You won't mind doing that?"

"Not a bit."

"We've got an Olivetti portable in the orifice. Putting my tutor's hat back on, I'm sure it'll be valuable experience for you."

"Where are the others – I mean Professor Blair and Fabia?"

"They're opening a grown-ups' trench nearer the stone circle. They might let us have a look at it some time. Now come and see what your gang have been doing."

We went back up to the top of the hill, where everybody was standing about looking hot and drinking out of plastic canteens of water. Somebody yelled "Yoohoo!" and Fabia approached up the path, wearing a straw hat.

"We'd better wait till she gets here," said Pete. "And then give her a sitrep."

"Situation report," said Malcolm, looking at me as if I might not know what that meant. Which was true, I didn't. But I did now.

"Hullo, everybody," said Fabia, walking up to the trench. "So what have we got here?"

"It's quite exciting, it could be a – " began Pete, but she talked over him.

"I'd like to hear from one of our acolytes." She looked at them and nobody spoke. She pointed at Derek. "How about you, Ginger?"

"Well, we've uncovered what could be part of a metalled road or track in a line from our stone circle along the route of the supposed cursus."

"Let's have a look at it." She stepped into the trench. In a few places, a rough stone pavement was revealed. "Hmm. Better than nothing. We expected to find this, didn't we? Who's recording it?" Gavin, the blond one, raised a pencil. He was holding a board with some paper pinned to it.

"What's a cursus, anybody?"

"Usually a double line of small stone posts. They can go on for miles," said Malcolm.

"Och aye, the noo!" said Fabia, mocking his accent rather badly. "Ye're not wrang! Not always stone posts, though."

"Ditches and earthworks?" said Colin.

"Indeed. Dates, anybody?" She looked around. Her gaze fell on me and I realised I should have done some more reading up.

"The Neolithic!" said Colin.

"And when did that happen?"

"Three thousand years ago."

"Really?"

"I mean – 3000 BC!"

"That's more like it. Any finds?"

Derek held out a tray and she picked through it. "This isn't bad!" she said, picking up a flint arrowhead. "Make sure Gareth gets it. You'd better all knock off now and get the finds squared away in the barn, and write up your reports. You'll need to hand those in at the end of the week, so no slacking."

She shoved the tray back at Derek and set off back down the field.

"As she says!" said Pete. "Did we say there's a little library in the telly room? Text books as well as James Bond and Love Story!"

Everybody was picking up their stuff and going back down the field. I found myself at the back of the parade with Pete.

"Just write something about the pottery you've been washing," he said. "I'll give you that reference book."

"Thanks."

"You can copy someone else's notes about what we found today," he said. "And tomorrow you can trowel with the best of them. Don't mind Fabia, her bark is worse than her bite."

"That's what people always say."

"Yes, it's lazy isn't it? Let's just say she has an unfortunate manner."

The others launched into "Hi ho, hi ho, it's home from work we go!"

Back in the kitchen we made tea and ate biscuits. Pete gave me the pottery book and said "Now, who's on dinner duty?" Fortunately it was two of the boys and he showed them where all the supplies were.

After tea he showed us the barn where Gareth and Jonathan were setting out finds in little plastic bags with typed labels. There were more maps and photos round the walls, and some stills from the TV programme. I nipped into the telly room and found a basic book on prehistory with some chronologies. I suppose if I stare at it long enough something might go into the old brain. I took the books back to the dorm and wrote in my official dig notes journal. The other girls were there doing the same. Nadine put on a plastic bath hat and went to have a shower.

"You know if you don't wash your hair for three weeks eventually it cleans itself?" said Donna.

"I wouldn't like to try it," I said.

"You'll stick to Wood Nymph?" She must have seen the shampoo bottle on my locker.

"Yes, I like the adverts!" They're soppy, but I like to feel protected by dryads. "Is there anything else we're supposed to be doing? Actually, can I borrow your notes on what you did today?"

"Feel free." She chucked her notebook over. She hadn't written much and I quickly copied it out.

"Just like school," she said.

"Isn't it," I said. "Like the convent, anyhow."

"You went to a posh convent?"

"It was a boarding school and the girls there were pretty snobbish so I suppose it was a bit posh."

"Where was it?"

"Surrey."

"Lucky for some. Better than a comp."

I gave her the book back.

"I expect we should lay the table like helpful elves," she said. "Where's Gail got to?"

We went out into the yard, where Gail and Derek were patting one of the ponies.

"Come, come, come to the cookhouse door!" said Donna and we went into the kitchen. She organised us to set the table and fill water jugs. Gavin and Colin were standing over the stove.

"Smells nice! What is it?" asked Nadine.

"We've made a lot of rice," said Gavin. "There a list of menus and how to cook them."

"They think of everything."

"Looks like Bridget - she's drawn smiley faces all over it," said Gavin.

"This rice is soggy - I think I'll strain it," said Colin.

"You need to stir the mince - it's starting to burn," I said. He handed me a wooden spoon and I stirred it around in the huge battered frying pan. There was room for us both because the stove was enormous too.

"I hope there's lots of ketchup!" said Donna. She picked up the handbell which was on the counter, and rang it vigorously outside the door.

The others came in, and we doled out the food. Gail got a private bowl of grated cheese. Colin sat next to me again, and the tutors came and joined us – apart from Roland and Fabia. Perhaps their B&B gave them an evening meal.

"How did you get on pot-washing?" asked Colin.

"It was fun – there were a lot of schoolkids and we sang Old Macdonald."

"Just like Guide camp?"

"I never went on one of those."

"She went to a posh school!" said Donna.

"I had to leave when my parents lost all their money," I said. "And then I went to a local school and mixed with the plebs."

"It sounds like something out of Bunty or Judy!"

"Except it's usually the other way round – the slum kid goes to the posh school!"

"Did your parents really lose all their money?" asked Colin.

"No, not really. We moved. I didn't mind leaving the convent, except then I had to start all over again with new people."

We had moved, but I don't think it was to be near a day school for me.

"So what A levels did you do?"

"Classical civilisation, art history and botany – but that wasn't till after I'd left school. I did them all at Regent College, where I am now."

"I see you've taken your rings off. Very sensible."

"Oh yes – I put them on a chain round my neck. I think I'll leave them there."

"And pretend to be single!" said Donna, and Malcolm said "Aye, aye!"

Just as I was about to ask Colin what A Levels he'd done, Fabia and Roland came in and everybody shut up.

"I see you've had a busy day," said Roland. "Found a flint arrowhead! And a pavement! Well, keep looking. There's a theory that the cursus was used for ceremonial games and sporting contests, rather than just processions. Including archery. And the bottle-washing is coming along well, thanks to child labour. Some people collect Victorian poison bottles, I'm told. Well, everyone has to have a hobby – even Gareth. He turns them into arrowheads! We'll have a knapping session later, and Pete, could you dish out this list of lectures? You may even have to give some of them. No peace for the wicked, eh?"

And they exited. Some of the others said they'd go to the pub again, but I stayed behind and went to ring Mike. I told him I was loving it, sort of. We said good night, and I put the list of lectures into a folder and lay on my bed and turned on the radio and read the prehistory book to the strains of Nights in White Satin. It was pretty dry. Gail was hanging about too and we made some cocoa and went to bed.

CHAPTER SEVEN

Donna and Nadine came back later when we were already asleep, and blundered about getting into bed and giggling. I got up and went to the bathroom, and they apologised for waking me. They soon fell asleep, but I stayed awake and heard the howling noise again. It was musical, and rose and fell. Whoever was making it went to sleep themselves eventually.

So, the next morning was the same as the first, except it was grey and overcast. Nadine did her hair up with one of those leather things you put a spike through, and put on a Celtic-inspired necklace. Pete came in while we were eating porridge and said I could do some trowelling but he hoped I'd read the pottery book.

"I'll read it next," I said. "I've been boning up on the eras. I get the lithics confused."

"Palaeo, Meso, Neo!" he said. "Palaeo is really, really old and primitive. Meso is after the Ice Age, smaller, finer tools. Neo people were sophisticated and farmed and made refined tools – just like us, really."

"The Neolithic is still going on!" said Colin.

"Except that the 'lithic' bit means stone," said Malcolm.

"You can all find your way up to the dig site, can't you?" said Pete. "We'll break at about 10.30. Bring some water, though apparently it's going to chuck it down later and we'll have plenty."

"Can we drink the water out of the tap – that we were washing pots in?" I asked.

"Probably fit only for cows!" he went off again.

"Did you go to the pub again?" I asked Colin.

"No, I stayed behind like a good little boy and wrote up my notes and read one of Roland's books. Those old gods were nasty pieces of work, weren't they?"

"Yes, all rather gory. I think I've read that one."

"We've got the joy of a lecture on it, too. But apparently there's a folk evening at the pub tonight, I think I'll go to that."

"Ah, the good old days! We had to make our own fun," said Gavin. "We can still sink a few pints while the rest of you are warbling away. Were you a choirboy, Colin?"

"As a matter of fact I was," he said, going rather pink.

"Colin the choirboy! Come on, let's go on our merry way."

We went out into the yard, where two girls in green jerseys were wheeling bales of hay on a sack trolley. They said "Good morning!" and we said hello and went on up to the site. Pete and Bridget were already there, looking at a map. Pete gave me a trowel and told me to copy the others.

"We want to get this whole area cleaned back," said Bridget. She explained that meant you scraped off a layer of soil so that you could see what was underneath. Nobody found any more flint arrowheads, but Nadine found some charcoal, and a clay pot which might contain a burial, and Bridget was very excited about it. They dug out the whole thing and put it in a tray packed in old newspapers and she said they'd send it off to be X-rayed.

"You reckon a cremation?" asked Donna.

"Yes – ashes and fragments of bone," said Bridget.

"But are they – human?" said Gavin in a spooky voice.

"All civilisation is caused by alien astronauts," said Malcolm.

So we carried on the rest of the day, and the pot-washing children came and went. It started to spit with rain. Supper was brown rice and beansprouts, made by Donna and Nadine.

"Are you coming to the hostelry?" Colin asked me as the others prepared to go to the pub. I said I would.

"Watch out, it'll be full of local yokels," said Gavin.

I thought I might walk with Nadine and Donna, but they paired off with Gavin and Malcolm respectively and went on ahead, and Gail said she'd go to bed and read. So I went with Colin, who said things like "By Jove, by Jove, by Jingo!" and the others laughed at him.

Colin and I found chairs at a table with some other people in the singing half of the pub. Donna and Nadine and the boys played billiards in the other bit. Gareth and Jonathan were already there, sitting in the corner.

Three men sang some sea shanties in harmony and they were rather good. Everybody joined in the choruses, and Colin turned out to have a nice voice, though he sounded a bit posh. I kept quiet – I didn't think my high squeak would fit in. Most of the singers were men, and people got up and did things from the "English Book of Penguin Folk Songs" as usual. Over the other side Donna and Malcolm were fighting over a billiard cue.

In one of the breaks, a bloke on our table asked us: "You'll be staying up at the Grove?"

"Yes, that's right," said Colin. "We're archaeology students working on the dig."

"Oh, ar? We saw you come in the other night. We usually get hikers and ramblers. They get lost on the moor and have to be rescued!"

"I expect we'll be doing that too!" said Colin. The man said he was Martin, and his wife, in a blonde beehive hairdo, was Pamela. We introduced ourselves.

"We had some of your lot here before," said Martin. "Diggers. Close on 20 years ago. We even got on the telly!"

"They were digging too near the stones," said Pamela. "The stones don't like that."

"Load of superstitious nonsense!" said Martin.

"We didn't have all this trouble with the noises before that," said Pamela.

"What noises?" I asked.

"Up on the moor – howling and groaning. And people see things in the mist – a walking shadow."

"Sounds like the Brocken Spectre," said Colin.

"But the stones look after their own," insisted Pamela.

"Yes, that's what they said on the TV programme."

"They're supposed to go walkabout once a year," said Martin. "That's the time to grab the treasure! But don't get your hopes up. They never found any treasure last time. Don't believe they ever will."

People began singing again. When it was getting quite late I said to Colin: "If we sneak out now we won't have to walk back with the others."

"Why, what have you got against the others?" he asked, but he came with me. Unfortunately the others saw us going out and yelled stuff like "Going for a snog?"

As we walked up the avenue in the dark Colin said: "They're a bit cliquey, don't you think?"

"Just a bit."

"Understandable, really," he said. "They've all been at Blackhampton for two years and know each other really well. And they belong to some kind of archaeological club."

"An 'arch soc'?"

"Something like that – but I gather this one has been going for a couple of hundred years. It was started by one of those types who wanted to revive the Druids, but it became more normal over the years, like things do. They've even got a club-house in London somewhere where you can stay, and dine, and read in the library."

"Why don't you join?" I thought it sounded up his street.

"You have to be invited."

"Had you met the others before?"

"No, we befriended each other on the train, if you can call it that. You're a first year, aren't you?"

"That's right."

"Have you found it easy to socialise?"

"On the course? No, it's not like it was when I did A levels at the same place. Though actually my mates were third-years, and I knew some of them already."

"So they've left now?"

"Yes, we're still friends, but it's not the same."

"And you're in the middle of London – no campus, I suppose?"

"Oh, no. Just a canteen. And no 'socs'!"

"Apathy Soc and the rest! They usually fizzle after a few meetings. But then you are married."

"Yes, and I've got a part-time job, so I'm not lonely."

There was a faint wail from the moor.

"Did you hear that?" I said, stopping and listening.

"No, what?"

It came again, and died away.

"Oh yes. We heard it in the night. Probably bitterns."

"Don't they boom?"

# 43

We went on up the dark avenue of trees. We could see the silhouette of the house at the end, with one lighted window high up. I wondered if I should have tried harder to make friends at Regent. It was easy before, once I'd met Christine on modelling gigs and she turned out to be doing history there – or so she said. What was next year going to be like?

"What did you think of the folk night?" asked Colin. "You could have joined in."

"I like listening to men singing. We go and hear the police choir at Christmas, and sometimes they do other concerts."

"Of course, your husband's a copper. How did you two meet?"

"Mike was looking for a misper – a missing person - who'd got in with a druggy crowd, and he came to the hippy boutique where I was working to ask if we'd seen her. So anyway, we got talking, and he took me out to dinner, and we started going out, and here I am."

"What happened to the missing girl?"

"Oh, she turned up eventually."

"Should he have taken a witness out to dinner?"

"Oh dear, probably not."

"It gave him an excuse to see you again, I suppose. So was all this before you went to university?"

"Yes, I've done everything the wrong way round!"

We'd reached the stable yard. "I expect I'll get five minutes of peace and quiet before the others get back!" said Colin. "See you tomorrow! Sleep well!"

And we went our separate ways.

CHAPTER EIGHT

The next day we carried on "cleaning back", and the boys and
Donna and Nadine wielded spades and exposed some more earth.
I did a bit of inefficient spading away of the stuff we'd scraped
off and putting it into piles or "spoil heaps". Pete said I could
sieve it all later.

"Fun to come!" said Colin.

It had rained in the night, and it was cloudy and a cold breeze
blew off the moor. We worked away, making clinking noises as
our trowels hit rocks. We uncovered some more of the stone
walkway, and found potsherds and human teeth and possible
worked flint while the knees of our jeans got muddier.

It started to rain, but we carried on, mopping up puddles with
huge sponges. Soon there was no point going on as the rain was
turning the trench into a swamp.

"This is ridiculous!" said Nadine, her hair plastered over her face.

"Archaeology is such a dry subject!" said Colin.

"Right! We've had quite enough of this!" said Pete. "Let's make a
run for the tent." So we picked up our trays and scarpered to the
tent, which was still full of children and teachers. I said hello to
the children and looked at their table of potsherds.

"What do you think?" Pete asked the teacher in charge. Rain was
coming through the roof and some of the children looked rather
blue. "We're packing up, why don't you?"

The teachers thought that was a good idea. We waited while the
children put their anoraks on to see if it would "slacken off", but
it didn't, and in the end we all set off down the field, carrying
our finds. We put them in the barn, where Gareth and Jonathan
were working, the children left in their minibus, and we went to
change our clothes and sneak a hot shower. I brushed my hair and
left it down and hoped it would dry. We hung our wet jerseys in
the boiler cupboard and Gail said: "I wonder if you could make
yoghourt in here?"

We had sandwiches and packet soup as usual, and Pete and
Roland came in again.

"Good morning, campers!" said Roland. "Or is it afternoon? Since
rain has stopped play, I suggest you have a look at Malison Grove,
next door. The owners have generously opened their doors to you
scruffy herberts, and you don't have to pay. If anybody asks, refer
them to Mrs Collingwood – she's the housekeeper or manageress
or something, and lets out this generous accommodation. You can

get tea and buns in the café, the gardens have been restored and I gather there are pony rides though of course in a monsoon that doesn't apply. If none of that appeals, there are finds to wash and sort. Just remember to wipe your muddy boots on the mat!" And he went out again.

"And Gareth has arranged some entertainment for this evening," said Pete. "At least, he's going to lecture on flint tools, which comes to the same thing. In the lecture room after supper. Off you go to the stately home. Look out for the ghosts!"

"Are there really ghosts?" asked Nadine.

"All old houses have ghosts, don't they?" he said. "This one has lots. Headless horsemen, weeping ladies. The guides will tell you all about it."

"Shall we go?" I asked Gail, who was sitting next to me. She said OK, and Colin said he'd come with us.

"I suppose we might as well go too," said Nadine to Donna.

We got jackets and hats and set off, and Derek trailed silently behind us. It was just a short walk to a side door for the public - the grand front entrance looked unused. There was a desk and a little shop and a café, with middle-aged people dressed as Victorian servants. There really was a mat, so we wiped our feet on it and Donna explained we were the students.

"We've been expecting you!" said a lady in a white bonnet affair. "Mrs Collingwood told us all about you. This was the servants' quarters - butteries and breweries in the days before supermarkets! You can have the run of the place, most people have been put off by the weather. Now here's a plan and a leaflet each, and I hope you enjoy it! If you have questions, there are plenty of people to ask."

"I thought you had to be at least 40 to be let into one of these places," said Nadine, as we set off.

"Sh! She'll hear you," said Donna. Soon we came out of the servants' bit and down a corridor into a hall with a flagged floor and a fireplace and some oak furniture. It reminded me of Harpsden Manor, where I'd spent rather too much time with occultists and stoned hippies, until I found the way out.

"The medieval great hall is through here, ladies and gentlemen," said a man in Georgian costume with knee breeches. We went in and looked about at the old weapons and stags' antlers on the walls.

"Look, it says about the ghosts," said Nadine, reading the pamphlet. "There's a weeping woman in black who you can't catch however hard you try."

"If I see her I'll probably be running the other way!" said Donna.

"Psychic research was popular in Victorian times, wasn't it?" said Nadine. "Anyway, this girl was determined to make the ghost speak, but it was just always out of reach like a mirage and then it faded into the wall."

"Just as long as she keeps out of the stables," said Donna, pretending to shiver.

We wandered around cosier rooms with tapestries, cupboards full of china, Regency sofas with fraying seats, and people in historic costume posted at doorways. There was a library with old books, and tattered silk wallpaper and a piano. It was rather cold. I examined some books in a glass-topped table, open at engravings of monstrous creatures and Greek gods, and when I looked up the others had moved on.

I opened a door and found myself in a dark corridor leading to a staircase and more passages. I went down one lined with framed prints of buildings and old maps, but it was so dark you could hardly see them. There was a faint smell of damp and mould. Then I had a bit of a shock – there was another of the pictures from my modelling days, the one where I was standing in a field in Victorian clothes, holding a straw hat and looking sulky. It was the one my old enemy Gilles had up in his office at the sinister firm – but surely it had got burned when the building was struck by lightning and attacked by wolves?

But he'd bought it in an art gallery, so there must have been lots of copies. I wondered if the owners of Malison Grove had salted their art collection with stuff that just looked as if it had been there for centuries. Anyway, my picture was in a dark corridor and I hoped none of the others would ever see it. I turned back and soon found myself in one of the main rooms on the ground floor. Here were more family portraits, and a big oak table, and my fellow-students being addressed by a bloke dressed for a Victorian shooting party.

"Is this another of your number?" he said as I came in and joined the others. "You haven't missed too much, dear. I'm sure your friends can fill you in. And now these" he pointed to the portraits of a man and a woman in ruffs and jewellery and elaborate clothes "These are the Lord and Lady Malison of the 17th century. Like the previous Lady Malison, they were rumoured to dabble in the dark arts. See the book Lady Malison is resting her hand on – probably a copy of Culpeper's Herbal that can still be seen in the library. And these are their descendants, painted by Lely – or 'school of'!"

The party moved off, and I stayed looking at Lord and Lady Malison. I know Elizabethan portraits make everyone look rather pale and gaunt, and the artists weren't awfully good at getting a likeness, but they looked just like my parents, who I hadn't seen since I was about 18.

Lady Malison had a sad expression and fairish hair and a brooch pinned to her bodice: gold, with rubies and white enamel. It was like the one my mother used to pin onto the lapel of a smart tweed jacket she'd made herself, and that she said was a family heirloom. I began to feel conspicuous, so I joined the group in front of the Lely.

"Doesn't he look a berk?" muttered Derek to Gail, indicating the guide, who was talking about the effects of light falling on satin drapery. Finally he said: "And that concludes my little exposition." "Thank you so much," Gail said.

"I'll leave you to enjoy the rest of the room." And he went into the next one, where there were some damp people in raincoats looking at the tapestries, and we could soon hear his voice droning on. Colin was over by the book case which filled the end wall.

"The Sworn Book of Honorius!" he said. "I wonder what that's about? How provoking, the book case is locked!"

"They used to buy books by the yard, didn't they?" said Derek. "I'm sure they never read them."

"You must look at this picture – you missed it," said Donna, taking my arm. She hustled me past Lord and Lady Malison to a dark corner on the other side of the window.

"The guide told us all about her. It's the previous Lady Malison – the original witch! And who does she remind you of?"

I looked at the portrait. It was a bit like the ones of Lord and Lady Malison, but from an earlier time. The woman in it had long black hair, with part of it coming forward over her shoulder. She was wearing the brooch, and holding a book. She had thin eyebrows, a pointy nose and yellow-green eyes.

"Don't you think she looks awfully like you?"

"Everybody looked like me in Tudor times," I said. "It was the way they painted people. It was fashionable to be pale."

"They used white lead as make-up," said Nadine. "It was poisonous. But she's got your hair and eyes – even ears!"

"But look at the later portraits – they gave everybody the fashionable face. I'm surprised they didn't notice."

"They just wanted a record of their clothes," said Derek. "To display their wealth and status."

"Now I want to see the upstairs," said Nadine, "And the four-poster beds where Lady Thing was ravished by the Duke of Whatsit."

"I'll catch you up," I said, and they left me alone looking at the portrait of myself. But then someone behind me giggled and said: "Such utter tosh they spout!" I turned round to find a girl dressed as someone from the 30s – very Biba in a floaty cream dress with orange flowers.

"The other guides? How much was tosh?" I asked.

She gasped and put her hand to her mouth. "Oh jiminy cricket! You can see me! Most people can't."

"Oh – you're...?"

"That's right. It's not like in the booklet, there aren't any headless horsemen or ladies in black. Come up to the gallery where we can chat – there's nobody about. I've been dying for someone to talk to."

"OK," I said. "Where is it?"

"Go up the main staircase and turn to the left – I'll meet you there!"

She pointed to the door into the hall and when I looked back she wasn't there any more. Ghosts are like that – you don't see them come and go. I hurried through the hall and up the staircase.

CHAPTER NINE

At the top of the stairs was the long gallery, as she'd said. There were bookcases and cupboards, and chairs and tables pushed against the wall. I walked to the end and sat down on a window seat. The rain striking the leaded panes turned the view into a green blur.

"Oh, there you are!" said the ghost from behind me, and she came and sat in the seat with me. "We used to have tennis courts down there. And I'm sure the sun shone all the time. So, have you met some of us before? You didn't seem very surprised."

"Yes, a couple. We used to meet in Lyons in Oxford Street. So you're a Malison? Why did you say something was 'utter tosh'?"

"Oh, everything the guides say! Half the things downstairs were bought in a sale. When Croft Hall was burned down they carried a lot of stuff out onto the lawns and saved it, pictures and books and china."

"I think I remember the story."

"And the man who bought our house got hold of a lot of it. There were some rather good pictures and he pretends they are past Malisons. Some of the paintings he's put up are even fakes! It was the Croft Hall lot who sold their souls to the devil, not us! We've been boringly respectable for generations."

"So what were they called? The Croft Hall lot?"

"Oh, what was their name? Something funny like Bampfylde. No - Blanchflower. But he kept our things - look on that shelf, there's Rupert's old Meccano set! And our croquet set is in that box. And the fairy books, and Biggles, and my old school stories. Did you ever read the Chalet School? And he's stopped the roofs leaking. Opening the place to the public was a clever idea."

"It all must have cost a lot."

"Yes, he seems to be a millionaire or something. He's called Mr Dominus, and he lives here. I'd tell you all about him, except I can never get into his rooms. He doesn't mingle with the visitors, he leaves that to those idiots dressed in my grandparents' old clothes."

"What was it like back then?"

"Well, it was lovely for a while. There were lots of us, and my parents gave house parties, and the place was always full. I was the youngest. My brothers and sisters and their friends did a lot of amateur theatricals, they were always dressing up, and playing charades, and dancing to the gramophone. Mr Dominus has kept our old gramophone and all our records – the ones that didn't get broken! He even plays them sometimes."

"So then what happened?"

"Well, at some point I..."

"I see."

"I left the earthly plane, as the spiritualists say. I used to come and tease them when they were holding séances. It was fashionable. More fun than bridge!"

Ghosts never go into much detail about the afterlife, and I've learned not to ask. She went on: "My sisters got married, and my brothers, well, the war, you know. And then the American soldiers came. In the end, the place went to some cousins. Every time the roof sprang a leak they'd go up and put a bucket under the hole, and they ended up living in the kitchen and the housekeeper's room. And everybody's things and clothes were still around. And they had nothing really to do. Anyway, they left too, and the house was sold."

"It sounds rather sad. I'm Anna, by the way – what's your name?"

"Joan."

"Hang on, somebody's coming."

"Oh yes – well, DO come again. It's lovely to talk."

"You can tell me more about the old days, and the Malisons and the Blanchflowers!" I looked out the window again, and heard her say "Toodle-pip!" as Donna thundered up the stairs calling "Yoohoo!"

"Here I am!" I said, getting up and walking towards the staircase.

"Come on," said Donna. "I've had enough of this morgue!"

"What happened up here?" said Nadine, looking around.

Donna consulted the pamphlet. "They walked up and down on rainy days, and played games and danced – that was in Elizabethan times. We'd better go – it'll be closing time soon."

"Hadn't we better find Gail and Derek?"

"I think they went to look at some old kitchens," said Nadine.

"Or so they said," said Donna.

We went downstairs and back to our quarters and sat in the telly room watching Nationwide until it was time to cook dinner.

"Not much to write up today," said Donna, seeing Gail writing in a notebook with PTL written on the cover.

"I'm making notes about the house," she said.

"What does PTL mean? Please take lettuce? People teach Latin?"

"It stands for Praise The Lord," said Gail. "We're on cooking duty, Anna, shall we go?"

Gail took charge and told me what to do. Mainly I chopped up a lot of cabbage and she fried it with raisins, and boiled a vat of brown rice. The dish was OK with grated cheese, and yoghourt and chutney tipped over. For pudding there were apples, bananas and Kitkats.

While we were clearing up, Jonathan came in and said "Come along, everybody, it's time for Gareth's lecture and I know you don't want to miss that."

I got a seat next to Donna, Nadine and Jonathan.

"How did you like your trip round the stately home?" asked Jonathan politely. Gareth was faffing about with slides and saying "I wooooon't be a minute" in a northern accent. The boys laughed and said "Nooooo you wooooon't!"

"It was quite fun," said Nadine. "Why can't we sleep on those four-poster beds?"

"It might be somebody's bedroom," said Donna. "People still live there, you know."

"Not the Malisons, though, they died out, didn't they say?" said Nadine. "Anyway, we saw this picture that looked exactly like Anna, and it was of a famous witch!"

"You don't have any noble blood, do you, Anna?" asked Jonathan.

"Not that I know of," I said. Joan hadn't said the Blanchflowers had titles. "I thought it just looked Gothic."

"Yes," said Jonathan. "I know the one you mean. Back then they painted everyone with almond eyes and fine brows."

Roland and Fabia came in and sat at the front. Roland was wearing a safari jacket and a matching hat with a zip pocket in the brim. I wondered what you could keep in it apart from bus tickets or some spare cash.

"Simmer down everybody," said Gareth. "Now I intend not to go on for too long. I'll just baaaasically give you a few points about flint artefacts – let's hope we'll find some more, as such! And maybe next week if the rain keeps up you can all have a gooooo at making some. We'll need a squad to measure the stooones in the circle at some point, too, I believe."

"Thank you, Gareth, it's all under control," interjected Roland.

Jonathan went up to the projector again and put up a lot of slides with drawings of various types, and photos. Gareth explained them, and the boys laughed every time he said "As such". It was quite dull.

I read the pottery book in bed that night, while Nadine read a paperback. "What's that about?" asked Donna.

"It's called Still She Wished for Company," said Nadine. She put it face down on her locker and turned her light out.

"Isn't that a folk song or something? I thought we'd had enough of those." Donna turned out her light as well. Gail was already asleep.

"Something comes down the chimney in bits," I said.

"I suppose it's time for the Beast to start up howling again," said Nadine.

"Someone in the pub told me they never heard anything before the dig with Sir Finamore Whitelock," I said.

"Yes, I saw you talking to the local yokels. Did they say 'ooh ar'?"

"Not quite."

"Is it a ghost story, Nadine?" asked Donna.

"The book? I think it is, sort of. I'm not sure. The past and the present get mixed up. I hope those ghosts stay next door and don't come into the stables."

"Have you ever seen a ghost walk through a wall?" asked Donna.

"No, I haven't," I answered truthfully.

A faint howl came from the moor and Nadine sat up. "You're our witch, Anna. You do something."

"What can I do?"

"Use your powers! Chant a spell!"

# 53

"Oh, OK. I think there are some in Roland's book. I'll look them up. Goodnight."

I lay in the dark, listening for sounds from the moor, but heard only the rain on the roof. So was the picture that looked like me my mother's mother or my father's? Perhaps she wasn't a Blanchflower at all. Is she me? Am I really 300 years old? Have I just forgotten it all? There is a Lethe potion in the recipe book my mother left for me – I copied it all out, along with the odd bits of paper stuck in it, which might be even older. I gave the real book to my lawyers to put in the bank.

The River Lethe was the river of forgetting in Greek mythology. When you arrived in the afterlife you said "I am the child of earth and starry heaven", and the guardians let you drink the chill waters of Memory. The waters of Lethe were next to a cypress tree and you were supposed to avoid them.

But what if you wanted to come back? Am I her, returned? If I can't have children I can't be my own grandmother, and besides, I remember being little, when we lived in a village in the woods. And I remember being 10 and going to the convent, and meeting my old friends Murray and Elspeth again. They remembered me from primary school where we were all about six. I'm just me. I'm really 22. I fell asleep to the sound of rain.

CHAPTER 10

We fell into a routine quite quickly. We trekked to the village for chocolate and cigarettes, and the boys found an old table tennis set and put it up in one of the empty stables. They're organising a tournament, so that lets me out. I looked in the other stables, that used to have horses or ponies in, in case anybody had left a whole Victorian plate or an apostle spoon lying around. I didn't find any treasures, apart from an old blue windcheater hanging behind some sacks. I brushed the cobwebs off it and tried it on. The sleeves were a bit long, but otherwise it fitted. It might keep out the rain better than the cagoule, which was useless, so I borrowed it.

I finished the book on pottery and started again at the beginning. That was when I rang Mike to send me my Tarot cards and a few more paperbacks. I wonder if they'd notice if I nicked some books from Malison Grove? I'd seen some PG Wodehouse in the long gallery.

I needed the windcheater as we did a lot of trowelling in the drizzle and got taken to look at the trenches the grown-ups are digging near the stone circle. Bridget was mopping its floor with a sponge and squeezing it into a bucket as Roland pointed out various features. "British archaeology is all stains in the soil!" he said. We plodded back in the rain and Pete said Fabia was setting up a sieve for the spoil heaps and I could do that.

The others were trowelling at the other end of the trench, and Fabia and I struggled to put up the frame to hang the sieve off. She had on a felt Stetson with a scarf round the crown and her glasses were getting misted up.

"Damn this thing!" said Fabia, as the construction collapsed a third time. "Do we have to use it?" But Pete came up with a hammer and some wedges and soon it was much steadier. He brought us over some trays.

"You can take them down to the tent as and when!" he said, smiling and leaving us to it.

"It's being so cheerful as keeps me going," said Fabia in a dreary tone. Then she added: "You won't remember, it was a radio show from the war."

She shovelled some of the earth from a wheelbarrow into the sieve and swung it from side to side. The earth fell through onto a tarpaulin, and some stones and other lumps remained.

"Basically you just pick through whatever's left, and keep anything that looks interesting," she said. "I'll do it with you for a bit."

So we stood in the rain, rocking the sieve back and forth and picking stuff out of it, mostly without speaking. I held up a piece of flint.

"Yes, that's a possible," she said. This went on for a while, and I felt rather awkward. So to break the silence I said: "You'd think midsummer would be hot and sunny, wouldn't you? Like when you were here 20 years ago."

"Nineteen years ago. Yes, glorious weather, fortunately for the filming. Bit of a shock to see my hair. We all set it in curlers in those days, apart from Jeannette. Hers was too long, and straight, like yours. You're lucky you missed all that. Painful to sleep on. Have you ever had it cut?"

"No, my mother wouldn't let me."

"How Victorian. Do we think this is anything? Fragment of burnt wood. It can go in the tray. It wasn't long after the American army left. You know they were stationed here during the war."

"Thank goodness for the showers, anyway. But I expect you have a bath in your B&B."

"Oh, all mod cons."

"Was Jeannette the other girl in some of the programmes?"

"Oh yes, Miss Liu or Wu, something like that. She had rich parents in Hong Kong who sent her over here to school and university. She wasn't really part of our set, but Sir Finamore picked her for the programmes. I expect the Beeb wanted a bit of glamour. If they could see us now! How about you – is this how you imagined spending your student years? Slave labour in a downpour?"

"I hadn't really thought about it. I did A Levels and then they said when not do a degree? So did Jeannette become an archaeologist like the rest of you?"

"No - she didn't stick it. Actually she upped and left the dig after a week or two. Always worried about her manicure – probably just wanted to be on telly and it wasn't what she expected. We lose a lot of girls - change their major to history and then get married and have sprogs. Now I'm going to leave you to it. I'm dying for a fag. And maybe a large gin. When you've got some stuff together, take it to the tent and wash it, and then you can take it to the barn and help Gareth with the labelling."

"OK."

She slouched off down the hill and I carried on until everybody had a break.

"Having fun?" asked Gavin.

"Time of my life," I said unsmilingly.

"If wet, in the vicarage!" said Colin and for once everybody laughed.

Pete came over with the students' finds trays and said: "Let's take all these down the tent."

"Just an excuse to get into the dry!" said Malcolm.

So I picked up my trays and we went off. We said hello to the kids and the teacher on duty and put everything down on a spare plastic-covered table. Pete had a look at what the children had washed and told them they were doing a grand job. "Anna, you can do some more sorting when you have a moment. Did you read the pottery book?"

"I liked it so much I've started again at the beginning."

"With Anglo-Saxon shelly ware!"

"My favourite. Actually I like these bits with pictures on."

"I found THIS one!" said one of the little girls, showing me a miniature soup tureen with a transfer print on the side of a boy playing with a toy horse, and I admired it.

Pete filled me a plastic bowl from the tap and I started scrubbing the stuff from the trench, while he got a box full of clean pottery and put it down next to me and started going through it.

"Probably been occupation here for millennia," he said. "It was a sacred site, and pilgrims had to stay somewhere. Now if we could find some round houses..."

"Aren't there some up on the moor?"

"Yes, there are, hut circles, a village, we'll look at them soon. You can only get there on foot."

"You weren't on the original dig, were you?"

"No, I was a working archaeologist by then. Sir Finamore loved his students. He was the kind of guy who had acolytes."

"There's nobody like that at Regent," I said. "Our lecturers are all rather boring. It was more fun doing Class Civ, but the person who taught it has left."

I had known people with acolytes - Gilles, for example - but I probably shouldn't mention them.

"How are you fitting in? With most of them coming from Blackhampton - and speaking of people with acolytes..."

"You mean Roland?"

"Yes, he's dying to become Sir Finamore the Second."

"I'm getting on OK," I said.

"How are the girls?"

"Gail is all right, but she's a bit of a missionary."

"One of the born-again lot, I hear."

"Is that what they are? I used to be a Catholic, but she doesn't think much of them! The others think I'm posh because I come from Surrey and went to boarding school."

"They want a handle to tease you with. Don't let it get you down. I notice you don't go to the pub often."

"I'm not much of a one for pubs really."

"Anyway, don't mind the boys. Boys will be boys."

"They're like the boys at secondary school."

"I hope you found a few nice ones back then?"

"Just a couple. I met one in a café."

"Do tell!"

"We weren't supposed to go because it had a jukebox and bikers went there. So we met some bikers and my friend Lynn is married to one of them now."

"Well, that's not very exciting! Anyway, the boys probably tease you because you're married and not available crumpet."

"Not what?"

"It's usual on these trips. You know, miles from civilization, boyfriends or girlfriends left behind, equal number of girls and boys. And of course Gail's out too, she thinks it's a sin, so Donna and Nadine can take their pick. And there are plenty of haylofts, if you fancy the idea. They've even got hay in them."

"Really, how do you know? But I think they paired off at Blackhampton – Donna with Malcolm and Nadine with Gavin."

"Fair enough. And Bridget has a husband and some dogs, and Roland and Fabia have been together for ages, and Gareth has a wife and kids, and Jonathan isn't interested. And you wouldn't consider an old crock like him, would you? But you didn't put your rings back on."

"I thought they might get damaged."

"I hear your husband's a policeman?"

"You are a terrible gossip, aren't you?"

"Colin might be out of the running too, I hear he used to be a choirboy." He made a limp-wristed gesture.

"I don't think I know any gay people," I said. "Oh yes I do. Ianthe – one of my friends from the hostel."

"Did she try and convert you?"

"No – just told me not to get married and to have a career instead. She's got very Women's Lib. And then I kind of fell into archaeology. Anyway, what about you? I mean, are you married?"

"Oh, I'm an incurable romantic. I'm onto my third wife, or at least I was before we parted."

"Do you have any children?"

"A few – they're grown up, though. I got married too young, like you. But you don't have any, unless you've put them in an orphanage for the duration?"

"No, we haven't got any."

"You've got plenty of time. How old are you?"

"You are nosy, as well! I'm 22. I'll be 23 soon, my birthday's after midsummer."

Soon it was time for the kids to go, and we followed them down the path with the clean finds. We put them on a trestle table, and Pete went to pick over some of the other stuff, and Jonathan came over to me.

"Hello, Anna!" he said. "Now what have we got here?"

"It's what came out from sieving the spoil up in the students' trench."

"The cursus, yes. You know it leads to some barrows at the other end?"

"We haven't really had time to look at them."

"They could be next on the agenda, if the owners give us permission. We're still not really sure what these straight tracks were for. People used to think they were drove roads – for cattle and sheep, you know. Now, let me talk you through the procedure. You've washed everything, oh good. That's point one!"

And he showed me how to record everything in an exercise book, and write labels with the date, and put things in little plastic bags WITH their label.

"Even little bits of charcoal?"

"Yes, it'll all go in the record. If there's a big enough deposit, we can put it under the microscope. If we find out which tree this is from," he said, holding up a small black chunk, "it might tell us something. The students are turning up a lot. Almost more than we can deal with."

"Ritual!" called Gareth from the other end. "Sir Finamore was right."

"Yes, probably ritual deposits – you know they sacrificed precious objects, sometimes bending or breaking them first. And any pottery goes to Pete – he's I/C potsherds."

Jonathan got me a stool and I started work. I didn't mind this part, organising it all. He stayed nearby, working on some other things and writing on index cards in very neat script.

"How does it feel to be back?" I asked. "You were on the original dig, weren't you?"

"Yes – lurking in the background, and trying to dig up a megalith!"

"Did you really, or was that just for the cameras?"

"You remember the legend? That there's a gold hoard under one of them?"

"The BBC would have liked that!"

"Wouldn't they? And the British Museum. But all we did was rock it a bit and tip it sideways."

"Which one was it?"

"Perhaps Roland remembers. The Archaeological Society made us put it back where it was, as it was. Of course, sometimes megaliths fall over, and interesting deposits have been found. What did you think of the programme? It's a relic itself by this time. Seems like the Dark Ages, even if it was only 20 years ago. Those old cameras were huge!"

"I was looking at the fashions – the 50s are coming back."

"There's a vogue for reviving the past, isn't there? Nostalgia, they call it. Have they reached the 50s already?"

"Fabia looked pretty, and the other girl?"

"Jeannette, yes, she didn't stay the course. She'd been sent over from Hong Kong to a posh boarding school and then her parents thought she ought to go to university. Perhaps archaeology was undersubscribed."

"Did she go back home?"

"I expect so – she just packed her bags and left and we were a man short."

"You mean she sneaked off?"

"Someone probably drove her to the station. Now, how about that tea?"

Gareth came over from the other end and we had tea with chocolate biscuits.

"You'll have to get us another lot of finds tomorrow," said Gareth, looking out of the bar door at the muddy puddles. "But maybe it'll clear up."

"Roland and Fabia are turning up quite a lot too," said Jonathan.

"But they're too grand to wash, sort and label."

"There's something you could do, though, when you've finished with those," said Jonathan. "Come and have a look at this."

He indicated something covered with a cloth, on a little stand underneath one of those magnifying glasses that people use for embroidery. He took the cloth off to reveal a large lump of rusty-looking mud.

"It looks like an old battery," I said.

"Perhaps it is! Except it came from an early occupation layer up near the circle. By the weight it ought to contain some metal. When you've got a moment, you could start scraping away at the dirt with a toothpick and a paintbrush. Have you ever done anything like that?"

"I've done some restoration, china and textiles. I wouldn't mind trying."

"We'll arrange it. But only when we're here – we need to supervise. Don't get too excited – it may just be slag. Which will be interesting in itself, of course."

"Of course. Couldn't you just soak it in a washing-up bowl?"

"We don't know what's inside it – it might be some material water would damage! It might even include some cloth. Don't forget it's Roland's lecture this evening – he'll want the full complement. No disappearing off to the pub!"

"What's he lecturing about?"

"His pet theory about ancient religions – I hope you've read his book?"

"Yes, a couple. Lots of blood and gore."

"It sells copies. No worse than turning it into a televisual experience."

"But doooon't say we said so," said Gareth. "We have to be respectful to the Lord High Panjandrum!"

They were all about the same age, but Roland was a Prof, and Gareth and Jonathan seemed to do the menial jobs and not have titles. So we carried on until nearly dinner-time, and it was quite interesting. I was glad I'd got a special job to do.

\*\*\*

Roland's lecture was about early ritual, with rather a lot about a sacred grove hung with rotting corpses.

"We rely for this information on early writers such as Saxo Grammaticus and Adam of Bremen," he explained. "Saxo was keen to point out that Odin was a 'false' god. It all took place at Gamli Uppsala, which was also the location of the Thing of all Swedes, held until the Middle Ages."

The boys laughed.

"It gets better," said Roland. "It was part of a festival called Disablot."

More laughter, and he put up some slides of old engravings. "This is what Saxo called 'ghastly and infamous'. 'There even dogs and horses hang beside human beings', he tells us."

Whimpers from the girls and Bridget.

"The Romans were not impressed: 'The whole Gallic race is addicted to religious ritual', wrote Julius Caesar. 'Consequently those suffering from serious maladies or subject to the perils of battle sacrifice human victims. Some weave huge figures of wicker and fill their limbs with humans, who are then burned to death when the figures are set afire.' Slide please, Jonathan. 'They suppose that the gods prefer this execution to be applied to thieves, robbers, and other malefactors taken in the act, but in default of such they resort to the execution of the innocent.'"

Colin put a hand up.

"Yes, Colin?" said Roland.

"What about gibbets? I mean, heads were displayed on Temple Bar in the 18th century, by Civilised Man?"

"I think you mean 'enlightened'. I don't think any researcher has traced a connection – but the field is open if you're looking for a PhD subject."

He carried on and it all got even more grisly and everybody took notes.

CHAPTER 11

"There's a parcel for you!" said Donna at breakfast a few days
later, handing me a big box wrapped in brown paper. "Don't you
want to open it?"

"I'll open it in the dorm," I said. "I asked Mike to send me a few
things. Nothing very exciting."

"Who's Mike?" asked Malcolm. "The bluebottle you're married to?
Does he wear a helmet?"

"And nothing else!" said Gavin.

"He's a detective sergeant," I said, getting up. Back in the dorm I
cut the string with some nail scissors. Inside were my Tarot cards,
my crystal ball, some more detective stories, and the book where
I'd copied out my mother's magical recipes. I hoped Mike hadn't
looked inside. There was a letter as well.

"Sweetheart," it read. "Here are the cards, I found them
wrapped up in black velvet like you said. The book was with them
so I put it in too in case it's the instructions. And I thought you
might like the crystal ball! It got rather dusty, I can't keep up
your standard of cleaning. Can't wait for the summer to be over
for a change – or could you come for a weekend? Isn't there a
holiday at midsummer? We could go to Camber Sands again, or
maybe in September before your term starts. Hand in hand they
danced on the strand, by the light of the silvery moon. See – I'm
going spare with nobody to talk to. Ring soon! Love you lots." And
a row of kisses.

I locked the stuff in my cupboard, but left the paperbacks on the
top. Having the recipe book made Mum feel nearer, and I'd
written quite a lot of class. civ. notes in the back which might
come in useful if the girls were really frightened of ghosts.

The day was like the others – I sieved, and sorted pottery, and
washed and labelled, and spent about an hour picking gently at
the lump of mud that may contain a mystery object or nothing.
They found lots more flint blades which got passed up the line to
Gareth, who drew them and photographed them and identified
the stones they were made of. I nipped down to the village at
lunchtime (it's only about 10 minutes away) and bought some
sweets and a Woman's Own. I was reading it in the dorm when
the girls came in before dinner to tidy up.

"Knitting patterns!" said Donna. "How can you be a feminist and
knit?"

"'You must have a gilet!'" I read. "Actually I'm rotten at
knitting."

"What's a gilet?" asked Nadine, brushing her hair. "Oh, just look at my nails!"

"A sleevess cardie."

"Let's have a look – my God, what a frump!"

She chucked the magazine back at me.

"How can you read that tripe? The stories – all about finding the man of your dreams and becoming a domestic drudge."

"Sounds OK, apart from the drudge bit," I said. "I don't actually read the stories. We used to buy it at the convent for the problem pages and try and work out what on earth they were talking about."

They laughed at that, and when Nadine had finished filing her nails the two of them went off to play ping pong.


\*\*\*

The next day I went to the dorm before dinner to have a quick shower and wash my hair. When I came out in a dressing gown and a towel round my head Nadine was sitting on her bed with her back to me, with her face in her hands. She quickly sat up and blew her nose.

"Are you OK?" I asked, towelling my hair.

"Oh, I'm fine really. It's nothing."

"Is it a man?"

"You're very blunt! Perhaps you're assertive after all! No, it's nothing."

I carried on brushing my hair, and Donna came in. She looked at Nadine and said "Y'all roight?" in what she thought was a Liverpool accent. Nadine said, "Honestly, I'm fine. Just a fit of the weeps!" She got out her makeup kit and applied some Mary Quant Starkers nude foundation and drew her eyeliner back on.

"Probably PMT," said Donna. "And we're all pretty tired. Try an Evening Primrose capsule. You really have to take them for a week before, but you can have these, I can get some more."

"Thanks," said Nadine, taking the bottle. "Perhaps it's this place! It's getting me down, what with the rain and the ghosts and the howls!" She laughed rather shakily.

"You haven't seen any ghosts, have you?" asked Donna.

# 65

"No, but that old house is creepy if you ask me. Shabby and decaying and mouldy. And they said it had been renovated! God knows what it looked like before."

"Never mind! One more year and we graduate and go out into the big wide world!"

"One more year! I'd like a lot more than that," said Nadine. "I wish I could see into the future."

"Oh dear, you are feeling bleak!" said Donna. "Shall go for a couple of bevvies after dinner?"

"Actually Mike sent me my Tarot cards," I said. "They were in the parcel. Would you like to try it?"

"You do Tarot readings?" asked Donna, sounding quite interested in me for once.

"Yes – I started doing it in the hostel, or was it at school? No, then I just used ordinary cards. And tealeaves, but everybody has teabags now. I remember, I bought the Tarot cards at the Atlantis bookshop opposite the British Museum."

That was when I'd made up a spell bringing statues to life, never thinking it would work.

"Can we try it?" asked Donna and I said fine. Gail came in and got out a clean shirt.

"So exciting, Gail," said Donna. "Anna's going to tell our fortunes!" I got out the cards and pulled a spare locker over to use as a table. Gail stayed standing. Suddenly she said rather loudly:

"I have to tell you that it's Satanic and I won't be a party to it!"

"It's only a bit of fun!" said Nadine, though she still looked rather anxious.

"Honestly, I just get it out of the book!" I said, holding up the leaflet that comes with the pack of cards. "There is a picture of the devil, but it's just symbolic."

"I shall pray for you," said Gail, and picked up her shirt and went out to the bathroom.

"Oh no, she's going to put the kibosh on it now! Quick, before she comes back," said Donna.

"I can hear her chanting away in the shower," said Nadine. "But she seems to have got off with Derek – perhaps she won't be so holy for much longer. That's why they stayed behind the night we went out."

"Mike sent my class. civ. notes too," I said. "They say Ancient Greeks threw black beans out of the door at the restless dead. There are some beans in the store room."

"They'd probably sprout in this weather," said Donna. "And I thought the Ancient Greeks couldn't eat beans."

"That was Pythagoras."

"Didn't he have a theorem?"

"Do you want to be the querent - go first, I mean?" I asked Nadine, and laid out the cards while she sat on the end of her bed.

I shuffled them and she cut them, and I laid them out in the usual way – this is you, this covers you, this is the past and the future and so on.

"The Emperor! Probably Roland. 'Has total power over life and death'", I read from the book.

Nadine shivered. "I thought you were going to cheer me up! What about me? Tell me about me?"

"Here's the star – it means hope and optimism."

"She's got no clothes on - that looks like you!" said Donna.

"You'll have your turn in a minute, shut up!"

"It means light at the end of the tunnel and moving into better conditions. It points to fulfilment in every respect."

"Oh, goody! I hope that's not like the riddle of the Sphinx. I mean, what do the spirits mean by fulfilment? They might have different ideas."

"Aid us, O naiads and dryads!" I said. "Show us the truth that underlies appearances."

"Look out, she's going into a trance!" said Donna.

I turned up the Page of Wands, who stands in a desert with the pyramids in the distance, but as I looked at the card they turned into megaliths, and the Page turned into Gavin, with a dark-haired man standing behind him.

"I see a fair man guarding the triple gate," I said, and both of them giggled. "But there's someone behind him I can't quite see. He wants to pass through, but the fair man is in the way."

I turned up the Three of Swords, which is three swords piercing a heart. Even if a card looks grim, the book usually manages to give it a helpful message.

I pointed at it: "This could be a facing of facts, an argument, a telling of home truths that clears the air." They always say that being beastly to each other "clears the air".

"And here's the Knight of Cups – he has Mercury's wings on his helmet. That means protection. And I see..."

Gail came back into the room and made a lot of noise putting her stuff away. She sat with her back to us again. "Don't mind Miss Skeptical Attitude," Donna muttered.

"People think you are confident but you are really quite shy. I see you doing well in your exams and finding an interesting job," I said, making it up. I've never seen the future – maybe because it hasn't happened yet. "Perhaps nothing to do with archaeology. And you find happiness with a dark man whose name begins with a J. This may mean nothing to you now, but I'll leave it with you."

I gathered up the cards and was glad to see Nadine looked happier. I was sure she'd be better off with somebody else. Gavin might be good-looking, but he shouldn't make her cry.

"My turn now!" said Donna, so we went through the same procedure. I told her she didn't like to show her real feelings and found it hard to believe that people would care. "Too often, you blame yourself." I'd written a list of statements that would fit anybody in the back of the book. I turned up the Empress, but she transformed into a middle-aged woman standing in a kitchen wearing a flowery apron, so I said "Your mother would love it if you rang her."

"Not sure I've got anything to say to her," said Donna. "Well, thanks."

"I'll find those notes about ghosts," I said, riffling through Mum's recipe book. "Spirits cannot touch primroses. But there won't be any around at this time of year."

"Take one of those Evening Primrose capsules, Nadine, quick!" said Donna. "I've got some primroses in my pressed-flower kit, but I left it behind at Blackhampton. What else?"

"Oregano increases happiness and helps loved ones who have passed over."

"There's a packet in the kitchen!"

"Place one dried bay leaf in each corner of a room, cabbages are sacred to the moon, garlic…"

"Keeps off vampires, yes, we know. Perhaps the Beast is a vampire. And I'm sure Gail has a crucifix, haven't you, Gail?" She didn't answer.

"When attacked by wolves, use wolf's bane."

"Yes, wave some flowers at them, that'll work, I don't think! I wish I'd done Class. Civ., it sounds fun."

"I wonder what it looks like. There might be some in the garden. Oh, and it's terribly poisonous."

"Let's get the ingredients," said Donna. "Cheer up, Gail, just because you don't believe in witches!"

Gail turned round. "There ARE witches!" she said. "And they get their powers from the DEVIL!"

"This is all getting very medieval," said Nadine. "But let's get those herbs." So the three of us went into the kitchen, where Malcolm and Gavin were making Cornish pasties, and got the beans, oregano, basil and bay leaves.

"Oi, we might need those!" said Gavin.

"You don't put bay leaves in Cornish pasties," said Nadine.

"You do in mine," said Gavin.

"We're just doing a bit of a spell," said Donna. "We don't want the ghosties and ghoulies from next door coming and haunting us."

"They just make that stuff up to get more visitors," said Malcolm.

"What about the Beast?"

"I don't think dried bayleaves will work against HIM," said Gavin. "Are you coming to the pub later?"

"Might do," said Nadine, and we went back to the dorm. They put a bayleaf in each corner of the room, and scattered some dried oregano about.

"It doesn't smell of anything much," I said. "Fresh is better - there's bound to be some in the gardens. It grows wild."

I flung a handful of black beans out of the door, chanting: "By marjoram I expel thee, by Allium Sativum I command thee, by Laurus Nobilis I deplore thee, Depart and do not bother me."

"That sounds impressive," said Donna.

"I did botany A Level too."

"I expect birds will come and eat them," said Nadine. "Still, jolly for the birds. Where's Godly Gail? Disappeared off with Derek again, I bet."

"Did the Ancient Greeks really believe all this?" asked Donna.

We ate the pasties, and Malcolm told a revolting anecdote about a casserole that people kept adding to until it putrefied. Then the girls and Gavin and Malcolm went to the pub, Gail and Derek wandered off hand in hand into the drizzle, and I played ping pong with Colin and he beat me.

CHAPTER 12

The next day it wasn't actually raining, just grey and damp, so Roland sent us all up onto the moor with Gareth and Pete, saying we had to go some time and why not take advantage of a break in the April showers.

"Wear comfortable shoes!" said Gareth. I put on plimsolls, jeans, a cardie and the windcheater. Donna and Nadine laced their feet into walking boots. We set off, passing Roland and Fabia and Bridget in their trench, which they don't say much about. Then the stone circle came into view, half surrounded by stunted oak trees on the downhill side. We stopped and went "Wow!"

"Come on, chaps!" said Pete. "You'll get quite sick of the stone circle when you've spent days plotting it. It's uphill all the way from here."

"This was a corpse road!" said Gareth, as we reached the top and turned north.

"Delightful!" said Nadine.

"The upland farmers carried the dead in coffins to the nearest church, which could be miles away."

"Why are there no churches up here? Too pagan?" asked Colin.

"They tend to be in villages, and they're in the valleys. The cursus you're digging up may be an early version of the road idea."

"What do we do if the mist comes down?" asked Nadine. "We might end up walking round and round in circles."

"I've got my trusty Ordnance Survey map!" said Pete. It was in a plastic pocket on the front of his army trousers. "And a compass." He was wearing a safari jacket covered in pockets, and a navy blue knitted hat.

"The corpse road – it comes in the Lyke-Wake Dirge," said Colin. "Do you know the Britten version, Anna?" And he sang a verse, rather well.

This ae night, this ae night
Every night and all,
Fire and fleet and candlelight
And Christ receive thy soul.

"Colin's off again!" said Gavin.

"That's nice," said Pete, who was bringing up the rear, probably so that none of us got lost. "You could put guitar chords to that."

"I hope the Bridge of Dread is not on our route," said Colin.

"It's not marked on the map," said Pete. "But we should come to the hut circles if we keep on going this way."

We trudged on, past spiky bog grass and small dark pools.

"There's a bottomless pool up here somewhere, isn't there?" asked Colin.

"It dried up in a drought," said Pete. "It's really quite shallow. You don't want to believe everything you hear."

"We're almost at the hut circles!" called Gareth from the front. When we got there, they were rather unimpressive, just rings of stones with a gap for the door, but he explained they had turf roofs and looked like yurts.

"The weather was nicer in the Neolithic and people grew crops up here," he said. "We could try a bit of field-walking! Those walls are actual field boundaries."

We wandered about looking at the ground, but only found a few stones with holes in, which we pocketed.

"You certainly have to use your imagination," said Nadine, walking into one of the huts. "You'd get a decent view, though." We looked around at the moor stretching far away. The sun shone feebly, floating in a patch of clouds.

"Might be time to break out the sandwiches," said Gareth.

"Swap you a ham and lettuce for a date and cream cheese, Gail," said Donna.

"These stone walls are hard on the bum," said Nadine.

"We should really be eating acorns," said Colin.

"Aren't they poisonous?"

"Not if you soak them first. It's why the Druids worshipped oak trees, you know."

"Plenty of oak trees in the wood," said Gareth. "You could try making acorn stew."

"I can't think why we haven't already," said Nadine. "I bet they taste foul. I don't suppose there's a rubbish bin up here."

"No, we'd better take all our paper bags – shove them in your rucksack," said Gareth. "And then we'd better move on. Up ahead you can see the tor where a witch lived – it really is one of the highest points on the moor."

It was a huge pile of boulders and we had to make quite a long detour round it.

"What did she want to live all the way up here for?" asked Donna.

"She conjured up mists to lure travellers into bogs," Gareth explained.

"What for?" asked Nadine.

"I expect she ate them – she wasn't a vegetarian," said Malcolm.

They walked on together and got ahead. Donna and Gavin pushed past, saying "Oooh, Surrey, I mean sorry!" Gavin looked back at us and said: "We'll have to keep an eye on those two! Getting far too friendly."

"Cheer up!" said Colin quietly as they caught up the others. "Where's your sense of humour?"

"I refuse to laugh when anybody says 'pint'. Or 'fart!'"

"Or 'wally'! Or is it 'prat', now? Do people still say 'right on'?"

"No, they stopped ages ago!"

"I'm going to start keeping a list."

Pete came up behind us and showed us where we were on the map.

"Do you ever feel that none of this is real?" asked Colin, looking around at the misty landscape.

"None of this?"

"It's just a front, and we don't know what's really going on."

"Colin, you're barmy! Though I suppose it does look a bit unreal," said Pete. "Come on, let's try and catch the others up."

"It's not fair, they go hiking at the weekends," I said.

"I'm a Young Rambler myself," said Colin. But we hurried and closed the gap between us.

"I think you might say the mist is coming down now," said Pete.

It grew thicker and thicker. It didn't exactly swirl, there wasn't enough wind, but I could only just see Gareth at the head of the crocodile.

CHAPTER 13

"Let's stop here for a breather," said Gareth. "I want to point out the three counties you can see from here. The view's amazing, don't you think?"

Everybody laughed. We were surrounded by a thick grey blanket.

"Look, here's a giant hole with a stone in it," said Donna. It was about her height, with paths leading off from it into the murk.

"The villagers passed their children through the hole when they had whooping cough," said Gareth. "Look through it and you can see into other realms. The same goes for those hagstones you've been picking up."

"Sometimes called Adder stones," said Malcolm. "Or even Odin stones."

We took it in turns peering through the hole, but we could only see another stone set up in perspective.

"Let's pass Anna through it," said Gavin. "Nobody else would fit."

"I've been inoculated," I said and they actually laughed.

"Oh look, Gavin," said Malcolm. "The footprint of a gigantic hound!"

"I can't see anything," said Pete. "Oh yes – visitors probably bring their dogs up here." He peered at his map, which was in a plastic envelope. "Good thing this monument is marked on the map. I'll find a more direct route. This way!"

He pointed to a path, and we proceeded down it. The others got ahead again, and I walked behind with Pete. We slogged on for quite a way, seeing nothing but gorse bushes and sheep and the occasional moor pony.

"Shame we didn't bring a thermos!" called Gareth faintly from in front.

"What did they sing as the Titanic went down?" wondered Pete. "Abide With Me? Colin can lead us. Colin!"

There was no answer. The boys began to sing rather raggedly, and Gail joined in.

"Have you got a Colin up there?" shouted Pete.

"Thought he was with you! Better count heads."

We bunched together, and no Colin appeared. "We'd better shout," said Gareth, and everybody shouted "Colin!" over and over again.

"Shush!" said Pete. "I thought I heard heavy footsteps. Isn't that him over there? Colin! Yoohoo! Shut up, everybody."

It was very quiet. There were faint ticking and trickling sounds, and then light, quick footsteps.

"That you, Col?" asked Malcolm.

"Only a sheep!" said Gavin, as one appeared down the track.

"What have you done with Colin?" Malcolm asked it.

"Colin, you have changed!" said Pete. The animal looked at us blankly, then bounced away over the tussocky grass.

"We'd better retrace our steps," said Gareth, so we went back to the stone with the hole, and shouted some more.

"He's just disappeared, like old Dr Hickmott," said Malcolm.

"Who was he?" asked Pete.

"A distinguished Pearmanite. Went out for a packet of fags and never returned."

"Probably had another wife and children in another town."

"Or the next street."

Gavin suggested splitting up, but Pete said we'd better stay in a bunch. The two tutors conferred.

"He can't really come to any harm. The mist will probably lift soon," said Gareth. "Basically, the main thing is to get you all home as quick as poss, and then ring the police."

So we set off again. As we went downhill the mist thinned. I looked back, and the cloud was sitting on top of the moor. We descended the steep hill to Malison Grove.

"On a clear day you can see the gardens," said Pete. Donna held her hagstone in front of her eye as if it was a telescope. "Can't see a thing. You try."

"What can we see? The realms beyond?" said Nadine languidly. She held hers up as well. "Not a sausage. That wood is in the way."

I was further up the hill. I looked through my hagstone and saw the lawns in bright sunshine, with little figures moving around, wearing long dresses and ruffs.

"What can you see?"

"Just the former inhabitants of Malison Grove."

"How do you know they're former?"

"They're wearing Elizabethan dress." Is there a word for telling the truth when you know no-one will believe you? It was probably Joan's sisters and friends playing charades.

Gareth led us down towards Roland and Fabia's trench, where Bridget was bent over, wearing unflattering dungarees.

"Hail, wanderers!" called Roland. "We expected you long ere this."

"You must be tired out!" Bridget raised her head from the dirt. "It's time for tea, anyway."

"Sorry, we're one short, Roland." said Gareth, rather sheepishly.

"Don't tell me you've lost one of them!" barked Roland.

"Yes, I'm afraid so."

"Well, what are you going to do about it?"

"I suppose if he doesn't turn up soon..."

"Don't hang about, ring the police now!"

"It's quite clear now, though," said Bridget

"It's still thick up on the top," said Gareth. "I'll go and ring them."

"Looks like carelessness!" said Fabia. "Roland, we'd better pack up here."

"Oh dear, I have put up a black," said Gareth as we went on down towards the stables, with Bridget following, tidying her hair with muddy hands. We flocked into the kitchen and I collapsed in a chair.

"Bags first for the shower," said Nadine.

"Did you have a good time before the mist came down?" asked Bridget.

"We saw the Hound's paw print, didn't we, Malcolm?" said Gavin.

"Did you really?"

"Yes, up by the holey stone. What's it called?"

"Just the Hole Stone, according to the map," said Pete.

"Perhaps it was a lost dog!" said Bridget. "Poor little thing."

"This one wasn't little. There must be a whole pack of them, judging by the howls," said Malcolm.

"I do miss my labradors. Did you pick up anything? Do any field walking?"

"Just these stones with holes in," said Nadine, putting her collection on the table.

"Can I have yours?" I said, getting mine out of my pocket. "I'm so used to washing finds." Donna gave me hers as well, and Gareth came in to report.

"Well, the local constabulary took me seriously. They said kids are always getting lost on what they called these 'outward bound' trips, trying to do seven tors in a day in a rainstorm and ending up with hypothermia. They're going to go out with torches and Alsatians."

"You're much later than we expected," said Bridget. "When you've showered and changed your footwear, why don't we go down the village and get fish and chips? I'll rejig the cooking rota tomorrow."

"Excellent idea!" said Pete, and we all scattered. I put my plimsolls to soak in a basin and washed the stones and laid them out on our windowsill.

"Looks quite pretty," said Donna.

"They ward off witches and ghosts and demons," I said.

"Oh, whoopee! We'll be OK then."

"I feel almost human," said Nadine, spraying eau de toilette on her neck. As we went out into the yard, where the others were gathering, Colin strolled in, muddy but still smiling.

"Well, where have YOU been?" said Pete. "We've got the plod out looking for you with bloodhounds. Or was it Alsatians? Gareth – you'd better call them off."

"Righty-ho!" said Gareth. "Glad to see you, mate. I'll catch up." And he went into the office to call the police.

"We're just off to the chippy," said Pete. "Do you think you can make it?"

"After a while, there doesn't seem any reason not to keep on walking," said Colin. "I think I lost you at the giant Polo mint." So we headed for the village and he came with us.

"Didn't you hear us calling?" asked Pete.

"Which way did you go? I was trying to go back the way we came, but I think I went north instead of north. I just heard a faint wailing, and a lot of barking."

"That must have been the police dogs."

"I had no idea where I was. Perhaps I was pixy-led. There are supposed to be pixies up on the Moor, along with everything else, aren't there? I listened for a stream - you can always follow one because they flow downhill, sometimes off the edge of cliffs - but I couldn't hear one, so I just carried on. I shouted for you occasionally. I saw a lot of sheep footprints and I thought they would lead me to a farm, but no go. There were dog footprints as well - the Hound obviously! - and an unfortunate sheep that had met an untimely end."

"In the Great Grympen Mire?" asked Pete.

"No, it had been gnawed by something. Well, the Hound has to eat."

"Ooh, yuk!" said Nadine.

"Then I thought I saw you, Pete, so I called out, but whoever it was didn't answer."

"Sure it was human?"

"He was far away - a bloke-shaped shadow in the mist."

"The Yeti!" said Gavin.

"Anwyay, he moved away and I followed. I thought he might be a shepherd or a farmer and lead me back to some sort of civilisation. I think we curved round in a sort of detour. There were lots of outcrops and then we were back at the hut circles. The mist dissolved, but I lost sight of the bloke. I decided I might as well go on going downhill even if I ended up miles away. If I hit a road I could always hitch back. But then I realised I was coming down the hill behind the house and it was plain sailing from there. I hope you weren't too worried."

"Gareth's just worried about his job," said Malcolm. "I don't think Roland's any too pleased."

"Lo, yonder - the Poseidon Fish Bar!" said Pete.

There was cod, coley, skate and rock on the menu, so we ordered cod, chips and pickled gherkins, which we ate sitting on benches by the wall of the churchyard. "If it's not shrouded in mist, we can have a look at the stone circle tomorrow," said Pete. "We ought to get on with surveying it, anyway."

While I was writing my report in the dorm, and my diary, I made up a quick spell and wrote it down. If the stones could move, and go down to the river to drink, I'd rather have them on my side. And they probably wouldn't look kindly on anybody who tried to unlock their secrets. I'd have to try and stay behind on my own so I could recite it.

CHAPTER 14

We headed for the circle with clipboards, tape measures, yardsticks and notebooks. I carried my stuff in a canvas shopping bag and Colin put his in a leather music case. The whole gang were there, apart from Bridget, who was trowelling in Roland's trench.

"They're pretty big, aren't they, these menhirs or dolmens?" said Colin, standing next to one. "Almost as big as Stonehenge, though not so shaped."

"That's what we've come to find out," said Roland, handing him a yardstick.

"I'm surprised they're not more famous."

"The family kept them under wraps – and the whole place was wooded until they were rediscovered in the 17th century. Now, get busy, folks! Jonathan will show you how to proceed."

We measured the maximum girth and height of the stones, and the distance between them, and plotted their position on a sketch plan. Jonathan took photos, and Gareth drew the megaliths, paying attention to their "facets".

"We're not short of granite here," he said. "No need to drag a megalith all the way from Wales."

"We had fun trying to raise one on an A-frame on Salisbury Plain," said Pete. "And pull it along on wooden rollers."

"That's what you always see them doing in books," said Nadine. "While Stone Age woman stayed at home in her round house."

"Toiling away spinning and weaving by hand," said Fabia. She was wearing a stripy T shirt and a knee-length denim skirt today, and espadrilles. I'd given up on looking presentable and was wearing jeans and a white sleeveless shirt.

"I suppose they cleared the trees," said Colin. "Vandalism, really."

"The Vandals were much later," said Fabia.

"And I suppose the family weren't so keen after the BBC fiasco. See any carvings, Gareth?"

Gareth was peering at a stony surface.

"You won't see any in this light," said Roland. "We'll have to wait till the sun's low in the sky. We're so near midsummer that won't be till late this evening."

"Please don't remind me of the passing of time," said Fabia.

She had the book of the TV series with her, and leafed through it. "Here are the carvings we found, Gareth. Bronze axe heads, like at Stonehenge."

"It's not terribly clear," said Gareth, looking at the old photo. "With the eye of faith…" He peered at the stone. "I wonder if a torch would show them up? Were they all axe heads?"

We broke for elevenses, and Derek produced some dowsing rods and started pacing back and forth with them. They're two bent copper rods that fit loosely into metal slots that you hold in your hands.

"I doubt if this is on your syllabus, Derek," said Roland.

"Won't you keep an open mind?" said Derek. The rods crossed, and moved in and out.

"Not so open that everything falls out the other end!" said Roland.

"You'd need to stick some markers in the ground for a proper survey," said Gareth.

"Anybody got any lolly sticks?" asked Malcolm.

"Can I have a go?" asked Nadine. "Can anybody do it?" Derek handed her the rods and she walked about while they crossed and uncrossed.

"What are we looking for here, anyway?" asked Malcolm.

"Like proper archaeologists, we won't be surprised at anything," said Pete. "But I doubt we'll come across a pyramid."

"This has been a sacred site for thousands of years," said Roland. "We're turning up some very interesting post holes."

"Ritual," said Gareth. "Bound to be ritual."

"Very Spears Games," said Fabia, holding out her hand for the rods. "Don't they do Ouija boards too? Where did you get them?"

"Small ads in the back of the NME," said Derek.

The students all took a turn with the dowsing rods. If they crossed, that meant you'd found something. They crossed with most people at a spot near the central slab.

"This was the altar," said Gavin. "Perhaps we're detecting blood from sacrifices."

"Or perhaps the stone just fell over," said Pete. "And it isn't a sacrificial slab after all."

"They may all have been repositioned," said Colin. "Wasn't one of the Malisons an antiquary?"

"Yes, he commissioned some engravings of the stones – they're in the book," said Gareth. I picked it up and looked for the picture – it showed the stones looking much bigger and more jagged, with some gentlemen in hats and knee breeches in the foreground.

"Do you want a go?" asked Derek, handing me the dowsing rods. I passed the book to Colin and took the rods and walked up and down like the others had. I soon worked out how to make them cross or lean out by very slightly moving my hands.

"Look, the rods are going wild!" said Nadine. "You've got the power, haven't you?"

"They're just very sensitive," said Roland.

"But she told our fortunes. And she looked through the hagstone and saw Elizabethan figures on the lawn!"

"Really," said Roland in a plonking tone of voice.

"Yes," I said, "They were wearing ruffs and scarlet dresses."

"Practising archery?"

"No, just dancing about."

"Well, you're full of surprises," said Fabia. "It must have been the staff – they love dressing up, but I didn't know they pranced about on the lawns."

"Elizabethan dancing," said Roland. "I believe some people take it up as a hobby. Well, as long as it keeps them amused."

I gave the dowsing rods back to Derek.

"We could do a proper survey this evening," he said.

"I don't really like it, though," said Gail.

"It's just a natural phenomenon. Farmers use it to find water."

"I still don't think we should do it. It's like yoga, it might open your mind to dark forces."

"Well, if you don't like it, we won't."

"Surely yoga's just trendy PE," said Roland.

Donna laid her hands on one of the monoliths. "There's a theory, isn't there, that walls and places absorb the energy of everything that's happened there, like a tape-recording?"

"You've all been reading too many paperbacks," said Roland. "May we resume operations?"

Derek put the dowsing rods back in his rucksack, and Fabia peered at her clipboard through her glasses and walked back to the stone she'd been measuring, kicking over Jonathan's tripod in the process.

"Must you put everything right in my path!" she snapped.

"Awfully sorry, Fabia," he said, and painstakingly set it up again.

"How did early man draw straight lines?" asked Donna. "Like from here to wherever the processional way ends? Was it lines of energy in the ground?"

"Probably equipment like this," said Gareth, who was taking measurements with a protractor and a plumbline. "Or a long bit of string. Baaaasically, Early Man was no fool."

"Do you think stone circles like this were actual temples?" asked Colin, walking off with the end of a tape-measure. "They could have had roofs, like the round houses."

"A bit draughty with the wind whistling through the gaps," said Nadine.

"Like a giant Wendy House?" said Fabia, making notes on her clipboard. "And I thought you were all second years."

"You should hear my theory about Silbury Hill!" said Colin.

"I can't wait."

"When they excavated, they found it was made of layers of chalk and turf. A layer of chalk, a layer of turf and so on."

"They never found the king on a gold horse they were looking for!" said Gareth.

"So obviously some of the time it was covered in chalk, and gleaming white, and then they covered it up in turf again. Why?"

"I'm sure you're going to tell us."

"It has a moat, doesn't it? And sometimes the River Kennet floods, and the moat's full of water. And it reflects the hill, so you see a globe instead of just a hill."

"It would be a bit wonky – Silbury Hill is more of a cone with a flat top."

"But what if it was in one if its chalk phases? The moon! Obviously!"

"Just don't put it in your dissertation."

"I've given away the ending now."

"Less of the chat, boys and girls!" said Roland, and we toiled on.

"It's rather a good theory," I said to Colin. "There are lots of tales about people disappearing into white castles, too."

"Don't say that to Roland, he hates Robert Graves, and the White Goddess and all that. He prefers to make up his own theories. Probably wildly jealous of Graves being so popular."

"You seem in a good mood, despite getting lost yesterday."

"It was quite fun in a way. Anyway, I've decided there's no point trying to impress this lot."

"So you might as well laugh at them? What a clever idea."

"Still, the archaeology bit is fun!"

"I've got the feeling we're only here to do the boring jobs."

"Yes, we just do as we're told. Do you think Sir Finamore really meant to dig up the stones one by one?"

"Someone would have stopped him. What about the Malisons?"

"They were fairly moribund at that stage. But what about those Druids turning up? Surely they were actors?"

"I see what you mean. So it was all a set-up? Jonathan didn't seem to think so. He said they shut down the dig."

"Well, he would say that, wouldn't he? What would you have done if you hadn't come here? Gone on holiday somewhere?"

"Mike can never get away for long. We're always talking about a fortnight in Greece or somewhere, then we end up going to Camber Sands." I never went abroad with my parents either – but I suppose it might be difficult for them to get passports.

"If you go again, walk along to Winchelsea – lots of archaeology on the beach! Peat cuttings abandoned when the sea came in."

"We will another time. Thanks for the tip."

At lunchtime we ate off the "sacrificial slab". Colin went over to Roland and hung about while the great man conferred with Fabia.

"Well, any more questions?" he said to Colin at last.

"What do you think of this idea that Stonehenge was a giant computer?"

"Another crackpot bandwagon!" said Roland. "Don't waste your time on it. It's a pity you're not one of my students. We aim to beat the romantic notions out of them."

"Are we going to dig here in the circle, like Sir Finamore?"

"The new owner is not keen. We can't even come near. He probably wants to open the circle to the public, too, and have trippers tramping all over it and eroding the ground and chipping bits off."

"But we could always test the acoustic properties."

"And how do you propose to do that?"

"Singing! Or ringing bells. Or beating drums."

"We could try hitting the stones with drumsticks," said Malcolm.

"The days have passed when ignorant peasants lit fires round them and smashed them up with crowbars," said Roland. "Or built them into cottages."

"Really, Roland, you shouldn't encourage them," snapped Fabia.

"Everybody had enough lunch?" said Gareth. "Shall we take a quick tour of the wood? It's part of the ancient woodland that once covered the whole moor."

"That's what they wanted the bronze axes for," said Colin. "To deforest the environment."

"Oh, go hug a tree," said Malcolm.

We followed Gareth and Pete, and Fabia joined us at the last minute, leaving Roland and Jonathan to their surveying. Under the lichen-covered trees it was shadowy, dim and quiet, and smelled of earth and dead leaves. We filed along a narrow path.

"Let's try this way," said Gareth, as the path branched to the right. "If we go straight on we'll just get to the gardens."

"It's quite sinister," said Nadine, climbing over a fallen tree-trunk green with moss.

"Roland likes to think it was a sacred grove," said Fabia.

"What were they used for?" asked Gail.

"Human sacrifice as usual," said Gavin.

"Cheer up, Gail," said Fabia. "Christianity got to the heathens in the end – circa the year one thousand in most cases. Earlier in Britain, of course, but it didn't take immediately."

"Like a vaccination," said Colin.

"Who rattled your cage?" said Malcolm.

"The entrance to the cave is along here somewhere, isn't it, Fabia?" asked Gareth.

"Yes – we never got a proper look, just posed around the entrance. The Beeb cut the last programme and we had to go. Let me see if I can remember where it was."

"We ought to plot its position," said Gareth. "And isn't there a central clearing?"

Fabia looked about her. "I remember that yew tree – it's somewhere around here."

The students cast about a bit, and Gavin climbed up the bank to our right and dived into some bushes.

"Could this be it?" he called, and we scrambled up to find him kneeling on the ground, holding the vegetation back to reveal a rocky hole in the side of the hill.

"That looks like it," said Fabia. Gavin knelt down and peered in. "Can't see a thing." Gareth handed him a torch and he shone it into the darkness. "Still can't see much." He put the torch down the front of his T shirt and crawled in.

"Look out!" called Gareth. "Mind your head!"

Gavin shouted wordlessly, and Fabia called "Are you OK?" There were scuffling sounds, and Gavin crawled out again.

"It's a dead end," he said. "It gets a bit bigger just inside, but then it just stops. And there's a hole in the floor. I put my hand on nothing and nearly fell in. I shone the torch down and it's quite deep, but narrow. Too small to get down. Too small for me, at any rate."

"Your forehead's bleeding," said Donna, dabbing it with a tissue.

"I hit my head when I lost my balance."

"It could be a bone cave," said Pete. "Where they disposed of their dead. Fair chance there'd be burials around it too."

"How about we dangle a camera?" asked Gareth. "If you wouldn't fit, Gavin, it would have to be someone..."

And they all looked at me.

"Good thing we brought the boiler suits and hard hats and ropes," Gareth went on.

"We'll talk about it later," said Pete. "Let's go back now. We shouldn't really have let you go inside, Gavin."

"You won't mind giving your body to science, will you, Anna?" said Malcolm.

I said nothing, and we retraced our steps.

CHAPTER 15

We carried on with our survey until the sun sank, and Roland said we could knock off. Donna and Nadine and the two boys said they'd go for a swift half before dinner. They ran down the hill past the grown-ups' trench, and the adults packed up and walked after them. It was Derek's turn to cook and Gail had swapped with Colin so they could be together.

"We can use my live yoghourt – it's solidifying nicely," she said. "And I'll check on the bean sprouts. They should be full of living energy by now."

"Before you go, Derek," I said. "Can I borrow the dowsing rods? I'd like to have another go."

"Be my guest." He handed them over.

"Well, I've got a pile of notes to write up," said Colin, waving an exercise book.

"All your theories?"

"I'm saving them for my best-selling paperback. Sure you don't mind being left up here all on your own? I could stay if you like."

"How kind, but I'll be fine. Nobody around but sheep."

So they all left me in peace. I had a look for some axehead carvings, but the sun wasn't low enough yet. I played about with the dowsing rods some more, making them cross and uncross, but they'd just been an excuse. I'd really wanted to read out my spell. I put the dowsing rods in my shopping bag and took out my notebook.

Pamela in the pub said the stones protected their own, meaning the hoard, probably. I walked round the circle, trying the catch them out swapping places behind my back. Then I stopped and intoned:

Hail, ancient carven stones!
Never to be overthrown!
Guard your ancient secrets well
Where the gold is, never tell.
And when hatred threatens love
Don't forget your power to move
Fill the wicked ones with fear
Always shall the truth appear
Whatever evil shall befall
Come and aid me when I call.

I might need help if the others plan to send me down the cave – but perhaps they were joking as usual. I put my notebook back in the bag and went over to one of the smoother stones. The sun was lower, but I still couldn't see any carvings. I ran my hand over the surface in case I could feel anything, and then a deep voice behind me said: "I knew you'd come."

I froze for a moment, then slowly turned round. Standing by the sacrificial slab was a tall, thin man with white hair, dressed in dark clothes.

"Gilles!" I said. "I knew we'd meet again one day."

"So did I," he said. "I summoned you once I knew I was safe."

"Why did you do that? You were only safe as long as I couldn't tell the police where you were! Though I suppose you can always disappear again."

"But I like it here. It's rather magnificent, don't you think? And as to why I should want to summon you, how would you like to be Lady Dominus?"

"You're 'Mr Dominus'! I should have guessed." His real name is Gilles Lemaitre, or at least he was calling himself that when I first met him, and we have shared a few adventures, not always on the same side. After that he became Mr Magister – and now Dominus. It means the same thing, if you've ever learned Latin.

"Yes, all this could be yours!"

"You're teasing me as usual."

"I'm perfectly serious. Have you left your policeman husband? I see you're not wearing a wedding ring."

"I was worried my rings would get damaged, digging."

"Digging? So you're one of the students?"

"That's right."

"I came up here because I thought they'd have all gone home by now. I saw them earlier from my tower, busy with measuring tapes. What do they hope to find out? Or are they treasure-hunting, like Sir Finamore? You've heard the legend, I take it."

"Yes, some people we met in the village talked about it, and the stones moving."

"It would be rather fun to find it, don't you think?"

"I thought you were a millionaire with a lot of ill-gotten gains. Though my friends and the staff got a payout, even if your investors didn't."

"Of course, some of your friends were working for me, weren't they, as well as you?"

"I'm glad you're still on the earth plane, anyway, and the djinn didn't get you. What really happened, the last time we met?"

That was when a rival witch called Dorinda was attacking his office building with a pack of wolves she'd liberated from the zoo, just as Gilles and I were trying to exorcise a djinn that he'd raised to help him escape from prison – where I'd put him – and couldn't get rid of. Well, it was partly my fault. I had to tell the police about the drugs and the kidnapping.

"Let me show you round the grounds, while I tell you the story," he said. We moved into the shadow of the trees.

"And I doubt if they'd ever make you a sir," I said.

"Oh, it's quite easy. You just get a lot of people to write in saying how marvellous you are and what a lot of work you do for charity. Don't you fancy having a title? Divorce is so easy these days."

"We never said 'till death do us part', but I meant it all the same."

"You still look about 16."

"Do I? I'd hoped I was a bit more mature."

"But with an old soul."

"Charming! You used to offer me untold riches and my heart's desire."

"Everything I have could be yours."

"Not so untold any more?"

"Riches are rather vulgar, don't you think?"

We came out of the haunted wood and through an orchard into a walled vegetable garden.

"I've restored this place, anyway," he said. "That's charitable enough. It was in a sad state. And it's the real thing, not like Harpsden." That was his Victorian Gothic place near Reading. "Here I really can be lord of the manor."

"It's a change of scene, anyway."

90

"And image!"

"I suppose all your modern sculptures and pictures got burned."

"Sadly, yes." He used to have a flat at the top of the office building he owned, with black leather sofas and a cinema screen. It had amazing views of London.

"Aren't you afraid of being seen? Somebody might recognise you."

"The authorities only have my mug shot – they take a portrait on arrival, you know. And it doesn't resemble me any more."

He meant that his hair had been black then. He isn't old – his hair turned white when he was being haunted by the djinn, which is a kind of Egyptian demon.

"Who said you can't disguise height?" I asked.

"Chesterton, wasn't it? Don't worry, the visitors and most of the staff will have gone. Oh yes, I have a few staff of my own. They're all genuine human beings. I'm not taking any chances after the last time."

"Do they come when you call them? And then do they go away again?" Spirits and demons don't, always.

"This lot go home to the village or the nearby town. And the courting couple aren't haunting the place this evening."

"No, they're doing the cooking."

"Do you get on with them all? How is it, living in a glorified youth hostel?"

"Most of them are OK. They're not really my type. I like the tutors best. Some of them."

"And you can always complain about them to your husband."

"I don't want him to think I'm not happy – he might tell me to come home."

"Why not take refuge with me? I've got some rooms on the top floor."

"Thanks, but I don't think so! Anyway, you were going to tell me the story."

We walked along gravel paths between flower beds, past a pretend temple and a sundial.

"VULNERANT OMNES ULTIMA NECAT," I read out. "My Latin isn't good enough for that."

"Every hour wounds. The last one kills," he translated.

"Not exactly cheerful."

"But that the dread of something after death..." He didn't finish the sentence.

We came to a small round pond with lilies and goldfish and a tiny fountain bubbling away in the middle. There were curved marble benches around it, pillars with pink roses climbing up them, and statues of Greek gods in the gaps.

"How do you like the Italian garden? Rather romantic, don't you think? The statues were brought back from the Grand Tour in the early 18th century. Here's Hermes, lord of tricksters; Diana, lady of the hunt and of the moon. Athena, goddess of love, and Hera, personification of wisdom. You'll find the rest of the pantheon scattered about the grounds."

"Who is the temple dedicated to?"

"I don't know – how about the four winds? Boreas, Zephyrus, Notus and Eurus."

He sat down on a white marble bench by the pond and I sat down too, but not too close. I noticed he was wearing a dark blue shirt with the sleeves rolled up, and a black scarf round his neck.

"When the lightning struck – if it was lightning – and the place caught fire," he began. "And you and Melusine ran for it, I thought I might as well carry on with the exorcism, so I finished the incantation. The smoke was so thick I couldn't see the demon any more, but I heard it run out of the room and down the stairs, so I went after it, down to the foyer. The glass wall was shattered. It jumped through the hole and I followed. The forecourt was filled with mist. There was another blinding flash, and I couldn't see the djinn any more, just Dorinda and her wolves dispersing right and left. I was alone among the spotted laurels, and fire engines and sirens were coming nearer, so I vaulted over the gate and made myself scarce."

Melusine was a girl who helped him defraud a load of people – she's never been heard of again. And once the police got into the building they figured out how the scam was worked.

"And you didn't want to meet the police."

"The whole enterprise was about to crash anyway. You can't go on robbing Peter to pay Paul."

"I'm glad you got out."

"The papers said that they were searching the wreckage for my remains, and that everyone else had got out through the escape tunnel. I was glad about that too."

"Yes, Mel was with me and Alan, and we told the firemen to look for you."

"Kind of you. And now come and look at the house."

"I saw it the other day."

"And the guides filled your head with a lot of nonsense. I know - I wrote some of it!"

We walked back along a pergola covered with roses and wisteria.

"And so the demon really is gone for good?"

"Yes, thank Thoth, Anubis and Bast. I don't see it any more. Procul omen abesto!"

"You told us to save ourselves. Perhaps it didn't understand."

"Perhaps."

"I hear you lay on pony-cart rides here as well!" I said, changing the subject.

"Yes, round the grounds. There was an old trap in one of the stables."

"You'll be setting up a zoo, next!"

"There are enough wild things on the moor. Haven't you heard them howling?"

"Not friends of yours, are they?"

"Not this time."

"But running a stately home - it's not very wicked, is it?"

He laughed. "Not very. I just fleece the public."

"But legally this time. Have you retired from being a wizard?"

"I've been pursuing some lines of research - perhaps you can help? I'd like to think the stones were on my side. I'm sure they'd do what *you* told them."

"Move aside while you look for the hoard? As long as you don't want to sacrifice me on an altar."

"Never! And now there's something I want to show you in the house." We went round to the side entrance. He unlocked the door and we crossed the hall to the room with the family portraits. I wondered if he'd heard me recite my spell.

CHAPTER 16

"I've moved all my books here from Harpsden," said Gilles, "And bought a few more, and there were some already here." I remembered those books – with engravings of demons, and stars and the zodiac, and naked people in baths, and in odd combinations. It probably all symbolised something.

"Here are past Malisons, some attributed to Lely. But these two are more interesting. They say their pallor was induced by their magical experiments."

"That's what the guide told us." I tried to look neutral.

"Actually these people's name was Blanchflower, not Malison, but keep that to yourself. They really were notorious witches in the days of Good Queen Bess. She passed a law against 'conjurations, enchantments and witchcrafts'. It looks better in Elizabethan spelling. They say that the book in Lady Blanchflower's hand is the book of recipes she inherited from her mother. That's one of the reasons I bought their portraits – and a lot of their library. I'm still cataloguing it."

"How did they escape being burned at the stake?"

"Perhaps they knew some cunning arts to avoid that fate – or had friends in low places. They even carried on being Catholics. But this is the one I really want you to see."

And he led me to the picture of my grandmother on the other side of the window. I said: "Yes, I've seen it."

"Perhaps you are a relation, or a distant descendant. Your surname was Lestrange, wasn't it?"

"Yes, before it was Savage."

"Even if it's a coincidence, I shall always have a picture of you," he said. "She was the mother of Lady Blanchflower. You see the book of spells appears in this picture as well. I've been looking for it among their collection, but it hasn't surfaced yet. They said she had the secret of longevity and forgetting."

It must be the actual book of spells my mother left for me, that's now in a vault in the bank. That's where I found the longevity potion that my parents gave me, and that they must have taken back in the days of Queen Elizabeth I, which I reversed in the ceremony in the British Museum. At least, I fervently hope that worked. I suppose 22 is a bit young to have wrinkles or bags under your eyes. How old was I when I did the spell? But I'd stuck at 14, so... I can't work it out.

"You wouldn't want to live for hundreds of years really," I said. "You'd have to keep updating your clothes, moving house and changing your name. Oh – you've done that. I mean, you'd have to move on before everybody you knew twigged that you never aged. And the future sounds ghastly – all flying cars and going to space and living on pills."

"And everybody wearing tunics, so unflattering – I shall insist on a toga! So, do the Blanchflowers remind you of anybody?"

"Not really," I said, looking at the pictures of my parents again. "The guides said there were ghosts too – have you seen any?"

"No, I made all of them up as well. The visitors like it. Come and see the upstairs. And there's a lot more we need to talk about."

We went upstairs to the long gallery where I'd chatted with Joan, and walked up and down on the creaking floor boards.

"Have you told your husband about any of our adventures?"

"Only the bit about the drugs. Sorry about that. I could have told him about the phony investment scheme if I'd understood it, but I was too dim to work it out."

"That was Melusine's brainwave – I hope she's living it up abroad somewhere on the proceeds. But you've never told your husband about your powers – he doesn't know you're a witch?"

"No." Nobody does. Apart from a few ghosts. And the coven in Haslemere.

"Or not yet. What about your fellow students, do they suspect?"

"I read the Tarot cards for them, and did a few spells to keep off ghosts – they believed those stories the guides told. And they're afraid of the howling on the Moor – at least, I think that's why Nadine was crying."

"Maybe someone had broken her heart."

"Maybe. You know, nobody talks like that any more, it's odd. They don't talk about 'love' any more."

"Make Love Not War? Love-Ins? Free love? All over? So what do they do?"

"They pair off like people used to. I mean, like when I was at school. This lot have. But they think magic is only something like dowsing, or ley lines, which are all rot."

"Yes, it's fashionable, isn't it, all that? Makes it easier for you and me to pass without notice. But you wouldn't like your husband to know about your – parallel career? You must have concealed quite a bit."

"I haven't worked out how to tell him, if I ever do. I don't know what he'd say. I keep expecting it all to just fade away, but it doesn't."

"Of course I know quite a lot about what you did before we ever met, through our friends in Haslemere. Your university might take a dim view."

Again I thought of that naked ceremony in a winter wood. I'd been briefly involved in a coven in Surrey, where we lived before my parents vanished. And the witches were friends of Gilles, as I later found out. Some people let it all hang out in the Summer of Love, but everybody seems to have gone back to being conventional, and they're as shockable as they ever were. It's odd that people can say everything's going to change, and then it just goes on being like before, and nobody even comments on it.

So I said: "And you wouldn't like the police to know where you are?"

"They dole out heavy sentences for drug-peddling, and even more for fraud. This house is an improvement on a prison cell."

"Like I said before, I don't like the idea of anybody being shut up. Oh, Lawrence got out, by the way! Did you pull some strings like I asked you to?"

"What's he up to now?" he asked, avoiding the issue.

"He's gone back to selling clothes – I model for him from time to time."

"I've still got that artistic photograph of you in a field. They were on sale in poster shops, so I bought another copy."

"Yes, I saw it in a corridor," I sighed. "And there's even one in the pub."

"I've talked with our friends from Haslemere. Oh, they won't give me away."

"No, they keep a low profile. And they wouldn't want anybody to know what they got up to."

"In a way, being a suburban witch is cover in itself, these days. But they wouldn't like people to know they were serious. And they know my power to raise demons. I thought they might lead me to your parents, but they moved, and then moved again, leaving no forwarding address. You don't talk about them – do you know where they are?"

"Actually I don't."

"What does your husband think about that?"

"He pretends to think they're criminals on the run."

"What do you think?"

"I think they must have some good reason for disappearing."

"Do you miss them?"

"I miss them terribly. And my friends."

"Do you ever go back?"

"I've been back once or twice - I ran into Charles. He was the one who gave me all that info about demons. And I've been to people's weddings."

"So Charles did that research! You know, the coven were very angry with him for leaving?" I hoped they hadn't done anything to him - but then he knew how to protect himself."

"He's a geography teacher now. They didn't like me leaving either. But once was enough."

"Yes, you could have done a lot for them. That was why they passed you on to me."

"I think I worked that out."

"And of course Charles wouldn't like to lose his job."

"No - his new school would be shocked."

"And you kept your mouth shut before - I imagine there's a lot you didn't tell the police. And aiding and abetting a felon is a crime. You wouldn't like prison. I didn't. Have we reached an agreement?"

"You mean, we'll just blackmail each other again?"

"Yes, why not? It worked before." He smiled.

"All right, then."

"We're friends?"

"Friends."

He held out a hand and I took it. He held on to mine, so I said: "I'd better go, they'll be wondering where I am."

"Will you make something up about where you've been?"

"I do that all the time. I'm a terrible liar."

"You're probably a very good liar by now."

We went downstairs again and he saw me to the side door.

"Drop in when you're passing!" he said. "I really mean it, unlike most people."

I walked back to the stables, thinking. There was a lot I'd have to keep from the adoption people, too. Gilles is a villain, and a wizard, and he tried to use Ursula in a ceremony on Parliament Hill before I stopped it and took her home, but he is one of the few people I can talk to about all that. Just him, and a couple of ghosts. He's an old friend, or enemy, or Nemesis – as in fate you can't escape.

I went into the kitchen to see if there was anything left to eat, and found Gail, Derek and Colin washing up.

"Where have you been?" asked Gail bossily.

"What are you pondering?" asked Colin, wiping a plate with a blue checked towel.

"The inevitability of Fate."

"Now THERE's a question! Do you think it's inevitable?"

"No – because the future hasn't happened yet."

"That's very profound," said Derek seriously.

"I just mean you keep bumping into the same people."

"Just a coincidence."

"There's no such thing as coincidence," said Derek.

"And no such thing as an accident," said Gail. "We've kept you some dinner in the bottom oven." She produced it – it featured thinly sliced mushrooms and tasted strongly of Marmite.

"So where have you been really?" she asked, getting out the instant coffee.

"Have the others gone back to the pub?"

"What do you think?" said Derek.

"I got talking to one of the staff in the gardens. He showed me round. I never got a chance to see them the other day."

"Yes, they are beautiful," said Gail. She and Derek exchanged a look.

"You want to look out for people like that," said Derek.

"Yes, that's what I thought, but anyway, it was fine," I said.

"Nothing creepily sinister went on?" asked Colin.

"Nothing at all," I lied.

"Well, we've got Gareth's workshop to look forward to!" said Derek. "He's going to teach us how to knap tomorrow. And we get to play with bows and arrows too."

They disappeared off to the gardens, and Colin and I watched telly.

CHAPTER 17

At breakfast I got a letter from Mike (he writes to me a lot and I write to him), saying it would be my birthday soon after midsummer and we could go out to a posh restaurant, and what about finding somewhere new? I wrote back that I really wanted to go to the revolving restaurant in the Post Office tower but it was probably frightfully expensive. I keep telling him I'm having a marvellous time apart from the rain and the mud. I'll tell him about the people when I get back - I've got to put up with them for a few more weeks.

The boys went to put up some straw targets in the field for the archery demo. Gareth was still setting up in the barn, so he said: "Talk amongst yourselves! I'll be 20 minutes or so yet."

While he was clearing tables and laying them out with stuff, the others went to brew up. I was following them when I remembered I'd left the shopping bag with my notebook and the dowsing rods up at the circle. I went round the front of the house, and up through the wood, and picked up my bag from where I'd left it at the foot of one of the stones. I hoped the dowsing rods wouldn't rust.

I came back via the gardens, and detoured to the lily pond where I'd talked to Gilles. I was glad the djinn and Dorinda the witch hadn't got him. I'd met them both when they were trying to raise demons and acquire the riches of the earth, or something. Dorinda ended up in prison, too, though she had nothing to do with the drug-dealing side of the business. She was furious with Gilles for escaping, and not getting her out as well, and that's why she attacked his office building with storms and mist and a pack of wolves.

I looked at the goldfish, and listened to the little fountain burbling, then went over to the statue of Hermes. He has always been my protector, and he saved me from Gilles and his otherworldly minions once, in an underground carpark. I was forced to be a trickster, and to aid and abet felons, and I'd stolen some money from the hippies to get a train home from Harpsden, so I was a thief as well. I picked some pale pink roses, using my penknife, laid them at his feet, and scarpered back to the barn, where everybody was clustered round Gareth. I got out my damp notebook and tried to look interested.

"Come to the front, Anna, so you can see!" said Gareth, and the others made room. "You haven't missed much! I'm just about to talk you through these." He'd laid out some flint knives and arrow-heads, and he told us all about them and what era they were made in. The early ones were big and chunky and he said they were "hand-axes". I didn't see how you could hold them in your hand without cutting yourself, but he explained they probably used a bit of leather as a grip.

"They used to butcher mammoths with these!" he said, making chopping motions.

Some of the tools were really beautiful. There was a spear-head made of red stone that looked like a leaf, and delicate arrowheads with barbs. There were minute pieces called "microliths". He passed them around and let us have a closer look. Then he showed us some he'd made himself, some out of flint and some out of coloured glass.

"You could turn them into a mobile, or jewellery," said Nadine. "With a bit of silver wire."

"How can you tell them from the real thing?" I asked.

"You can't really," said Gareth. "Except a fake would have no wear, and it might be made from the wrong kind of stone for the location. Some people are not above salting the mine."

"And then do they sell them?"

"I believe they do. But doooon't let me put ideas into your head!"

Then he produced some lumps of flint and showed us how to "knap", on a bit of leather on your knee, "retouching" the edge with a deer's antler. Then he gave us each a piece. We produced a lot of rubbish or "debitage", and he told us to study it as we might be finding bits.

"This black stuff is from Grime's Graves in Norfolk," he said, "And this white stuff is what we commonly call chert."

Of course I was hopeless at knapping and my piece of flint ended up shapeless and then broke in half. Gareth gave me a flint tool to draw and I got on better at that, doing the facets in pencil and then going over it all with ink. Then we had another demo from Jonathan – how they attached axe-heads to hafts, and arrowheads to shafts, and spear points to spears. "They used cornus or viburnum for the shafts, or reeds," he explained. "Here are some I made earlier."

"Did you make the arrowpoints as well?" asked Gareth. "Very nice. Why don't you show them how it's done?"

"What was your PhD about, Jonathan?" asked Malcolm. "You know, the one you never finished."

"It wasn't about flint knapping," said Jonathan mildly, and went on demonstrating how to make glue by cooking birch bark in a saucepan over a Camping Gaz stove, and attaching the arrowhead with raw sinews. We soaked the sinews to soften them, and I got my hands covered with the sticky black glue, and my arrowhead fell off. The made ones seemed quite secure, though, and the sinews had dried. While we were doing that Jonathan made a couple of beautiful leaf-shaped arrowheads which Gareth admired.

"I'm not giving them to you, Gareth," said Jonathan, putting them in his pocket.

"You're big on reconstruction at Blackhampton, don't you?" asked Gareth.

"They call it experimental archaeology these days. Roland's very keen on it."

"He made us join Archery Soc," said Nadine. "But I can never be bothered to turn up."

Pete came over and picked up a finished arrow. "Are you going to try these for real?"

"After lunch, I think. Come and join us," said Gareth.

After some sandwiches and Nescafé and fig rolls, we all went up to the field, where Jonathan was waiting for us next to the targets. They were set up in the direction of the barrows, down a bit from the trench.

"We haven't got time to go through the whole bow-making process, but have a look at these," said Jonathan, handing some out. "See how they used the properties of yew – heartwood on one side and sap wood on the other, so that it acts like a spring."

We admired the ready-made bows and lined up to shoot with them. He had even made wrist-guards out of bone, stone and leather thongs.

"Like bracelets! Can I keep one?" asked Nadine.

"I'm afraid not," said Jonathan. "There are some leather gloves you can borrow – but of course they're not authentic."

Roland and Fabia appeared on the skyline and came down to watch.

"Quite like school sports day!" said Roland.

"Spectators please keep a safe distance," said Jonathan, and they sat down on the bank, Fabia pulling her denim skirt over her legs. We put on the wrist guards and Jonathan showed us how to fire the arrows.

The boys went first, and were frighteningly good at it. Gavin hit the bullseye and Roland clapped slowly and said: "Well done, that boy!" Malcolm collected the arrows from the straw target and Gavin pretended to aim at him, but Jonathan quickly pushed his arms down.

"Never, never let your gun, pointed be at anyone," he quoted.

"That's true for guns, I suppose," said Gavin.

"Goes for these as well."

"We don't want any accidents," called out Roland.

"Useful in tribal wars," muttered Malcolm.

Donna wasn't too bad and hit the target several times. Gail and Nadine were more feeble, and Colin's arrows went wide. Then it was my turn and I could barely draw back the bow at all.

"We should have made a child's size one," said Jonathan. He helped me draw back the bow, putting his hands over mine, while the boys catcalled. I let go the string and the arrow fell limply to the ground.

"If at first you don't succeed!" said Gareth, so I tried again a couple of times, with the same result.

"Never mind," said Malcolm. "They'll find you another job under cover - like a nice cosy cave full of dead people!"

"Why don't you have a go, Roland?" said Gareth.

"I used to be quite good at this," he said, coming over and taking one of the bows. He hit the target several times.

"Well, shall we call it a day?" said Gareth, as Roland retrieved the arrows.

"But you and Jonathan haven't had a turn!" said Fabia. "Come on!"

"Division of labour, you know," said Gareth. "I'm just a humble flint knapper. Still, I've been watching you others."

He took the bow and and managed to get a couple of arrows into the target. Then he handed it to Jonathan, who shot three arrows into the target without fuss, but missed the bullseye.

"Adequate but unimpressive," said Fabia. "And you're supposed to be the expert!"

Jonathan started putting the arrows into their holders - I supposed they were quivers.

"We could have a tournament, like with darts," said Malcolm.

"Yes, if you want to get some modern kit," said Jonathan. "My reproductions are fragile, you know."

"Don't be such a wet blanket!" said Fabia. "You can always make some more. And if it'll keep the kiddies amused…" She got up from her campstool and joined us. "Anyway, my turn now!"

Jonathan handed her the bow, and got some arrows out again. "Not bad work!" she said, looking at them. "What an excellent technical assistant we have!"

She shot off a few arrows, most of which hit the target.

"My wrist really hurts!" said Nadine. "Do these guard things work at all? The string keeps hitting my arm when I let go of it."

"It's sinew, not string," said Jonathan. "Your stance probably needs adjusting." We got another demo and more catcalls. Then the tutors urged Pete to have a go, and he said "But I'm a pottery man! I've never done this in my life!"

"You're setting a bad example!" said Fabia. "No excuses accepted." So Pete took a bow from Jonathan and loosed off an arrow, but it hit the ground.

"Aim higher!" said Jonathan, and Pete got one to stick in the target and everybody cheered.

"I thought Jonathan was a lecturer like the others," I said to Malcolm.

"Roland and Fabia scaled the dizzy heights after Sir Finamore fell off the twig, and Jonathan was lucky to get the tech. asst. job. You have to publish, and have leadership qualities. Roland's a natural leader. But Jonathan's good at this kind of stuff. We do quite a lot of it."

"Building round houses?"

"That sort of thing, and how they lived and so on. The girls do spinning and weaving and dyeing, and make our clothes. We'd better clear up. You can carry some light quivers, I expect?"

Gavin picked up one of the targets. "Shame we can't leave these here."

"Would you mind putting them in the tent?" said Jonathan.

The other students went back to their trench, I helped Jonathan carry the bows and arrows back to the barn, where he shoved them rather carelessly into a cupboard.

105

CHAPTER 18

It poured down the next day and we lingered over breakfast. I got two letters, one from Mike, and one without a stamp in a handwriting I didn't recognise. Who else knew I was here? It turned out to be a note from Gilles giving me his phone number. Mike said he missed me like anything and was sitting by the window eating spaghetti hoops on toast. Pete put his head round the door and said they were having a confab in the office and further details would be released as and when they were available.

Colin said "Flaming June – flamin' 'orrible!", and in a minute Pete came back and said: "Put on your wet weather gear, and come into the barn." So we did. The windcheater wasn't much good against a downpour, so I got a bin bag and cut some armholes and a headhole in it with the kitchen scissors, and put it over the top. In the barn, everybody was standing round a table piled up with ropes and hard hats and orange boiler suits.

"Are we all here?" said Roland. "Since it's tipping down we thought we'd have another look at the cave. Some of us will be in the warm and dry, and the rest of us will be under the trees. Jonathan, you'd better bring that bumbershoot." Jonathan unhooked a golf umbrella from where it was hanging on a peg, and stood leaning on it.

"Do you need us all?" asked Gareth.

"Yes – we need several people on the rope, and bring some trays. Got your camera, Jonathan? This is the smallest boiler suit we've got." And he held up an orange garment. "And are you all wearing wellies? Good. Anna, climb into this. Sorry, you'll have to remove that very chic creation you're wearing."

There were sniggers at that. He handed out some more boiler suits to Gareth, and to the boys, and doled out hard hats. I supposed I'd just have to be a good sport and go along with it. I took off the binbag and got into the boiler suit.

"I don't think there's a suit to fit you, Pete," said Roland. "No size extra-large!"

Donna helped me roll up my sleeves and trouser-legs, I put my wellies and hat back on and we filed off through the field and went round by the ridge and the stone circle. I was glad I didn't have to march past the front of the house looking a complete berk. Jonathan held the umbrella over Fabia and the rest of us just got soaked as we filed through the circle into the dark wood.

"The entrance to the underworld," said Roland, as we scrambled up the bank to the mouth of the cave. "A dim place of restless shades."

"I'll remember not to eat anything," I said. The more you eat in the Underworld the longer you have to stay, and the same goes for fairy food.

Jonathan pulled up a couple of the bushes that were covering the entrance, and tore down some of the ivy. Pete handed me a hard hat with a headtorch. I gave my own hat to Donna to look after, and buckled the helmet under my chin, and Pete showed me how to turn the torch on. The boys were uncoiling the rope and looping it round a tree trunk. Pete and the lads would be on the other end.

They put a loop of rope over my head and arms, and Jonathan hung the camera round my neck. "It's very simple, and the flash is automatic. Just press this button."

"Don't worry about quality," said Roland.

"And take these," said Bridget, shoving some plastic finds bags into my pockets. "In case you can grab any finds. Or a soil sample, even."

"Sounds rather medical," said Malcolm.

"Oh, earth, then!" said Bridget, crossly.

"I'll do my best," I said. Just for a moment I wondered how I'd got here, and whether I could just run away. Except I was tethered to a tree and wouldn't get far.

"You don't need to stay down there long," said Pete. "We'll pull you up the moment you scream."

"And if you don't scream after ten minutes, we'll pull you up anyway!" said Gareth.

"Maybe Sir Finamore found the treasure after all and stashed it down there," said Pete.

"He'd have come back for it," I said. "Wouldn't he?"

"He didn't have time, poor sod," said Pete. "Yell 'Pay out!' when you want us to lower you."

I walked towards the cave opening, and they fed the rope between their hands.

"You're going to come back a star!" said Roland, slapping me on the back rather painfully. The others were huddled under the trees, and Bridget and Nadine were sheltering under a bin bag, probably the one I'd been wearing. Fabia stood aloof under the umbrella.

I got down on my hands and knees and crawled inside. The passage didn't go very far – it widened out and I could see the slit in the floor. I peered down – there was a rough, narrow shaft, and then it opened out into a chamber. I sat on the left-hand edge of the slit, put my feet down it and shouted "Pay out!", and they called "OK!" and I started to climb down. It was a tight fit, even for me, but fortunately the walls were quite rough, with hand and footholds. After a bit my feet could only find air, and I was dangling on the rope. I proceeded in jerks, with the light from my torch bouncing off the wet rocky walls. After not much more of this my feet hit the ground and I shouted "Stop!"

"Are you on solid ground?" It was Jonathan's voice, sounding quite near. I looked up and saw his face peering down the hole.

"Yes!" I called.

"Have a look round! Take some pictures!"

The torchlight's narrow beam flashed on wet rock and yellow mud as I moved my head about. I thought I'd be methodical and try a panoramic sweep from left to right. There was rough rock behind me, and to my left piles of sticky mud with a few fragments of bones poking out. I pulled one of them out and put it in my pocket, and took some pictures. I dug out a handful of yellow clay and put it in one of the finds bags. Then I continued my sweep and the light hit a white dome and two black holes. I was staring into the eye sockets of a skull. I screamed.

I could hear Jonathan scramble out of the way, and they began to pull me up, but then I shouted "Stop! Pay out again!" Soon I was back on the floor. I looked about till I found the skull again – it was on top of an almost complete skeleton, slumped on a ledge in front of me. Water dripped from the ceiling and ran down the wall and down its face, which was the same yellow as the mud.

I took photos of the bones, then shouted "Pull me up!" again. I held my arms over my head so that I could grab the sides of the slit, and swarmed up it, scraping my knees and elbows. "Stop!" I called as I climbed out of the top. I crawled out of the cave entrance and the others cheered and clapped.

"Why did you scream? What did you see? Is it worth further investigation?" asked Roland.

"I screamed because there's a complete skeleton just sitting there."

# 109

"Wonderful!" said Roland. And the others went "Wow, really?"

"If we could only widen the cave mouth…" began Roland.

"With dynamite? It's all granite," said Jonathan. "Ask Gareth."

"And it would destroy whatever's down there," said Fabia.

"Have we got a bag of any description?" asked Roland.

"Jonathan brought his stuff in a rucksack," said Gareth.

"Excellent. Can we tie another rope to the rucksack? You'd better empty it out, Jonathan." He began turfing out the contents – notebooks and tape measures – and putting them in the side pockets.

Pete said to me: "Don't forget that whoever's down there has been there for hundreds – probably thousands of years."

"You want me to go down there and fetch it, don't you?"

"Well, it's a find and a half. It'll make Roland's day. And you'll get top marks for this module."

I handed the camera back to Jonathan, and crawled into the cave and down the hole again. "Forgive me," I said to the skeleton, before picking up its skull and putting it in the rucksack. I packed in a few of the other bones and sent the bag back up again. I moved my torch beam so as not to see the poor headless thing.

It was very quiet, and I thought about the hill above my head, and the people who were found crushed in the side galleries of an ancient flint mine. It wasn't quite the tightest place I'd ever been in – there was that underground carpark, and the houseboat Melusine set adrift with me in it. And at least here nobody wished me harm, and even if the rope broke they'd send down another one. I hoped.

The rucksack dropped down again and Gavin called: "You OK?"

"Just fine!" I said, and filled up the bag again. It took several goes, and I hoped I hadn't missed anything.

"That's it!" I shouted to Gavin, and he shouted back "I'll tell the guys to pull you up", and soon I was rising jerkily towards the hole and climbing up it. I crawled out again and Roland said: "You're a real trouper."

I muttered to Pete: "I'm not doing that again, ever, ever, ever."

"For a novice archaeologist it's rather a baptism of fire."

"Fire isn't quite the word!" said Roland.

"Mud's good for the complexion," said Nadine. "But you can scrub your face with this tissue." I took it gratefully.

They'd laid out the bones on the bin bag. "It's nearly all here, remarkable state of preservation," said Bridget, and they put it back in the rucksack.

"We've earned our lunch," said Gareth. "Then we can wash poor old Eric here and lay him out in the barn."

We went back through the sopping green woods, Jonathan carrying the rucksack with the skeleton. I headed straight for the shower. I chucked the boiler suit in too, but I remembered to take out the bits of bone and the handful of mud from the pockets first. I put on some clean clothes and took the bags into the barn, where Gareth was unpacking "Eric".

"I picked up a few bits of bone, too. And here's some mud. Why's it so orange?"

"Something ferruginous - iron-bearing. Maybe a spring. What formed the cave, we ask ourselves? It's just a skeleton, you know, we've all got one, just bones," he said, setting them out on the table. "And it's what we expected to find - just not a complete one like this. There's probably loads more down there." He peered at one of the plastic bags. "This looks like a section of human femur."

"Did they use places like that as graveyards, then?"

"At various times, yes."

"I'm not going down there again."

"Yes, it would be a bit mooch for you. Besides, you couldn't cope with the digging, and you're not really trained. Perhaps Roland will get some funding - it needs proper investigation, proper equipment. And some very tiny archaeologists. Shame we can't send children down mines any more! Perhaps there's another entrance? But you don't mind coming and washing it this afternoon?"

"No, I don't. It was the cave I minded. Did I get all the vertebrae?"

"I haven't counted them yet!"

"That must have been quite spooky," Nadine said when I went into the kitchen.

"It was - and painful. I've bashed my elbows and knees."

"You are brave."

**111**

"I'm not brave, I'm always utterly terrified."

"Well, if that wasn't enough to put you off archaeology for life!" said Colin.

"Hot, sweet, strong tea is the ticket!" said Bridget quickly.

"Or there's some Celestial Seasonings," said Gail. I opted for an ordinary Tetley teabag. At least it didn't have an uplifting mantra on the packet.

"It's probably a Piltdown skull chucked down by Sir Finamore," said Colin.

"A whole Piltdown skeleton, you mean," said Derek.

"Turned out to be an orang-utan, didn't it?"

"Let's wash Eric this afternoon," said Gareth, coming in. "We should all share in the experience."

"Let me know when we can come and view the body," said Roland.

"It won't take long to lay him out. Give us about an hour."

CHAPTER 19

Gareth found a diagram in a book, and we followed it as we laid out the bones. Pete and Bridget had gone to type reports in the office. I think that meant he dictated, while she typed. Was it possible to be put off something for life? Weren't you supposed to pick yourself up and start all over again? Did I want to be doing this for ever, with people who played darts and went on about real ale and made jokes about bodily fluids? But perhaps I'd better just get my degree – and then what?

"What do we think, class?" asked Gareth, consulting the book. "Is Eric male or female? Has anyone measured the long bones?"

Gavin ran a tape measure over the femurs. "Sixteen inches."

"Let me just check," said Gareth, looking through the book. "Our other burials have been rather fragmentary. Seems rather short for a man."

"Wasn't everybody shorter in the olden days?" asked Nadine. "Look at their beds."

"They slept sitting up," said Donna. "They thought only dead people lay down."

"Wasn't that in Tudor times, though?"

"Now, we're supposed to look for something called the sciatic notch," said Gareth. "Where's Fabia? She's good on this stuff. Anyway, it's good training. Have a look at the picture, Gavin, and compare it with the pelvis."

"This is the auricular surface," said Gavin, pointing at the pelvis. "That must be where it articulates with the head of the femur." He picked up the leg bone and tried to make it fit.

"I don't think that's quite respectful, Gavin," said Gareth. "I'm beginning to think this is a lady. Have a look at the book, everybody. Any thoughts, Jonathan? You've seen a few skeletons in your time."

Jonathan came over from the other end of the barn, looked at the bones for a bit and said: "I think the students should have a go at working it out," and went back to his bench. So we all had a look at the diagram, and the "sciatic notch" did look wider than on the male pelvis in the picture.

"Not Eric but Erica, then," said Gareth.

"The femur goes into this hole here," said Derek. "It's like a puzzle."

"We ought to issue students with those Airfix human body kits."

"I think we ought to pray for whoever it is," barked Gail.

"Do you expect us to down tools and say the twenty-third psalm every time we dig up some bone fragments?" said Malcolm.

"If it makes you feel better, Gail," said Gareth. "Your first complete skeleton – a bit upsetting."

Gail recited in a slightly choked voice: "For I am persuaded, that neither death, nor life, nor angels, nor principalities, nor powers, nor things present, nor things to come, Nor height, nor depth, nor any other creature, shall be able to separate us from the love of God, which is in Christ Jesus our Lord."

"Amen!" said Roland, coming in with Fabia. I went over to Gail and said: "That was beautiful. Where's it from?", and she said "St Paul".

"We never did him at the convent," I admitted.

"What do we think?" asked Roland, walking round the table with the skeleton lying on it, now neatly arranged. Fabia stood on the other side and we drew back a little.

"We're of the opinion it's female," said Malcolm.

"Very good."

"Actually, what's this thing sticking in the shoulder blade?" said Derek, peering at it through the ribs, which we'd laid on top of it.

"I think we may have a cause of death," said Gareth, lifting off the ribs. There was a lump of something sticking out, looking like part of the bone. He ran his fingers over it. "I do believe it's an arrowhead."

"On the left-hand side – straight through the heart?" suggested Malcolm.

"And we'd just decided she was female."

"What can the skull tell us?"

"No brow ridges," said Derek, looking at the book. "It looks quite – is refined the word?"

"Gracile," said Roland. "It certainly doesn't look male."

"Nasal bone small and broad," said Malcolm.

"And high cheekbones," added Derek. "Or do all skulls look like that?"

"What do you think, Fabia?" asked Gareth. "This is more your province."

Fabia was silent for a moment, then she said: "I'm concerned about the state of preservation. There are fragments of tendon. It doesn't look to me like a body that has lain undisturbed for – if that's a flint arrowhead – maybe six thousand years."

"Were there any other skeletal remains, Anna?" asked Roland.

"There were little bits sticking out of the mud. I picked out a few and gave them to Gareth."

"They probably defleshed and disarticulated before depositing."

"What about carbon dating?" said Colin.

"The cave could have been in use for thousands of years as a burial place," said Gareth. "Could be someone else's scapula – though it matches the other one."

"If the entrance was always open...." began Malcolm.

"Anybody could have been posted down at any time," said Gavin.

"You know what this means?" said Roland.

"Yes – we'd have to report it to the police," said Gareth. "Come and have a look, Jonathan."

Jonathan fingered the butt-end of the arrowhead, and looked at it closely.

"Yes, it does look Neolithic, doesn't it?" he said. "Could the bones have been jumbled?"

"The shoulder blade had fallen to the floor," I said. "You'll see when you develop the photographs."

"So it may be a composite. It's a puzzler!" said Roland. "But we'd better follow procedure. Don't want to get into any trouble with the rozzers, or our funding bodies, if you'll excuse the pun."

"How about a second opinion?" asked Gareth.

"Good idea, I'll phone Margaret at London University and see if she can pop down for the day."

"Who's Margaret?" I asked, when they'd gone out.

"She's the top physical anthropologist there," said Gareth. "She's worked with Roland before. She'll be thrilled. Still tipping it down, I see. But there's find-washing and labelling to be done, and piles of stuff in the tent still to be gone through."

Gail said: "Can we put a sheet or a blanket over the skeleton?"

"Of course you can," said Gareth. "But Jonathan, you'd better take some snaps first."

So Gail went to get a clean sheet, and Jonathan started clicking away, and Donna and Nadine said they'd write up their notes in the café at the Grange, and have some coffee walnut cake. "Why don't you come with us, Anna, you'll have lots to write."

"Yes, I fancy sitting somewhere in the warm."

"Good thing you're not claustrophobic!"

"How do you know I'm not? How can you go cave diving?"

"Oh, we don't really, we were just having you on!"

I bought some postcards in the shop – views of the house and garden, and the portraits of "Lord and Lady Malison". I've got a photo of my parents I took with a Brownie 127, and Mum left an old album for me to find, and there's a picture of them in there with different names. The lawyers put that in the bank, along with the recipe book. They never liked being photographed. I wondered if Gilles had worked out why they disappeared. I wrote a PC to Pauly at Junk and Disorderly in case he forgot about me.

\*\*\*

Next day it was fine for once, so it was back to the trenches. I did some trowelling, and sieved some spoil heaps and occasionally raised my head and looked up at the moor and breathed fresh air and listened to the birds calling.

"Curlews!" said Colin. "Also called peewits."

"Funny we never hear the howling in the daytime," said Nadine. "Oh, here's another burnt patch."

"Whatever it is, it's nocturnal," said Malcolm.

"Loads of animal bones," said Nadine, scraping. "Stone Age picnic."

"The Beast's victims," said Gavin.

As we came in for lunch Fabia and Roland were driving away.

"They're just taking Margaret back to Eldritch station," said Gareth, coming into the kitchen. "She says it's a teaser, but the skeleton looks recent, so I've rung the local plod again."

"Didn't they even offer her a sandwich?" asked Pete, buttering a slice of bread.

# 116

"They'll stop at a pub on the way. She's a bit grand for cheese sarneys."

"She must have got a very early train."

"She came down last night and stayed in Eldritch."

"I wonder when they'll turn up? The police, I mean."

"They said they'd be here right away."

"Well, I suppose they have to treat the body as a body. Have you taken plenty of photographs?"

"Yes, Jonathan took some snaps."

We went back up to the trenches with Bridget and Pete, and carried on as before, but soon all the trays were full, and Pete helped me carry them down to the barn. When we came in through the old barn doors, which look out onto the fields, Gareth and some strange men were standing around the table with the sheeted skeleton.

"This must be they," muttered Pete, putting our trays down. "Let's stay and see the fun. Pretend to be working."

"You've brought me a lot of muddy finds!" said Jonathan. "Well, you can jolly well wash them here."

"Wanted to be in on the act, didn't we?"

"Gareth's doing the honours," said Jonathan.

Three of the men were wearing ordinary clothes – brown suits and green pullovers – but there were a couple of constables with a stretcher. I filled a plastic bowl under the tap, found a toothbrush and started scrubbing.

"That must be the forensic pathologist," said Pete, pretending to tidy things.

"What's he doing?"

"Drawing back the sheet. Now Gareth's showing him the arrowhead, I think."

"Most remarkable!" said the pathologist. "Have you ever seen anything like this before?"

"A flint arrowhead?" said Gareth. "The students are turning them up practically every day. We had a go at making some."

"With any success?"

"Some of the students caught on quickly. It's a hobby of mine."

"Really. Can you show me some examples?"

"He's getting out his collection," said Pete.

"I see. Can I take one of these for comparison?"

"I suppose so. Why not take several?"

"Thank you. Now we've brought a stretcher, but I'm wondering if boxes wouldn't be better."

"You'd have to lay her out again. She's a she, we think."

"Let's have a look at that pelvis – I think you're right. Did you make a guess at height? But we recompose the departed all the time."

"Oh, yes, of course you do. We struggled a bit, following the book."

"You've done a good job!"

"We thought she was about five foot four. I'll find you some boxes."

"Thank you. Yes, there's a formula you can use with the length of the long bones. We'll have a good look, and let you know what we think – probably tomorrow. Did you find anything else down there?"

"Just a few fragments of bone – you can have those too if you like."

"Yes, we'd better take them. Well, we'll be in touch. Careful – she's fragile. Got any packing?"

"By the way," said the other plainclothes man. "You'll tell all your crew to keep quiet about this, won't you? Don't want the press getting onto it before we've got anything to give them. Should we have a word with the head bod?"

"He's near the stone circle," said Gareth. "I'll pop up and keep him posted."

"Right. We can talk to him tomorrow. Meanwhile keep away from the cave."

"Will do."

"Well, they're boxing her up and taking her away," said Pete. "Show's over for tonight."

I looked round – they were going out with the boxes.

"Where will they take her?"

# 118

"To the morgue in Eldritch, I suppose."

"Well, I'd better go and tell Roland the glad news," said Gareth.

CHAPTER 20

Next morning I was helping Jonathan bag and label things when the phone rang in the office, and Gareth answered it. "It's the police – they want Roland to ring them back," he said, putting his head round the door. "I'll go up and fetch him."

"There are some boxes and packing material to go up to the tent," said Pete. "We need to pack up all those Victorian potsherds - but I want to hear what the police have to say, don't you?"

"I could nip up with some boxes," I said. "Roland won't get here for a bit."

So I made a few journeys with boxes and bags of packing material, which is like the stuff you put in hamster cages for bedding. The tent was empty – the children had gone when their term ended. As I came back in from the last trip, Pete said: "Oh, there you are! You missed all the fun. Roland was trying to tell the law their job. We could hear him yelling down the blower from here."

Gareth shook his head. "He's not happy. He came and told us all about it. Dramatic find like that – might even get into the papers! It probably will now, though, in a different way."

"So they do think it's recent?" I asked.

"Yes, they say 20-30 years. It's their pidgeon now. They'll be back soon – to look at the 'crime scene'. Roland told them we'd taken pictures, but they want to see for themselves."

"I expect they'll start looking up missing persons cases," said Pete.

"Yes, they mentioned that, and something about conditions in the cave, re the preservation and skeletonisation."

"Did Roland tell them about the dig and Sir Finamore?"

"Yes – when he was telling them how we knew about the cave. They even wanted to interview Sir Finamore, but Roland explained he'd keeled over with a heart attack shortly after they stopped filming."

"I knew he'd died suddenly," said Pete. "Were you all still here?" He turned to Jonathan, who'd been working away quietly as usual.

"Yes," said Jonathan, putting down his felt-tip. "We were staying in the old stables, and he was upstairs in our flat over the tack room. Roland was with him."

"That must have been a shock," said Gareth. "Biscuit, anybody? You must have been about the same age as this lot."

"Yes, we didn't really know what to do. The BBC people had packed up and gone. We called 999 and the ambulance came and took him away. Fabia had to ring Lady Whitelock. We all went to his funeral, back in Blackhampton."

"That must have been tough on Fabia," said Gareth. "I mean, what do you say?"

"He died in our flat!" said Pete. "Still, I suppose it's changed a bit since then."

"Not much," said Jonathan. "Same curtains."

"I hope it doesn't spook you out," said Gareth.

"It would be hard to find a building of any age someone hadn't died in," said Jonathan, turning back to his work table.

"Who lived in the big house in your day?" asked Pete.

"The last of the Malisons – mainly in the kitchen. One of them had a model railway in the gallery. And the gardens were all overgrown."

"Sounds rather romantic," said Pete. "But I suppose they have to spruce these places up if they want to make money out of them. Well, do you fancy boxing up some of the rubbish dump?"

So we went up to the tent. There were a lot of old marmalade jars, ginger beer bottles and inkwells stacked around, not all of them broken. I'd already sorted most of the sherds into types, and centuries.

"What's going to happen to it all?" I asked, as we packed it away and wrote on the lids with a Magic Marker.

"We'll give it to Malison Grove and they can put the best bits on display."

"That would be a fun job."

"They could tell the history of the place."

"What about the bones?"

"I'll get the boys to put them in sacks, and there's bound to be a cellar or a buttery they can stash them away in, over at the big house."

"They'll love that."

"There's lots of this blue and white figurative – why don't you slip a few bits into your pocket as a souvenir?"

"I already have. No – not really! I do like these, though." And I picked out the little dolls' soup tureen, and a green piece with a bird on it.

"Very good taste. I can see this jug – I think it's a jug – in an Edwardian bedroom."

"We sell a lot of those bedroom sets." I put the sherds in my pocket.

"Just when everybody's got bathrooms and doesn't use them any more. What do they do with the potties?"

"Plant bulbs in them."

"We can't leave the boxes here – they'll get damp. We'll shlep them down to the barn and I'll ask Mrs Collingwood where she wants them."

Jonathan and Gareth gave us a hand, and we were stacking the boxes in a corner of the barn when a car drove up outside.

"It's the police again," said Gareth, looking out of the window. "We'd better form a reception committee." He went out into the stable yard and Pete and I tagged along.

"Good morning!" said the plainclothes man from the day before. There were two others, one with a camera, and some constables. "We met yesterday – Inspector Forrester. As I told Professor Blair this morning, we'd like to have a look at where the discovery happened. Now you say the remains were found in a cave? I must say I didn't know there were any around here."

"A cave, that's right."

"So you didn't actually dig her up?"

"No – you said she was just sitting there, Anna?"

"You found her?" He turned to me.

"Yes."

"All by yourself?"

"When you see the cave you'll understand why, Inspector," said Pete. "The entrance is tiny. We let her down on a rope."

"Really? How deep is this cave? Sounds more like a pothole. We'll need to take photographs. And any you've got."

"I took some when I found her," I said. "Of the skeleton and the whole cave, really."

"Right. If you give us the film we can get those developed pronto."

"I'll get the camera," said Jonathan, who had come out behind us. "There are some shots of the skeleton on the table, too."

"Were you all present when this discovery was made?"

"Yes, we were," said Gareth. "The entire team, students and all."

"I think we'd better assemble you all again. Is Professor Blair around?"

"They're up near the stone circle," said Gareth. "It's not far from the cave. We can pick up the students on the way if you like. If you want us all to come with you?"

"That's right. Let's get going, shall we? Can I just take your names?"

We gave them, and the sergeant took notes. Jonathan slung the camera round his neck. Followed by the constables, we went up to the ridge, where Bridget was supervising. Everybody stopped and looked at us as we approached.

"This is Bridget Porter, she's in charge up here," said Gareth.

"Right, I'll take over from here," said the Inspector. "Good morning, Madam. I'm Inspector Forrester and this is Sergeant Clavering. It's about this find you made, of the recent skeleton."

"Of course," said Bridget. "We were expecting you."

"We'd like to see where the discovery was made, and I gather you were all present? I think you'd better all come with us. And is Professor Blair up here somewhere?"

"Yes," said Bridget, "If we go this way we'll meet him. It's the most direct route, anyway. Come along, everybody."

"I suppose we'd better do what the law says," said Malcolm, laying down his spade.

"And you don't want to miss the fun," said Colin.

"Right! Where to now?" asked the Inspector.

"Follow me!" said Bridget. "This was some kind of ceremonial road – we've made a lot of interesting finds. Probably ritual deposits."

"Any flint arrowheads?"

"Quite a few, and other tools. Some of them are rather fine."

"Well, we'll go into that later."

Colin fell in beside me. "Well, this is exciting!" he said. "I suppose it's a murder investigation now?"

"I suppose it is."

"I hope this doesn't mean we have to stay at the weekend. I was going to be hopelessly square and visit my parents."

"They said the skeleton had been there 20-30 years. So maybe they only want to talk to anyone who was here 20 years ago."

"Did they? Well, that lets me out."

As we approached the trench where Roland and Fabia were trowelling, Roland rose to his feet and Gareth ushered the Inspector into the presence. As we came up, Roland was saying: "Surely you don't need us all."

"We might as well reconstruct the crime – or the discovery," said the Inspector. "And then of course we'll need to talk to you all – especially this young lady." He indicated me. I suppose he'd forgotten my name. "So this is the famous stone circle? Very impressive."

"Lived here all his life and never seen the sights," said Colin. "Like Londoners not going to the Tower."

"I've never been to the Tower!" I said. "And the circle isn't open to the public."

"I suppose you could look at it from the moor. And there isn't a fence here."

We entered the trees and filed along the narrow path, the Inspector and Roland at the head and two constables at the back.

"So how did you know this place was here?" asked the Inspector.

"We found it on our original dig, 19 years ago," said Roland. "We were investigating the wood for signs that it might have been a sacred grove."

"The wood's private too, like the circle," said Gareth.

"How long has that been the case?"

"Decades, I should imagine."

"We can follow our footprints from the other day," said Roland. "Here they are, going up the bank."

So we all climbed up to the mouth of the cave. The photographer took a lot of pictures – I wondered if he was snapping all of us discreetly.

"It's pretty low and narrow!" said the Inspector, peering in. "Now, can you just explain how you went about the procedure?"

Roland explained about the ropes, and who'd been involved: "You see we didn't get a chance to investigate after the Beeb pulled the plug on the series."

The Inspector sent one of the thinner constables inside with a torch to look down the hole in the cave floor. Jonathan fiddled with his camera, winding the film on.

"So, a medium adult can get that far," said the Inspector, as the constable crawled out and put his helmet back on. "You're next, Richards." He indicated the photographer. "Get some shots through the hole, there may be something else down there. But I don't know how the hell we're going to get it out, unless…"

"I'm not going down there again," I said.

"Don't worry – you can leave it to us. We wouldn't want you tampering with the evidence."

The photographer emerged in his turn. "I've got a few shots with the flash," he said. "I might be able to rig up some way of poking a camera down there."

"Our pictures should be on this film," said Jonathan. "Of the skeleton in situ and when we'd laid it out on the table."

"Thanks," said the Inspector, taking it. "Did you see anything else down there, Richards?"

"Just a lot of ancient-looking bones – fragments, though, sticking out of the mud."

"Yes, we've got a few of those. We'd better get back to base. Have you got an office we can use?"

"How about the lecture theatre?" said Pete.

"That'll do fine. We'll want to talk to you all in turn. Shall we go?"

"Do you mind if we tidy up the trenches on our way? We've left our tools lying about," said Bridget.

"I don't see why not."

So we returned the way we'd come.

\*\*\*

"Is there somewhere you can all wait?" asked the Inspector, as we stood about in the yard.

"I suppose the kitchen, or our flat," said Pete.

"All right, just stick around so you're here when needed. Sergeant Clavering – take everybody's names, and then come and join me. So where's this lecture hall? You come with me, young lady."

"It's this way."

I set some chairs around the table that's usually at the front, and he moved the blackboard out of the way, and the Sergeant came in with his notebook.

"Right," said the Inspector. "I'm assuming you're one of the students and not one of the schoolkids they've had up here helping out."

"Yes, I'm a student, and my name's Anna Savage, like I told the sergeant." I was getting rather tired of "young lady".

"Very well, Miss Savage – "

"Mrs."

"Mrs?"

"Yes, Mrs."

"How long have you been married?"

"Five years, I think."

"So you're a bit older than the other students?"

"Yes, I suppose they're all about 19 or 20."

"It matters at that age. We'd better take your address."

I gave it to the sergeant.

"And what does your hubby do?"

"He's a detective sergeant, in London."

"So you're used to police procedure?" They smirked at each other. "Now – can you tell us how you found the body?"

I launched into the tale, and the sergeant took it down in shorthand.

"Did Professor Blair lead you to the cave?"

"No, Fabia remembered where it was."

"So she was on this famous dig, too?"

"Yes, her and Jonathan. And we only found the chamber when Gavin crawled into the cave the other day. They never investigated the cave back then."

"Gavin?"

"He's the one who looks like a Viking, sir," said Sergeant Clavering.

"So I suppose you lot know all about flint arrowheads? Keep digging them up?"

"Yes, and we made some, and then we had a go shooting with them."

"With bows and arrows? Like cowboys and Indians?"

"Yes, at targets."

"I see. Was anybody supervising?"

"Yes, Gareth and Jonathan."

"And was it the first time any of you had fired off an arrow of any kind?"

"The Blackhampton lot do it as part of a re-enactment. It's called experimental archaeology. But I'd never done it before and I don't think Pete had."

"I suppose it would be quite easy to let one of these things off by accident. If you weren't used to it. Do you fancy having a go, Clavering?"

"Yes, if we can borrow a set?"

"Do you keep the archery gear around somewhere?" asked Inspector Forrester.

"Jonathan put everything away – you'd better ask him."

"So when was this original dig?"

"I can't remember exactly – they turned the TV programmes into a book. There's a copy in the barn. But Roland will know."

"We'd better talk to him next. He looks as if he's about to go off bang. But perhaps he always looks like that. Would you fetch him for us, Mrs Savage?"

## 127

I said I would, and I went. Their questions had been a bit random, but I supposed it was "just routine".

CHAPTER 21

Most of the others were in the kitchen, smoking and drinking tea, but they said Roland and Fabia were up in the flat, so I went to find them. The tutors were all there in the cosy little sitting room, doing the Times crossword. As I went in, Roland was saying: "Of course it's all about the criminal these days. Poor little things have unhappy home lives or neurotic traumas or some such fashionable drivel. But what I say is, what about the victim?"

"Have the police done with you?" Pete asked me. "Who do they want to see next?"

"Roland."

"Your turn, Roland!" said Pete.

"Oh, good!" he said, getting up. "I'd like to talk to them about their dating evidence."

"Stay a minute!" said Pete to me, as Roland stumped down the stairs. "What were they like?"

"Just like normal policemen."

"I suppose you know a lot of them."

"Yes, I do, but when I meet them they're usually off-duty and more friendly."

"Do you think they'd mind if we got on with stuff?" asked Gareth.

"Not as long as they can find you when they want to interview you, I suppose."

I supposed they were done with me for the moment, so I had some tea with the others, and Roland came out, and Fabia went in next. The boys were playing cards at the end of the table and the girls were reading books. I went and wandered round the gardens with the visitors for a bit, and when I returned there were still a few people left in the kitchen and Bridget was saying: "I wonder if the policemen would like some sandwiches? I'll make a lot."

"They'd probably like some tea."

"I took them in some about half an hour ago."

"Next victim!" said Colin, coming in. "Who hasn't been processed yet?"

Derek got up. "Take this plate of sandwiches with you," said Bridget. "And ask them if they want more tea. We'll call it a late lunch."

She put plates of sandwiches on the table and we came and got them. Colin came and sat by me.

"I suppose experimental archaeology was just getting going back then," he said to Donna and Nadine, sitting opposite.

"Back then?"

"When they did the original dig. Though there was none of it in the programmes."

"It all gets a bit much at times," said Nadine. "I'm not the most brilliant cook. Donna's eel chowder wasn't bad, though. But I signed up to dig, not to weave. And I can't get the hang of spinning."

"Surely you just need to work out how it was done?"

"Oh no, we have to make all our costumes. Well, that's the idea. Roland would hate me to tell you, but we had to cheat, otherwise half of us would have been in the nude. There's a Weaver's Guild in the town and they made most of our fabric for us while we pretended to be ever so interested."

"They even spun and dyed the yarn for us," said Donna. "It was quite fun learning about that. Onion skins and roots. The colours are really subtle. And the Guild ladies loved it."

"But I wouldn't touch the animal skins – eugh, the smell!" said Nadine.

"Still, you could see why they needed so many flint scrapers," said Donna. "For tanning leather."

"That was the fun part," said Gavin.

"Well, you cheated too," said Nadine. "Getting those fur pelts from Sweden – or was it Canada?"

Pete came in and said: "We haven't forgotten anybody, have we? The police are packing up, and they told me to tell you all the gossip ban is still on – no chatting with your families, OK? And Roland wants to address us – stay put, I think the coppers are still in the lecture hall. Would you ring the handbell, Donna?"

So she did, and the rest of the compliment trickled in, Roland and Fabia last.

"I think we've all been processed now," said Roland, looking round at us. "And you're all up to speed. Our wonderful policemen think the body is of recent date, and I must admit they made a case. So today has been a bit of a washout, dig-wise. Let's take it easy this afternoon – diggers stand down. Write up your notes and amuse yourselves. Gareth and Jonathan can always do with a hand. Write postcards home, but be discreet. I hope none of you have rung the Daily Yell with the thrilling story of the Corpse in the Cave?"

"Just the Guardian, but it wasn't political enough for them," said Colin.

Roland ignored him and went on: "Meanwhile, I've had one of my brainwaves."

"Don't strain yourself," said Fabia.

"Eldritch, our benighted market town, boasts a pizzeria, would you believe? And I thought it would be jolly good fun if we all went there this evening. They even have wine, though it may be Algerian rough red or German grape juice. What do you think?"

"We'll have to redo the cooking roster," said Gail.

"We can just let off the lucky pair. Agreed? Right, minibus at seven. Jonathan, you can drive. That means you can't drink." We all said "OK" and "Great idea", and the tutors went out.

"So, it's not just a skeleton, it's a 'body', now," said Colin, as we mooched out into the yard.

"Could it be medieval?" asked Donna. "Or Tudor? Were there any clothes?"

"I didn't see any," I said.

"So she was entirely naked," said Malcolm. "Victorian perhaps, like Maria Martin in the Red Barn. The police will have to go through a lot of cold case files of missing persons. Could take them months."

"But shot with a neolithic arrow? How late did flint-knapping go on?" asked Donna.

"The Civil War, really," said Malcolm. "Forget it – we've got the afternoon off. Anyone for table tennis?"

The others dispersed, and I went to the dorm and wrote Mike a long letter about it all. Then I sneaked into the office – nothing is ever locked. The phone was on the desk, which was covered in old yoghourt pots full of pens, and rubber-band balls and paper-clip chains. I rang the number Gilles had given me and he answered. "How nice to hear from you!"

"Did you see the police swarming around?"

"I did. Mrs Collingwood said they came to see something you'd found, but that's all she was told."

"I thought you ought to know, I found a skeleton in the cave in the wood..."

"YOU did?"

"The others were there. We were investigating the cave. And they reported it to the police. You have to, you know, in case it's recent. So they came and took it away, then they came back today and they say it IS recent, and they talked to us all."

"How recent?"

"About 20 years ago. They'll probably want to come and talk to you."

"Mrs Collingwood has a standing order to say I'm away."

"Oh, good."

"But how did you find it?"

"The entrance to the cave is very narrow and nobody else would fit. They let me down on a rope. That was what I minded most, really, not finding the skeleton."

"And how did they retrieve it?"

"They made me go back and get it. I'm not going down there again, though."

"I should hope not. Where are you speaking from?"

"The office. Oh, they've left a policeman behind, I'm not quite sure why. I'd better go now. They'll wonder who I'm talking to and we were told not to talk to anybody."

"Well, goodbye! And thanks! Avoid caves in future – they're full of gorgons, hydras and chimeras dire."

I hung up, and walked into the village to post my letter and postcard.

CHAPTER 22

In the evening I put on clean jeans and a shirt, and one of the skinny-rib cardigans Lawrence had given me, and let down my hair. Nadine put on more makeup and did some back-combing, and Gail applied blue eyeshadow.

"There's no need to package the goods!" said Donna, who looked the same as usual.

"You seem to get on OK," said Nadine, looking at herself in a hand mirror. "Come on Gail, everybody back on the coach!"

"If it's Thursday it must be Belgium," said Donna.

"I wish it was," said Nadine.

Jonathan parked the minibus in a side street and we walked to the pizzeria, where Roland and Fabia were meeting us. It was like a normal restaurant, except the walls and ceiling were made of terracotta pink fake stone.

"I suppose it's meant to be a cave," said Colin.

"What's it made of?" asked Nadine. "Don't poke that stalagmite, Gavin, it might break."

"Chickenwire and plaster, I expect," said Pete, coming in behind us.

"Stalactites not stalagmites," said Colin. "They stick "tite" to the roof."

"Right ho, team," said Gareth. "That must be our table, and there are our Lords and Masters."

There was a long table down one wall, with Roland at the head and Fabia in the middle of one side. Roland raised a hand and we went over and found places to sit.

"This superlative brasserie wasn't here in our day, was it?" said Roland.

"It was just an ordinary café, don't you remember, Fabia?" said Jonathan.

"The past is a merciful blur," said Fabia.

I had a place next to Pete, with Nadine on my other side.

"Well, here we all are!" said Gareth, beaming.

"You do have a talent for stating the obvious, dear," said Fabia, and a waitress came and handed us menus.

"What did I tell you, a choice of plonk or plonk!" said Roland looking at the wine list. "Frascati might be the least nasty."

"Strictly speaking, only white wine is plonk," said Colin. "Vin blanc, you know."

"I'm sure we are all grateful for that public-service announcement," said Roland.

"What do you fancy, Anna?" asked Pete.

"Just the kind with tomatoes and cheese."

"That'll be a Margarita."

"Any drinks while we're waiting?" asked the waitress, getting out a pad and pencil.

"Beverages are on me!" said Roland. "Or at least, on the Foundation. And I, as its illustrious head, command you all to have a good time." Most of the men said "lager" and Bridget and Fabia ordered white wine.

"Don't you ever drink anything but Coke, Anna?" asked Gavin.

"Not all the time."

"Go mad! Let your hair down! Have a – what have they got? Riesling? It'll either taste like lemon juice or boiled sweets, but at least it's alcoholic."

"No, thanks," I said.

"You might lose your inhibitions," said Malcolm.

"Have they ever cut someone open and found an inhibition?" I asked.

Just then Roland tinged on his glass with a knife and bellowed: "Pray silence! A few announcements. As you know, midsummer's coming up, and I thought I'd give some of you a long weekend – Monday off, long enough to get home and see your parents, or loved ones. We can't spare you all, but here's a completely random selection. We won't miss..." He read from a list in his hand: "Gail, Derek, Colin, Gareth, Bridget, Anna, Pete."

"Thanks, Roland," said Gareth. "I haven't seen Rosie and the kids for weeks. Talking on the phone just isn't the same."

"Jonathan, you've never had any loved ones, so you can stick around and be useful."

"Yes, I've always got plenty to do."

I was just planning which train I'd get and what we'd do when Pete chipped in: "I don't think any of my wives want to see me – and I've got loads of notes to type up and lectures to prepare. I was hoping Anna could help me, she's a whizz on the Olivetti. And she's doing such good work on the possible artefact. It might be something we can impress funding bodies with."

"Good point," said Roland. "You don't mind, do you, Anna? The lucky few can be off on Saturday morning, and come back Monday night."

"I hope you don't mind?" Pete said to me and I said oh no that was fine. "Only if the Thing is gold, or finely worked, we can attract some press coverage and more money."

"Well, that's just great!" said Nadine. "It's like being told there's a school treat and getting all excited and then being told you're being kept in as a punishment."

Gareth said quickly: "So where's everybody going on holiday this year?"

"Walking the Pennines with a group," said Donna. "After this."

"Do you think I could get another weekend off, though?" I asked Pete. "It's my birthday after midsummer and I think we'll still be here."

"And you're making up your mind to be 19," said Fabia.

"I'll be 23. I'm a mature student."

"Thanks for making me feel about 100."

The waitress started handing out the drinks, and I asked Nadine if the Foundation members often had meals out.

"Yes," she sighed. "We socialise a lot. It takes up a lot of time. I wish I'd never joined the beastly outfit, but Gavin insisted."

"But isn't that the point of a club? Or a soc?"

"Not when you have to dress up as a Viking and make salutations to Odin and drink out of cow-horns."

"What, real ones?"

"Yes, the boys make them. Everything has to be authentic. Roland insists."

"Do you all belong?"

"Just me and Donna, and Gavin and Malcolm. Gail thinks it's all Satanic, and anyway, she wasn't invited. You know when you arrive at university and you just join everything because you want to meet people?"

"It's not really like that at Regent."

"With this lot, you have to sign up for the whole three years – or is it life? Roland and Fabia and Jonathan have been members for years. I think Sir Finamore was the head back then – oh, here's my pizza."

Hers was Hawaiian, with ham and pineapple.

"It was brave of you to turn down a drink," said Pete to me. "It's all 'have some Madeira, my dear'. They probably do it to you a lot, because you look so young."

"Not really. We mainly go out with Mike's colleagues and their wives, and they're used to me. There's a policemen's club with a bar, and we have parties there, and discos."

"Ever so suburban!"

"I suppose it is. Some of them do live in suburbs and have big gardens and kids. Well, that's OK."

"But you couldn't live there?"

"No. We'd miss London."

"Did you grow up there?"

"No. Actually both of us grew up in suburbs! Well, I lived in one for a bit."

"I wouldn't put it past them to spike your drink, either, so watch out."

"I hadn't thought of that."

My pizza came and the waitress went round the table spraying some dressing from a bottle onto everybody's food.

"What's that?" I asked Pete.

"Chilli oil," he said, holding out his plate. I quickly covered my pizza with my serviette and hands and said "No thanks!", and the waitress looked at me as if I was mad.

"Hot stuff!" sneered Malcolm. "Try it! You might like it."

"That's what they say about drugs," I muttered.

"So you never tried those either?"

"I don't smoke."

"There are always hash brownies."

"You ought to try living dangerously, Anna," said Gavin. "We can always call the waitress back."

"I just don't like spicy food."

Fabia, who'd been sitting in silence looking grumpy as usual, got to her feet and said "It's so stuffy in here!" and stalked out of the restaurant.

"Oh dear, in one of her huffs again," murmured Pete in my ear.

Bridget was looking concerned, and saying something to Roland.

"Perhaps someone should go after Fabia, though," I said. "She looked upset."

"She always looks upset. Odd to see her smiling in those TV programmes."

"Shall I see where she's got to?" asked Donna.

"It'll only annoy her more," said Roland.

"Not half as much as if nobody goes," Pete muttered to me. "But leave it for a while – she's probably just gone to the pub to down a few whiskies. Don't say I said that. I was thinking of somebody else."

Donna got up, and Roland said: "She'll come back in her own good time."

But Donna went out, and we all started munching our pizzas. We could see Donna and Fabia standing on the opposite pavement outside the bank, deep in discussion, Fabia with her arms crossed.

"Very defensive body language," said Nadine.

"They'll miss Roland's lecture," said Pete.

"Lecture?"

"After a few bevvies, you don't think he'll keep quiet, do you?"

"Of course, Christianity is just another sacrificial cult," said Roland, laying down his knife and fork.

"Here we go," said Pete.

"Piety will ever suffer persecution!" said Gail, who was sitting with Derek.

"We know all about your martyr complex, Gail," said Roland. "Well, passing swiftly on, or we may get a sermon from the other end of the table."

"A rival sermon – that would never do!" said Pete in an undertone.

"Who said that, Gail?" I asked her. "Were you quoting somebody?"

"St Paul again. He said we'd be attacked before Armageddon."

"Bonkers!" said Pete. "But well done for speaking up."

"Oh, Derek, I've still got your dowsing rods, they're in my – "

"If I have everybody's attention?" said Roland. "And you thought I'd just brought you for a meal out! Human sacrifice was known among the Druids, Celts and Odinists. The Druids believed in reincarnation. But the purpose of that was to make warriors brave – if you didn't fear death you would be all the more..."

"Bloodthirsty?" asked Pete.

"Courageous!"

"So sacrificing a human was some kind of proof?" asked Bridget, looking puzzled.

"Pythagoras taught that souls migrated, because if you just told people not to murder each other they took no notice."

"You might come back as a beetle!" said Gavin.

"And the idea made people kind to animals, as former people. At least, Pythagoras thought it would."

"What evidence have we that these people sacrificed humans?" asked Malcolm. "I know about the Aztecs, but..."

"Yes, the Aztecs did some pretty gruesome things, including flaying their victims and wearing their skins..."

Bridget's friendly smile dropped a fraction, and Nadine grumbled: "Must he go on about it just when we're eating?"

"I mean, isn't it like cannibalism?" asked Gavin. "It's always the next tribe that does it, but you can never find them?"

"And well done Gavin and Malcolm for asking the right questions," said Pete quietly.

"Yes, cannibalism," said Roland. "Some say it's a traveller's tale. And some say it's still happening. However, I'd like to use you as a focus group – I've got a TV series of my own under development, as you know."

"Wants to be another Sir Finamore," muttered Pete. "Modelled himself on the great man ever since."

"Did you mention Sir Finamore, Pete? Those theatrical trappings would never go over these days. That long hair and beard look ridiculous to us now."

I looked round the table and counted a high number of long hair and beard combinations.

"But I believe the time is ripe for a look at the way certain ideas have migrated through space and time. The Ancient Greek mysteries with their symbolic death and rebirth. Initiates actually spent the night in a grave! Rock-cut graves have been found in Mithraeums – they did the same. And the wolf cult – we know about Odin's wolves who will eat the sun and the moon at Ragnarok, and the Fenriswulf who will destroy the world at the end of time. Armageddon if you like, Gail. There was a wolf cult in many societies. Cohorts of young men lived as wolves for several years, raping and pillaging. Pits full of butchered wolf and dog bones have been found."

"Dogs too!" said Bridget, looking distressed. "Feral dogs?"

"No, it's thought they hunted with the dogs for a few seasons, and then sacrificed and ate them, to assimilate their fierce qualities."

Fabia and Donna came back in and sat silently down in their places. Fabia cut her pizza into slices and began eating it in her fingers.

"So what do you think, guys?" asked Roland, ignoring her.

"Human sacrifice and wolf cults?" asked Gareth.

"A programme on each, showing the universality."

"Like Mr Casaubon's *Key to All Mythologies*!" said Colin brightly.

"As I recall he failed to read the latest research, which was all in German, which he'd neglected to learn. If you remember your *Middlemarch*."

"It was on telly," said Nadine. "But she marries the handsome one in the end."

"Odin and his wolves – the wild hunt – were said to ride out at the winter solstice and might take you up with them."

"I've got a theory about British festivals," said Colin.

"You would have!" said Roland. "Well, let's hear the latest."

"Various customs have got moved around – Christmas customs got stuck onto Halloween – all that about zombies and vampires and demons really belongs at the darkest time of the year."

"Well, thank you for giving us the benefit of your research!"

"I'll write a book about it. All entirely speculative, like most paperbacks."

"Of course, the Vikings were pretty violent too," said Malcolm quickly. "All that about the blood eagle."

"That could have formed part of a human sacrifice," said Roland. "For those of you who don't know, the victim was dismembered while still alive, and his lungs were displayed on his back like a pair of wings."

Fabia put down her slice of pizza and stared at her plate.

"Victims were members of the royal family," continued Roland.

"But it could be a literary invention, or a mistranslation," said Colin.

"Many things COULD be," said Roland.

"I thought Odin's bird was the raven," Colin went on.

"Guess who's going to end up as an offering to the gods?" muttered Pete.

Roland began to chant loudly: "Ok Ellu bak, At lét hinn's sat, Ívarr, ara, Iorví, skorit. And the ravens were glad," he ended triumphantly.

"Any desserts?" asked the waitress, handing him a menu.

"The Druids, of course," carried on Roland, taking it from her. "We could do a whole programme on them. Strabo says some victims were shot dead with arrows in temples, or else burned in the famous "wicker man". Wouldn't that look magnificent? Without the victims, of course. The RSPCA wouldn't like that, would they, Bridget?"

"I saw that at an all-night horror screening," said Malcolm.

"You could add some legs of lamb – or venison – and have a feast," said Pete.

"Not a bad idea!" said Roland. "I'm sure the audience would love it."

"Can I take your dessert order?" asked the waitress and people asked for ice cream and rum babas.

"Some Roman authorities said the Druids were wise and kind and knew about plants and the stars," Pete said to me.

"They could have been both," I said. "Wise and kind AND they sacrificed people."

"That's an interesting theory – you should tell Colin."

But Colin had another question for Roland: "I don't really see the point. All these things, the mysteries, the Mithras cult. I mean, what was the idea of becoming a Mysteron?"

"There was always a reward," said Roland. "Want to succeed in business without really trying? Marry the girl of your dreams? Beat the neighbouring tribe in battle? You had to give the gods something back if they were going to help you. Anyway, more of this anon."

"There's always a catch," Pete muttered to me.

"What was that he was chanting?"

"Search me."

"Skaldic poetry," said Gavin.

"What about the bog bodies, they're popular?" asked Malcolm.

"Yes, see the Gundestrup cauldron," said Roland. "One of the Irish bog bodies was strangled, hit on the head, and had his throat cut, in quick order, then surrendered to the bog. And he seems to have been of high rank, and a willing victim. They chucked people into disused grain-storage pits and shafts, too."

"Grain-storage pits, now they're interesting," said Gareth. "The carbon dioxide given off by the germination of the top layer preserves the..."

"Why don't you prepare us a lecture on them?" said Roland.

"Good idea."

We had coffee, and Roland paid the entire bill, saying "It's all on the Foundation!". Then we shuffled out and back to the minibus. I was walking next to Pete, who said: "Nice dinner, anyway."

"The Foundation must have a lot of money."

"It does, thanks to the original Mr Pearman. Don't you know its history?"

"Colin and Nadine told me a bit."

"It was founded in the 18th or 19th century by Druid revivalists. And like all these societies, some rich bloke stumped up the cash, and they invested it, and now there's thousands there for the asking if you become one of the officers. It was a canny move on Roland's part, taking it over. He's got some flowery title – chairman of the board, or chief druid, or something! Oh no, we've lost Fabia again!"

Fabia was stalking off into the night, with Donna after her. We carried on to where the minibus was parked, and Roland followed us, still sounding off to Gavin and Malcolm about foundation sacrifices at Maiden Castle. We waited by the van, and just as Jonathan was saying "I suppose I'd better go and look for them," they came round the corner. Roland took Fabia's arm and said "Goodnight", and they went off to where their car was parked.

"Amazing the way she gets everybody running after her," Pete muttered to me as Jonathan drove us off, and the others started singing Swing Low, Sweet Chariot. "So anyway, the Foundation did some good work in the antiquarian line, studying the folklore of hoards and monuments, and surveying stone circles. They rather made a habit of that and their data is still used. The Druids are still around, of course, turning up in full costume at Stonehenge at the summer solstice – we saw them in the TV programme. But they're a different lot and hang out in Wales."

When we were undressing in the dorm I asked Donna: "Is Fabia OK?"

"She's all right," said Donna. "Just attention-seeking."

"And she's heard Roland's lecture on human sacrifice a thousand times," said Nadine.

For some reason I remembered the hippies, who thought it was all right to be pretty rude. They also had a rule that you never commented on what anybody did, and people often disappeared without saying where they were going or why. And they said they didn't have any rules. I must remember to give the dowsing rods back to Derek.

CHAPTER 23

Early on Saturday morning, Jonathan drove the chosen ones to Eldritch to get trains, and Roland came into the kitchen and said he wanted to go on surveying up at the circle.

"I'll need some volunteers – you, you, you and you. Fabia obviously, Gavin, Malcolm, Nadine, Donna. Jonathan can take some pictures and make himself useful. It should only take the morning. The rest of you know what you're doing? Good."

"Oh, I wish I'd had the weekend off, it's all right for some," moaned Nadine, pushing her chair back and taking her mug and plate to the sink.

"Not getting bored, I hope?" Pete asked me. "We'd better carry on in the barn." I said that was fine. Nadine and Gavin were putting stuff into the dishwasher and arguing in mutters. I heard a few words as I stacked dirty plates on the side: "Bet he wants to sound off some more... didn't bring the costumes for nothing... not like that... waste of time... cups go on the top!"

I left them to it, and went into the barn and turned on my Anglepoise.

"I hope they don't want us all to dress up," I said to Pete.

"As Ancient Britons? I can understand trying to reproduce the technology, but... Perhaps that's why they've all got beards!"

"Where's Jonathan?"

"He's fetching and carrying for Roland at the circle – he's got fewer minions than usual."

"So what did the police ask you?"

"Same as you, I expect. How we found the body and so on. I said 'What about potholers?' They wanted to know about the original dig and who was there, but I told them to ask Roland."

After lunch Pete and I worked in the office for a bit – he dictated from notes and I typed. After a while he said, "I've had enough of paperwork, let's see if the others have come back from the circle and dug up anything."

It was a still day, sunny and even quite warm. At the students' trench, Nadine and Donna were operating the sieve, and even Roland was wielding a pick. We made a couple of trips up and down with trays. Next time we came up, everyone was taking five, and Roland was leaning on a spade.

"I thought Fabia would be back by now," he said, looking along the ridge towards the stone circle. "What is the time?"

"About teatime, I think," said Malcolm. "She wanted to recheck some measurements. With all due respect they don't quite tally with the records."

"From 19 years ago? We were hamming it up for the cameras. No wonder they're a bit off. I'll persuade her to quit. Malcolm, you're in charge. Keep them up to it." And he set off along the ridge.

"She always vornts to be alone," said Nadine, imitating Greta Garbo badly.

We went back to the barn and carried on, with Jonathan flitting in and out as usual.

\*\*\*

It was my turn to cook, with Colin but he'd gone to see his "aged parents", so Donna said she'd help me. Nadine came and smoked in the kitchen and read Love Story while we were boiling rice and frozen peas. We added peanuts, raisins, red beans, chopped tomatoes and parsley, and everybody came in to eat it.

"Roland and Fabia not gone home yet?" Pete wondered. "Their car's still in the yard."

"Roland went to look for Fabia at the stone circle," said Gavin. "They can't still be measuring."

"Perhaps the stones keep moving about when they're not looking," said Malcolm. "They do that, you know, if you try to count them."

"Perhaps one's fallen over on them," said Nadine.

"Yes," said Gavin. "That one they tried to uproot. Stones never forget, like elephants."

"Perhaps they're revisiting the romantic scene where they first met," said Donna.

"Re-enacting it, you mean," said Gavin.

We all munched the rice and a green salad, and had apples and bananas and cheese for pudding, but Roland and Fabia didn't turn up.

"Well, it's the shortest night," said Pete. "Perhaps they're going to wait for the sunrise like real Druids. But you'd think they'd have warned us. And they must be getting hungry. Come on, let's see if they're still up there. Want to come, Anna? Anybody else?"

The boys said they were going to the pub, and Donna and Nadine said they'd go too. Jonathan had gone out again earlier, probably back to the flat.

"Let's go via the field," said Pete.

***

There were a few buckets and plastic sheets stacked by the spoil heaps, but no Roland and Fabia, so we set out along the ridge to the stone circle, with the moor on our right, where the sun was sinking. We walked on in silence until we could see the stone circle – and Roland, sitting on the central slab with his head bowed. Pete called out "Hi, Roland!", but he didn't raise his head. He was looking down at Fabia, who was lying on the grass at his feet.

"Stay there, Anna," said Pete. He went up to Roland and put a hand on his shoulder.

"She's dead," said Roland. "I went to look for her and she was here. She's quite cold."

Fabia was lying on her face, with the shaft of an arrow sticking out of her back.

"We'd better call the police," said Pete. "What a terrible accident!"

"Is that what you'll tell them?"

"Come on, you can't stay here." He tried to get Roland to his feet. "How long have you been here?"

"I don't know," said Roland, looking up and staring into the setting sun.

"It's about half past eight now."

"Someone should stay with her."

"Yes, but you come with us now."

"Don't leave her alone."

Pete looked at me.

"You go," I said. "I'll stay. You ought to ring the police as soon as possible."

So Pete hauled Roland to his feet and put an arm through his and led him into the path through the trees, where they quickly disappeared in the shadows. Fabia was lying next to the central stone, facing west, with her arms flung forward. I knelt beside her and held her hand. It was cold, and her hair was straggling into the muddy grass.

After a while I got up, and went to sit with my back against one of the megaliths, where I could see if anyone came up by the path or along the ridge. I hugged my knees and I listened out for footsteps, or the police arriving, but heard only birds singing, then a high-pitched howl from the moor. It was joined by a chorus, running up the scale and yelping down it. There was a low rumbling, and the megalith I was leaning against trembled. Then I heard faint police sirens, so I knew people would be here soon.

They came crashing up the path through the woods, and I got to my feet as Pete and the inspector and a lot of other policemen came out of the trees.

"Stay outside the circle, lads, we want to look for footprints," said the Inspector, and they started unrolling plastic tape. He and Pete came towards me, walking close to the stones.

"Are you all right, young lady?" said the inspector.

"Yes, I'm OK."

"Brave of you to stay up here alone."

"Not really."

"How long have you been here?"

"About half an hour, I suppose. Where's Roland?"

"There's a spare room in our flat, we've put him there," said Pete. "Gavin and Malcolm are trying to get him to eat something. Jonathan's looking after the girls – they're very shocked."

"I hope you haven't touched or moved anything?" Inspector Forrester asked me.

"I held her hand for a bit."

"How did it feel?"

"Cold."

"So you just walked over to her and back."

"Yes."

"You two join the others, Mr Beckerlegge. We'll be down when we've done the forensics up here. And then we can take this poor lady away. Off you go. Oh, better go with them, Smithers."

Pete took my hand, saying "I hope it wasn't too awful," and we entered the dark wood, with one of the constables walking behind us.

"I've never seen anybody who's just died before," I said. "But now I have. Poor Roland."

"He seems quite shattered. All the bounce gone out of him. I suppose they'd been together since the days of Sir Finamore. Funny they never got married. Sorry, I'm burbling. Must be the shock."

"That's OK."

"Whereas you've gone unnaturally calm. Nothing wrong with that. Poor Nadine is sobbing her heart out."

"I think she's quite sensitive, really. So's everybody, really."

"Shame we've got no medicinal brandy on the premises. I wonder if they've got some next door? I expect the police are talking to Mrs Collingwood, too."

"It probably just makes you feel worse."

"I wish Gareth and Bridget were here to fuss over us."

We went by the front of the house and Pete dropped my hand as we reached the kitchen. It seemed very bright inside. Nadine was sitting at the table smoking and Donna had an arm round her shoulders. Jonathan was sitting apart from them, down at the end. There was a policewoman standing by the stove and she said, "I'll boil another kettle, then, shall I?"

The constable who'd accompanied us stood just inside the door and took out a notebook.

"They'll want you all to stay while we investigate," said the policewoman. "I'm Eleanor, by the way," she said to me.

"I'm Anna, and this is Pete," I said.

"We wondered if they might have some brandy next door!" said Pete.

"Someone's talking to the manageress now. But the doctor will be along in a minute, we can get him to look in."

Nadine said: "I'm so sorry it was Fabia."

"Why don't you ring your mother? Would that help?" asked Eleanor, handing me a mug of tea. "Put in lots of sugar."

"Oh no, she'd be terribly upset," said Nadine croakily. "I'll call her tomorrow. I expect I'll have calmed down a bit."

"But can I make a phone call?" I asked. "Is it OK to say what's happened?"

"Yes, we'll be putting out a statement," she said. "Just don't give too many details. Where's the phone? You go with her, Smithers."

We went into the lobby by the office and I phoned Mike. Fortunately he was at home.

"Hello, sweetheart!" he said. "What gives?"

"I can't talk long," I said. "I just wanted to tell you there's been another murder. Same MO."

"Who – or can't you say? Is anybody with you?"

"Yes. It was Fabia – Professor Blair's girlfriend."

"Are you OK?"

"I'm just terribly sorry for them."

"I wish I was there."

"I wish you were too. And I promised to keep out of trouble!"

"It does follow you around. Where are you?"

"In the lobby, there's a constable with me. Everybody's in the kitchen. They'll want to come and talk to us soon. I'd better go."

"I'd come and get you – but they'll want you all to stay. Ring me tomorrow, at work, any time. Don't take risks, keep with the others. I'll try and find out what's happening. I love you!"

"I love you! Goodbye."

I put the phone down. I couldn't really ring Gilles, how could I explain it to Smithers? And Mrs Collingwood would tell him. We went back into the kitchen, and I sat down next to Pete.

"Talk to your husband? Feel better now?"

"Yes."

"Can I ring my mum now?" said Donna, and Smithers was sent out with her again.

"You know," I said quietly to Pete, "If the murderer came up the path through the wood, there'll be no way of telling now."

"Good point. We'd have walked all over his footprints. And I thought you weren't noticing anything. I hope it wasn't too grim, being there on your own."

I didn't say that I hadn't exactly been alone. Nadine was calmer, but still chain-smoking.

"Did you phone your parents?" Eleanor asked me.

"No, my husband. My parents aren't around."

"Sorry to hear that!"

"What about tonight?" asked Nadine. "Can we lock our door?"

"We'll leave some more constables, Miss," said Smithers. "And you'll be with your friends."

"I suppose so. I can't believe she's gone. I almost wish Gail was here! She'd tell us she'd gone to a better place."

"There is no death, only change," as an Agatha Christie character says, but Fabia really had gone, and it sounds like a platitude, so I said nothing. I wonder if my parents miss me? Perhaps living for hundreds of years makes you care less about other people.

So we sat there and Eleanor asked us what it was like studying archaeology, and Donna started talking about youth hostels, and we giggled weakly at incidents that weren't really funny. Then the Inspector came in again with Sergeant Clavering and another man, and said: "This is Dr Jones. Are you feeling better, young lady? Still in need of brandy?"

"These are better than brandy," said the doctor, handing Nadine an envelope. "Take one if you can't sleep. Everybody else OK? I'll be off then." And he went out. The Inspector pulled a chair up to the table.

"Take notes, Clavering. Now tonight I don't want to keep you all up. I just want to get a picture of where you all were this afternoon. We've got your names and addresses from the other day. But there don't seem to be so many of you as before." He looked round at us.

"Some of us got the weekend off. Gavin and Malcolm are with Roland in the flat. Has the doctor seen him?" asked Pete.

"Yes, he gave him a sedative. We gathered the other day that he and the victim lived together."

149

"Yes, that's right."

"I wonder why they never married."

"They were Bohemians in their day, I expect."

"So who went home for the weekend?"

"Gail and Derek and Colin – they're students. Bridget and Gareth, they're the other tutors."

Clavering scribbled in his notebook.

"Let's deal with you girls first. It's Anna, Nadine and Donna, isn't it? I hope you don't mind first names?" We said that was fine.

"Nadine, just tell me your movements this afternoon and you can get off to bed."

"We were all together most of the day. We did some more surveying at the circle in the morning."

"All of you?"

"Me and Donna, and Malcolm and Gavin, and Fabia and Roland were in charge. Jonathan came too to take photographs. After lunch we went back to our trench, and Fabia went back to the circle, and Jonathan went back to the barn, and Roland came with us because he said somebody ought to be in charge. And then later he went back to the circle to see what was keeping Fabia."

"And you can't see the circle from there?"

"No – the woods are in the way. It must have been different when the circle was built."

"And where were you two?" He turned to me and Pete.

"We were in the barn," said Pete. "Toiling away all day. No, I tell a lie, we were both in the office for quite a while. And we went up to the students' trench to collect more finds. That was in the afternoon. We made several trips."

"And Mr Leaf was with you?"

"He was in and out in the afternoon. I think he went to the office to get more labels and that sort of thing."

"And what time did Professor Blair leave you?"

"A bit before knocking-off time," said Donna.

"Didn't anybody have a watch?"

"We take off watches and jewellery."

"And were there any more comings and goings?"

"Well, obviously people sometimes go down to the stables to go to the loo."

"That was when you were in your trench?"

"Yes. And Malcolm went to get some biscuits. And Gavin took some finds down."

"But you girls were in sight of each other? Did you go to the powder-room together?"

"We did, actually."

"Just the once?"

"Probably a couple of times."

"And it's different for boys, of course. Probably just nipped into the wood. Right. So how long does it take you to walk down here from your trench?"

"Five or ten minutes."

"And from your trench to the circle?"

"About the same. Perhaps a bit longer."

"Thank you. So Mr Beckerlegge and Mrs Savage were together most of the time. Now I'll let you girls get to bed. Mr Beckerlegge can give me details about how and when you decided to look for Professor Blair and Miss Thompson."

We left them to it.

"What's he given you?" asked Donna.

"Some white pills," said Nadine, looking in the envelope. "I think I'll take one. I just want oblivion. For a bit. I wish I could just walk out and not come back."

"You don't, really," said Donna. "Where would you go? And the police would always find you." She went out to the showers.

"Do you think it's possible to start a new life somewhere else with a different identity?" Nadine asked me, picking up her wash bag. I could have said "I've known a few people who've done it and got away with it," but I just said: "I believe it is possible."

"How would you get a passport? You'd have to nick someone else's birth certificate."

"I suppose you would."

"They must have taken Fabia away. I heard a car drive off."

She went into the showers too, and came back with a glass of water and took the pill. We got into bed and turned out the lights. "Goodnight, everybody," said Nadine. I said "Goodnight", and Donna said "Goodnight, John boy". I lay awake for quite a long time. The police drove away at about two in the morning.

CHAPTER 24

Everybody was pretty quiet the next day, too. There were two constables in the yard, and the Inspector and his team drove up as we were eating breakfast. He came in and said, "Morning! Now we'll be around most of the day, but I suppose it's a working day for you so just carry on as usual – except for up at the stone circle, we've taped it off. And there are some constables at the cave. We'll be in and out, just ignore us unless we want to talk to you."

Pete came in while this was going on and told them, "Come in here any time and make teas and coffees. And there's a café at the Grove. And a shop and a chippy in the village, but I expect you know that."

"Thanks. We'll be fine." And he went out.

"Well, how are we all feeling?" asked Pete. "Take it easy, but I think work will take our minds off it. You'd better carry on with what you were doing. Any problems, ask me and I won't know the answer."

"How's Roland?" asked Donna.

"He insisted on going back to his B&B. Jonathan offered to drive him but he said he'd rather be alone."

\*\*\*

The police came into the barn later and asked Jonathan to show them where the bows and arrows were kept. The inspector tutted at the unlocked cupboard and asked if any were missing, but Jonathan said there weren't.

"Well, perhaps you didn't think of them as lethal weapons," said the Inspector. "We'll fingerprint them all, Clavering. There are five here – not one for each of you, then."

"No, the students took turns shooting at the target," said Jonathan. "I made some of these, and various Blackhampton students made the others. And the arrows as well."

"OK," said the Inspector. "Clavering, when you've done that, organise a search of the stables, and we're going to look at your sleeping quarters too." And he went out.

"Have you got something to wrap these in?" asked Sergeant Clavering.

They wrapped the bows and arrows in bin bags and tied them up with string, and Sergeant Clavering took them outside. He came back saying: "Who do the ponies and horses belong to?"

"The big house. There are some girls who look after them, and attach the ponies to a cart for trips round the grounds. And we've been told not to go near the horse," said Pete.

"Yes, it looked a bit frisky."

"Better consult Mrs Collingwood next door if you want to search the stables."

"Yes, apparently the owner's away. I'll talk to her, thanks." And he left.

"Of course it would be a good place to hide a murder weapon," I said to Pete. "In the stable of a skittish horse."

"Hasn't it been done? Or was the horse the murder weapon?"

"I think I've read that one."

"You haven't got any with you, have you? Detective stories, I mean. There's nothing here but historical novels and thrillers."

"I have got a few I could lend."

Clavering popped back again. "So which of you are the arrowhead experts?" he asked.

"Well, there's Gareth," said Jonathan.

"And you made the arrows the students were playing with."

"Yes, and they made some themselves, like I said."

Clavering looked around at the finds trays. "You're not short of arrowheads, are you? Can I take any of these?"

"I don't think so, they're finds from our dig and we're busy labelling and classifying them. We can give you a book, though. Didn't Gareth give you some arrowheads the other day?"

He got a book off the shelf and handed it to Clavering, who leafed through it: "And have you made all these different types? Some of them are quite intricate, aren't they? Must take a lot of patience."

"Well it's the only way, really, of working out how they were made."

"Thanks, I'll take this." And he went out again.

"Of course the only difference would be in quality," Pete said to me. "One arrowhead is much like another. Good grief, the others will be back this evening. I've got to think of something to say to them."

"They'll all be on the same train," said Jonathan. "I'm going to meet them at around half five."

"Good," said Pete. "I'd better come with you."

Suddenly there was an almighty bang, and we all jumped. "That sounded like a bomb!" said Pete, and we went out into the yard.

"Not to worry," said the constable on duty. "They took some dynamite up to the cave to enlarge the entrance."

"Without asking anybody's permission!" said Pete, crossly. "Roland will be furious. And what about the owner? What do they hope to find?"

"Some clothes?" I asked.

"Good point," he said. "But Lord knows what damage they've done. Well, it's too late now."

\*\*\*

Later Jonathan and Pete drove off to meet the train, and the others arrived back, looking rather stunned.

"Well, I'm not going to pretend I'm not shocked," said Bridget, as we gathered in the kitchen. "How are you all holding up? At least you had each other."

"Poor old Roland!" said Gareth. "I can hardly believe it."

"Will the police be back in force tomorrow?" asked Derek. "Are we going to close down the dig?"

"Yes, they'll be back, and I don't know."

"We'll have to see what Roland says," said Pete. "He's been incommunicado and I think they didn't want to bother him."

"How did it go at the station?" I asked him.

He dropped his voice. "I gathered them on the platform and said to come out to the minibus as I had something to tell them. They must have seen from my face something was wrong. So we went into the car park and I told them there'd been a quite ghastly accident, and poor Fabia was dead, and the police wanted to talk to them. And then I answered a few questions and Jonathan drove us home."

"I don't see any point in speculating," said Colin. "Leave that to the police. But why do they want to talk to us? Oh, I see – to work out if we could have got a train back and then gone again. Well, that's pretty far-fetched but I suppose they have to explore every avenue. How's Roland taking it?"

"He went back to the B&B."

"On his own?"

"I think I'll give him a ring, see how he is," said Pete, getting up.

While we were eating Penguin biscuits he came back and said: "Roland sounded not too bad, considering. And he's going to address you all tomorrow morning. I expect he's made a decision about whether or not to continue. After all, we've only got another couple of weeks. But the police aren't finished with us yet and don't want us to leave town, as they say."

I hoped they wouldn't want to search my locker. Where can I hide some Tarot cards, a crystal ball, a book of spells and an incriminating diary? I thought the others might stick around out of respect, or something, but the usual gang went to the pub, and Colin and I watched TV, and Gail and Derek went AWOL. I was asleep when the others got back.

\*\*\*

I woke early and got up as quietly as I could. Donna groaned, "What time is it?" And I said, "It's OK, I just can't sleep." I put the cards, the book, my diary and the crystal in my rucksack, and went out into the yard. The copper standing by the kitchen door said: "You're an early bird!"

I said: "Someone will be making tea in a minute. Or you go ahead - don't wait for us."

"Good idea," he said, and went into the kitchen.

I went to the stable where the horse lives, and looked in over the top of the door. He came and put his head out - he didn't look fierce. Quietly I said:

Creature of Poseidon hear me
I, Potnia Theron, command thee
Into thy domain admit me
Do not harm me, guard my hoard
Aid me when you hear my word.

I unbolted the bottom half of the door and went in, shutting it behind me. The horse stood aside and then returned to the doorway as I went to the back of the loose-box where there was some tack hanging up on pegs. I hung my rucksack on the end one. The heavy crystal ball thumped against the wooden panels. The horse was still guarding me, so I took the crystal out to see if it had anything to tell me. It was dark in the stable, but the crystal was glowing. I looked into it and saw stacks of cardboard boxes, like the ones we put finds in when they've been labelled and recorded. That vision faded, and I saw an attic full of old junk – a rocking horse and a lot of trunks and one of those dummies dressmakers use – Mum had one. The picture greyed into mist, and then the stone circle appeared. A huge megalith seemed to move towards me, and then the crystal filled with smoke again and the light went out. I put it back into the bag.

I moved up beside the horse and he made way for me. I shut the half door, and went to have a shower before the others woke up. I had told the horse I was Potnia Theron, mistress of animals – it has worked before. Poseidon is god of horses as well as the sea. People keep telling me I'm more powerful than other witches and wizards, but I don't know where they get that idea from. Other people in the magical underground, I mean. Perhaps it was because I knew things about them they didn't want anybody to know. And I cast a successful curse on somebody – I'm never going to do that again. I'd have to carry on with my diary on sheets of file paper and keep them in my handbag, or something.

When I came out of the shower Nadine was sitting on her bed, wearing a pale blue nighty with puffed sleeves.

"Have you been up for ages?" she asked. "I thought I heard someone get up, but then I fell asleep again."

"I couldn't sleep. I just wandered round a bit."

"Do you want one of these sleeping pills tonight? I've still got quite a few. Work like a charm."

"No, thanks. I'll be OK. Kind of you."

I'd washed my hair, so I sat on my bed detangling it with a wide-toothed comb while the others got up. We went to breakfast and I gave Derek back the dowsing rods. He said "Thanks, any time! Have any luck?" I said it was hard to tell. While we were eating muesli, the sergeant came in.

"Good morning!" he said. "I wonder if you'd all give me your locker keys? Or leave the lockers open, if you like. Just a precaution."

"I don't know what he thinks we've got hidden," said Nadine. "Perhaps I'll write some steamy love letters for him to find."

I propped my locker door open and left the key in the lock. There were some letters from Mike but they'd think that was normal. Then Bridget put her head in and said: "Roland's going to talk to us all in the lecture room in five minutes."

"I hope he's going to tell us we can all go home," said Nadine.

"I thought you were feeling better," said Donna.

We sat down on benches in the hall just as if it was a normal day, with the tutors in a bunch up at the end by the table and the blackboard. Roland came and stood beside the table and said "Good morning".

Colin stood up: "Roland, we just wanted to say how sorry we are about Fabia." We all made agreeing noises.

"Thank you, Colin," said Roland. "It was a terrible thing to happen. An accident, perhaps. But I'm sure the police will soon get to the bottom of it, and they say they don't mind if we continue the programme as planned. It will be the best way of taking our minds off this tragedy."

"I'm sure it will be for you, Roland," said Bridget.

"Thank you, Bridget. And I'm sure Fabia would have wanted us to go on with our plans, with the programme as outlined, in the best traditions of the Pearman Foundation. There's a lot to do before we close down the trenches and leave. And when the police have finished with us, we'll be able to say farewell to our friend and colleague in a fitting way. And now, I'm sure you all know what you've got to do. The police may get under our feet somewhat, but do your best to ignore them and carry on. You know what they're like - stuffy and bureaucratic and obsessed with routine."

"Pigs!" muttered Malcolm.

"Their greatest achievement so far has been to let off some dynamite at the mouth of the cave with the object of enlarging the entrance," Roland went on. "Unfortunately it worked too well, and the roof of the cave has fallen in, cutting off ingress completely. No need for Anna to repeat her daring exploits. Unless we - or another team another year - can find an alternative entrance, it will keep whatever secrets it contains. Pete - did you have something to say?"

Pete got up. "Yes, the police want to see those of you who weren't here at the weekend. Just to take details of where you were and who you were with. That'll be in here, but I suggest you wait in the kitchen."

So we dispersed. It was rainy and cold again, so I went to get my jacket. I felt it was mine now, and besides I ought to steal something from time to time to keep in with the god Hermes.

CHAPTER 25

There was a copper in our dorm, kneeling by my locker. I wished now I'd put Mike's letters in the rucksack.

"Don't mind me," he said. "We have to do this, you know."

"Yes, I know," I said. "Do you mind if I take some books?"

"Be my guest," he said. "Like detective stories, do you?"

"I like these old-fashioned ones," I said. He went to look through Gail's locker, and I got out a few detective stories and took them into the barn to give to Pete. Gareth was there, but not Jonathan.

"Oh, thanks!" said Pete. "These look good. Murder Must Advertise. That'll be a distraction, I'm sure."

"We'd better carry on, now," said Gareth.

"People always say that in books, don't they?" asked Pete. "And 'It's what she would have wanted'. Poor Fabia. She never seemed happy. Are you OK to go on with the Object?"

"Oh, yes. I meant to get my jacket as well, though. The policeman distracted me. He was going through our lockers."

"Well, I don't know what they expect to find," said Gareth. "I'm sure I've got nothing incriminating. Just pictures of my kids."

"I won't be a moment," I said. The policeman had gone, and I got the jacket off the hook by my bed and put it on. There was something in the pocket - the Victorian sherds. I put them in my locker, along with a stub of old pencil that must have been there for ages. I wondered if there were inside pockets, and found a deep poacher's pocket on the left, with what felt like a thin, bendy notebook at the bottom. I took it out – it was a passport. Jeannette Wu, born when and where, and her picture. So she couldn't have gone home to Hong Kong. I put it in my handbag and went into the barn.

"Pete," I said. "Do you mind if I don't work this morning?"

"No problem, why don't you take the morning off? We're all a bit upset."

"I just want to go into town – I need to get some more clothes. Mine aren't warm enough. I'll try not to be too long."

On my way out I picked up the book of the earlier dig. I put it in my shopping bag and walked into the village and got the bus to Eldritch. On the bus I leafed through the book, looking for

Jeannette. Roland looked very different with short hair and no
beard, and glasses with thick frames. Jonathan looked really
rather handsome and poetic, standing behind a smiling Jeannette.
Roland and Sir Finamore proffered flint tools in close-up.
Jonathan and Fabia were in the background, rather out of focus
but clearly holding hands.

Everybody got out in Eldritch's main square, and I asked someone
the way to the police station – it was just up a side street. Inside,
there was a high counter made of dark wood. I stood at it
wondering if I should ring a bell or something but then a
uniformed man appeared.

"Good morning, and what can I do for you?" he said, smiling at
me over the counter.

"I'm one of the students from the dig up at Malison Grove."

"Oh yes." He looked more serious now.

"Could I talk to Inspector Forrester?"

"Is it urgent?"

"It is, rather."

"All right." He lifted a flap in the counter and let me through,
and led me down a corridor. He knocked on a door, went in and
spoke to whoever was inside, then opened the door wider and
ushered me in to where Inspector Forrester was sitting behind a
desk.

"Good morning, have a seat. Thank you, Weston. Now, what's it
all about – Mrs Savage?"

I peeled off the jacket, and put it on the desk. "I found this
jacket in one of the old stables when I arrived. Mine let in water,
so I borrowed this one. It looks a bit old-fashioned, it could have
been there for years. And I just found this in the inside pocket."

I took the passport out of my bag and handed it over. He looked
through it, sighing.

"I suppose you guessed the body might be her," I said. He looked
at me and put the passport down on the desk. "I mean, after you
talked to Roland and the others and heard about the original dig.
You'd better hang on to the jacket as well."

"Yes, thanks. Can you keep this to yourself?"

"I can keep secrets. And I haven't told anybody, I came straight
here."

"What's the thinking down there?"

"We haven't really discussed it, but I'm sure it's occurred to people that she's the body. Have you looked at this?" And I handed over the book of the dig.

"I did have a brief look at it, yes."

"There are pictures of Jeannette – but only in the early part. It's arranged according to programmes."

"Thanks, I'll have a look at that. Now you will keep your mouth shut, won't you?"

"About the passport – yes, I will. I suppose you'll be contacting her parents, if you can find them. I suppose the university would have a record..."

"That would be the obvious thing to do, yes. Well, thank you for coming to us so promptly. And I mean it – no talking to your friends." He stood up and shook my hand, and went to the door and shouted "Weston!" and the policeman who'd let me in escorted me out again.

I checked the bus timetable and there was time to spare, so I looked around for a Woolworth's. In the school uniform section I picked out a grey jersey and a dark blue boy's windcheater. Hopefully nobody would notice that it was new and not as nice as the old one. And if one of us was a murderer, it wasn't a good idea to let anybody think I actually knew anything. I could trust Pete – I couldn't see him murdering anybody – but I couldn't be sure he'd keep quiet.

I found a phone box and rang Mike at work. I told him about finding the passport and taking it to the police station, and that the first body was probably the Chinese girl who left the dig early. I said they'd told me not to tell anybody, and he said that was a good idea and he'd keep an ear to the ground and to stick with a crowd. I bought a lucky Cornish pisky in a newsagent's, and a sandwich for the return journey. It was odd not to see any black or Asian people, like you do in London all the time.

\*\*\*

Pete was by himself looking at sherds, and I told him I'd done some shopping and rung Mike. He said Jonathan had gone up to Roland's trench and Gareth was on the hunt for biscuits.

"Did you start on any of the detective stories?" I asked.

"Yes, Murder Must Advertise. It's a hoot, as the characters would probably say. You know, we could have a go at detecting. I know

you didn't fire a Neolithic arrow into Fabia, and you know I
didn't."

"Unless you were mucking about for fun and it was an accident."

"Fun, at my age? And I could barely hit the target. And we were
together most of the time."

"Yes, if either of us went out it was only for ten minutes or so, or
we were in sight of the others."

"And wouldn't someone ask questions if you wandered about
carrying an ancient bow and arrows? You'd have to hide it
somewhere. I expect the police are drawing up a plan. Either all
of us could have done it, or none of us. If you or I had run up
there, fetched the bow from where we'd hidden it, happened to
find Fabia alone in the circle – and how would we know she'd be
there?"

"Didn't Roland say where she was?"

"Oh, yes, he might have done. How do people in detective stories
remember all this stuff? Anyway, we'd have come back red in the
face and out of breath and everyone would have noticed."

"In detective stories they always get the murder down to the
nearest five minutes, don't they? And they always make fun of
women's intuition."

"They get it out of the way early on!"

"I think they had rules – you're not allowed supernatural help, or
mysterious Chinamen, or forced confessions, or coincidence,
but..."

"In this one they're just playing about with a catapult," said
Pete. "And saying 'A games eye is a games eye.'"

"Oh yes, I remember that bit. Everyone was quite good at
archery, even the girls. Except Gail," I said.

"The Blackhampton lot have had practice. And you couldn't hit
the target at all, unless you were pretending."

"I wasn't - but you'll just have to believe me."

"I believe you – I don't think you're strong enough. And you
always say you're hopeless at tennis and ping pong."

"I could have been lying about that for years. Isn't there an
Agatha Christie where someone pretends she can't knit?"

"And they say 'It can't have been one of us, Inspector, it must
have been some tramp'."

Gareth came in with a biscuit tin and came over and offered us one.

"And I'm sure Gareth didn't do it," said Pete, taking a chocolate digestive.

"What didn't I do?"

"The murder."

"Well, I didn't, actually. I wasn't even here!"

"Good. And everybody else was up and down from the dig, and back and forth. Anybody could have nipped off for 20 minutes and nobody would remember now. And most of them could have fired the shot. Jonathan even made the things. It's disappointing! I was looking forward to working out a chart of who was where, when. We'll have to look at motive."

"Fabia wasn't always the kindest of people," said Gareth. "Poor girl."

"Didn't suffer fools gladly, as they say when people have died," said Pete. "Yes, everybody was on the receiving end, even Roland. Perhaps she made his life hell. I still think it could have been an accident. If I was the police, I'd ask the boys if they took the bows and arrows out again one evening, say, and left them lying about near the stone circle."

"They did say they wanted to have another go," said Gareth. "And I don't think the cupboard was locked – where Jonathan kept the gear, I mean."

"Perhaps someone just had a mad impulse," I said. "Wanted to see if it would work. Didn't mean to hit her. Certainly didn't mean to kill her."

"Do you think any of our lot are as crazy as that?" asked Gareth.

"What about Colin?" asked Pete. "He's pretty barmy."

"What if someone lived in a fantasy world?" I suggested. "Couldn't believe that anything he did could affect anybody in reality?"

"That's pretty far-fetched," said Gareth. "Though it would be quite difficult to kill someone with one shot. I mean it would be hard if you were trying to, but you might just be unfortunate enough to kill them by mistake. I expect the police are experimenting now. Not on each other, I hasten to add."

"And Roland seemed genuinely devastated," said Pete. "But I suppose you would be if you'd killed someone by mistake."

"Was Fabia always as... difficult as she's been recently?" I asked.

"I don't know – perhaps we should ask one of the Blackhampton lot. But they've all been a bit on edge this summer."

Somehow I didn't feel like telling them about finding Nadine crying in the dorm. I said: "The murderer could have fired from the trees at any point facing west."

"But then his footprints would be easy to find," said Pete. "I expect the police have looked. And we're assuming it's a he. I mean, you girls were in somebody's sight all the time."

"Most of the time."

"So if he did fire from the wood it would make more sense to go by the path – which was pretty trampled anyway. I suppose they could look at our boots, but we've all been up and down that way. And it's been raining pretty solidly. Yours are the only footprints that would stand out – the other girls are quite tall and probably have big feet. And everybody wears hiking boots or wellies. I expect the police are making plaster casts."

"They probably looked to see what size our shoes are when they went through our lockers. What about the arrowhead - could you tell anything from the kind of stone?"

"The ones made by the Blackhampton students used all kinds of stone," said Gareth. "The ones we've found here will tell a story about trade routes and sites of manufacture and so on."

"It's another blind alley," said Pete. "But what about Sir Finamore's students – did they make arrowheads? Though actually, what difference would it make? Do we know exactly when Fabia died?"

"She was quite cold when we found them," I said. "There's one thing we mustn't forget, though. Somebody here may be a murderer. So we shouldn't talk about any of it in front of the others."

"Good point," said Gareth, putting the lid back on the tin.

"And all this is just between ourselves."

"My lips are sealed!" said Pete. "As always."

CHAPTER 26

At breakfast Donna was dishing out the mail. I got a postcard of Broadstairs from Pauly at Junk and Disorderly saying "When are you coming back? Just got a load of mouldy old pictures you could clean. That cardboard box of oddments you made me buy - turned out to be full of old lace and a Coptic embroidery, whatever that is. Filthy. Needs cleaning. Hope having wonderful time. Gone seaside with the wife and kids." I had another letter too, with no stamp, and this time I recognised Gilles' writing. I went out into the yard to read it. I said "Good morning" to the policeman, and glanced into the loosebox to check on my rucksack.

"Look out for that one!" said the policeman. "The housekeeper from next door told us to leave him strictly alone - he's dangerous!"

I sat on the mounting-block - that's a stone for ladies in long skirts to get on their horses from - and read Gilles' note.

"More mayhem I hear," It read. "If you feel like getting away from your colleagues, come to the back entrance at 5.30 - I'll be waiting for you. No need to reply, just turn up, or not."

I went into the barn, which was empty, tore the note up into little pieces and buried it in a bin under some old newspapers and Kitkat wrappers. Then I wrote a quick PC to Pauly saying I missed them too and couldn't wait to clean embroidery, and stuck a stamp on it and put it in my handbag. I went on with my work - nobody expects me up at the trench any more. The others came in: Pete sat down to mark our reports, Jonathan made trips to Roland's trench, and Gareth examined flint artefacts through a jeweller's loupe and wrote notes about them.

While Jonathan was out of the room, Pete came over. "You know," he said, "We ought to chat to the people who were away. I'm sure the police are checking their alibis. But that's what they'd do in an Agatha Christie."

"Poirot just hangs about and lets people talk."

Jonathan came in with a stack of trays and Pete said: "Roland's not up there on his own, is he? In sight of the stone circle?"

"No, he's got Bridget with him," said Jonathan. "And Malcolm."

"Oh good," said Pete. "How does he seem?"

"The same old Roland. Back to form."

"Barking orders right and left? What have you got there?"

"Could you give me a hand with these, Anna?" asked Jonathan. "I hope you don't mind, you've become our chief bottle washer."

I went in to lunch early and found Bridget on her own slicing cheese.

"I never asked you how your weekend went," I said.

"What with everything," she said. "You had enough on your mind. I had a lovely time, thanks."

"Were your dogs thrilled to see you?"

"Oh, they were! Have I ever showed you their pictures?"

"I'd love to see them. What kind are they?"

"Olivia's a golden labrador, and Toby is just a mixture!"

"Did you have a long journey?"

"Quite long - Reading is just this side of London."

"How's Roland?"

"He *seems* OK," she said in a concerned voice, stressing the "seems". "Perhaps a bit more abrasive than usual, but really I can forgive him. Jonathan must be upset too - I mean they've all known each other since the days of Sir Finamore."

"He's a bit quiet - but then he always is."

"Bottles everything up - it's not good for anybody."

The others dribbled in, and I took a sardine and tomato sandwich and went to sit by Colin.

"I never asked you how your weekend was either," I said. "Or did I?"

"Oh, everything was as usual!" he said. "The aged parents were fine and we went for walks and cooked Sunday dinner and had cocktails with neighbours."

"Did you have to go far?"

"No, they live in Tavistock."

So presumably he could have come back - but how would he explain it to his mother and father?

"Are you an only child?" I asked.

"How did you guess?"

"I'm one too."

"I was sorry to hear about your parents. Was it a car accident?"

"No, but I don't like talking about it."

"Oh, all right. Did the police grill you all?"

"Yes, they did."

"They kept asking us how good everybody was at archery."

"Yes, they asked us that."

"It must have been a shock, finding Fabia. I hear Nadine was very upset. Are you all right?"

"I seem to be. And Pete was with me."

I wondered how I could tackle Gail and Derek. But surely if anyone had gone away for the weekend, then popped back to do a murder and rushed home again, they'd have thought of a cover story? Or even got their family to cover for them? And surely whoever killed Fabia must have spent some of the day stalking her and making sure she'd be alone? I wasn't being much good as a detective.

When five o'clock neared, I asked Pete if I could knock off at about twenty past, and he said that was fine. So I downed tools and went round to the back door just before 5.30. It led into the passageways where I'd got lost before and Gilles was waiting just inside, wearing a charcoal cashmere jumper and black slacks.

"Come in!" he said. "The visitors have gone, but there are coppers all over the place. Follow me."

He went into the "art gallery" and walked towards the picture of my grandmother, next to the wall of bookshelves. He put his hand on the spine of one of the books and a hidden door swung open. He stood aside to let me pass through to the foot of a stone spiral staircase. "Go on up," he said, pulling the door shut behind us. "Another time I'll show you the hidden door. All the book titles are imaginary – Snakes of Iceland, Wolves in Britain, The Origin of Tree Worship."

"But there were wolves in Britain," I said, climbing the spiral stairs while he followed me. I was glad I wasn't wearing a skirt. I was glad it wasn't dark. "And we hear howling on the moor at night."

"I've heard that too," he said. "Keep going, it's quite a long way up."

We went round and round and up and up. Small windows let in some light, and revealed odd views of the wood, the garden and the moor. At the top there was a wooden door with a pointed top and an iron ring for a door handle. "It's open," he said, so I went through into a room with several sides, and big windows with small panes.

"What brilliant views!" I said. "Like your old flat in London. You can see the stone circle and the Italian garden."

"And whoever comes and goes. I can even look at the stars through this." He gestured to a telescope in the window on the garden side.

"Didn't you have one in London?"

A door opened, and the housekeeper came in with a tray. She put it down on a black Chinese table and said "Will that be all?"

"Yes, thank you, Mrs Collingwood." And she went out the way she'd come.

"So are there some other stairs up here?"

"Yes, there are. But I thought you'd like the secret door and the spiral staircase. Have a seat." There were two low sofas facing each other, decorated in some old crimson embroidered fabric. I sat on one and he sat opposite.

"Who does she think I am? Mrs Collingwood, I mean."

"I told her you used to work for me before you went to university, which is even true. I should ask you to pour out, but you look too fragile to lift a teapot. It's Lapsang – I hope you like it."

"These are old," I said, accepting one. "18th century. Did they come with the house?"

"Most of the things do. I've just added to the collection here and there."

"But you haven't thrown anything away?"

"No – there's probably more to be discovered. I've never really excavated the attics."

"Are they full of old trunks?"

"Yes, and boxes and cupboards. You know the story about the couple who inherited a stately home? They told their friends one day they'd discovered a whole wing they didn't know was there!"

I sipped the smoky, milkless brew and accepted a Nice biscuit.

"I suppose you heard everything from Mrs Colllingwood?"

"I heard that there'd been another murder, committed in the same way, with a Stone Age bow and arrow. How do you feel? Were you all fond of Professor Thompson?"

"Nadine was in shock. They brought a policewoman who kept making us tea. Fabia was always sarcastic to everybody, and worked us pretty hard, but I'm sorry she's dead. Have you had the police over here too?"

"They've been talking to the staff, but none of them saw or heard anything. And they had a good look at all the old armour and weapons down in the Great Hall. I could have told them it was bought in the 19th century when it was the done thing to be medieval."

"Quite the wrong era, but I suppose they have to think of everything."

"When did it happen? Mrs Collingwood knew nothing about it until the police turned up early this morning."

"Yesterday afternoon, but we didn't find her until quite late. Pete called the police, and they had to look after Roland too. I suppose they didn't think of telling Mrs Collingwood, and the police just rounded us all up again. I don't suppose you saw anything? She was found in the circle."

"I was reading the *Clavicula Salomonis* at the desk overlooking the gardens."

"And I don't suppose you did it."

"I couldn't hit anything from here – and I've never tried archery."

"And your staff wouldn't know where to find a Neolithic arrow."

"And neither would I. Who found the body?"

"Professor Blair. But he didn't come and tell anybody. He just sat beside her. Then Pete and I went looking for them, because they usually come back and get their car and drive home to their B&B in the village and get dinner somewhere, but their car was still there."

"I see – so they lived together?"

"Yes. I suppose you could call Fabia his common-law wife. Or girlfriend. Is it OK to call someone a girlfriend when..."

"When they're an antique of 40-odd?"

"Anyway, that's why Roland was so upset."

"What happened then?"

"Pete took Roland down to the office to telephone the police."

"Didn't you go with them?"

"No – Roland wanted somebody to stay with Fabia. I didn't mind. It wasn't frightening."

"Really?"

"The stones rumbled and trembled, and there was moaning and howling from the moor."

"Howling for the dead!"

"You said you'd heard it."

"Yes, at night, and riding up on the moors getting lost in the mist."

"I meant to ask what's your horse called?"

"Gringolet - it's from the Morte d'Arthur." He pronounced the name in the French way, like his own.

"Does he know the way and get unlost?"

"Yes, probably better than I do."

"When Colin got lost he saw a black shape that he thought was a person – it led him to somewhere he recognised, and then disappeared. And I think Pete saw it too and thought it was Colin."

"Perhaps it's something raised by Sir Finamore when he disturbed the stones."

"That's what they said in the village! They seemed to know all about it."

"I feel rather disappointed that I've never seen it. But have you come up with a theory about the crime? Or rather crimes?"

"I can tell you," I said. "Because I know you won't talk to anybody else. Pete, one of the tutors and I are trying to be detectives. I lent him Murder Must Advertise. But I don't dare trust him with everything I know, or everything I've worked out."

"Because one among you is a murderer."

"Or may be. And Pete's a terrible gossip. They never really go into that much in books, do they? Pete still thinks it could have been an accident – or a prank that went wrong."

"Both times?"

"Even both times. I suppose the most obvious solution is that the same person did both murders, but why? And why so far apart? And here – in the same place?"

"How many of you were on the original dig?"

"Just Roland, Jonathan and Fabia. And Sir Finamore, of course, but he died when the BBC stopped the programmes."

"And now only Roland and Jonathan are left."

"But Fabia was shot after we found the first body and the police took it away. What if someone was copying what had happened? Or wanted to know how it worked? No, that sounds rather feeble."

"Could any of your fellow students have done such a thing? You said they were rather unsympathetic."

"Gavin and Malcolm are a bit wild. Derek seems fairly normal. And Colin's quite weird and the others bully him. At least Gavin and Malcolm do. And Roland. I still get on better with the tutors, apart from Colin."

"Weird in what way?"

"He comes out with impossible theories about Stonehenge having a roof and nothing being real."

"Perhaps he's been reading the existentialist philosophers."

"I think he's just teasing Roland, actually."

"What about the other girls?"

"Donna is rather sporty, and Nadine is quite feminine, and Gail's a Christian. Bridget is more matey than they are – she's another of the tutors. But there's one thing I haven't told anybody apart from the police."

"Do go on."

So I told him about the jacket, and finding the passport.

"Did you ever tell anyone you'd found the jacket?"

"Fortunately not. I expect people just thought it was mine, and I bought another one the same from Woolworth's."

"And you hadn't noticed the passport before?"

"No, it was quite flimsy, not like a UK one. It was down inside a kind of poacher's pocket that I didn't know was there. In books something's always sewn into the lining, isn't it?"

"What did you do?"

"I took it straight to the police. I think they'd already guessed she was the victim. They must have contacted her parents to see if she ever turned up."

"And you don't think she did?"

"I'm afraid she didn't. Poor them!"

"Let me know how you get on with your detecting. I'll do some research of my own - the black shape sounds interesting. It may be something inimical Sir Finamore raised by meddling with things he didn't understand. But surely you don't have to be a Miss Marple - haven't you seen any visions or received any messages?"

"How could I tell anybody?"

"You could say it was woman's intuition!"

"Yes - that might go down quite well. Or I could borrow Derek's dowsing rods and make them do what I told them. I wasn't sure about becoming an archaeologist, actually. I mean, would it be right to use magic to find out where to dig?"

"Do you think you could?"

"I don't know. I can't turn second sight on any more than I can turn it off. But anyway, I decided I'd do things the proper way."

"You could make your fortune - or your reputation."

"Everybody seems to want to have their own telly series."

"And what do you want?"

"Just a job. In a museum somewhere, I expect."

He took a book out of the shelves and laid it down on the carved Chinese coffee table, and sat down beside me.

"Do you remember this? Monstrorum Historia - it was in the library at Harpsden. Perhaps we shall find the black misty shape in here." He leafed through the pages - there were lots of pictures of demons.

"Mrs Collingwood is a human being, by the way."

"Glad to hear it."

"There are ways of making demons show themselves, but you have to find a black cat who is the firstborn daughter of a firstborn mother, or so the book says."

"You never had trouble seeing them before."

"Don't remind me. Operatio Nigromantica – periculosissima et
difficile enim est coniuratum dimittere."

We looked at more pictures of grotesque creatures, but didn't
find anything that fitted the description. There were rather a lot
of naked people, some with branches growing out of their heads.

"Symbols in a lost hermetic language," he said, turning over the
page to reveal more naked people sitting on each other's knees.

"I must go," I said. "They'll be wondering where I am."

He shut the book. "Can we meet again soon? You can keep me up
to date."

"The police want to keep us all here."

"You don't seem overjoyed at the idea."

"I'm not, very."

"I have plenty of spare rooms."

"They're probably haunted."

"The guidebook is unreliable on that point."

He opened the door to the spiral staircase and went down it first.
At the bottom he said: "Let me know what you discover. You
know how to find your way out, don't you?"

He stood in the doorway and watched me as I left.

## CHAPTER 27

I got back in time for dinner, and sat next to Gail, who was next to Derek as usual.

"I never asked you how your weekend went," I said to Gail.

"We just stayed with my parents in Basingstoke. It was fine."

"The police asked us about it," said Derek. "But I suppose they wanted to work out if we could have come back, murdered Fabia, and then gone home again."

"I've been praying about it," said Gail.

"I can't see why anybody would want to murder her," said Derek. "Did she steal somebody's theory and publish it as her own?"

"Discover something that disproved somebody else's theory?" Pete suggested.

"Or somebody stole her theory and she'd just found out?" said Colin.

"In books everybody has a motive," said Pete.

"Did she have any theories worth stealing?" I asked.

"She wrote a guide to the Neolithic monuments of Wessex," said Pete. "I think there's quite a lot of crossover with Roland's book on the area, but they've always worked together."

"She shared his interest in early ritual," said Bridget. "Of course, Roland's the big name when it comes to popular paperbacks, but in some ways her guides appeal more to the general public."

After dinner I looked on the bookshelves in the barn. There was a copy of Fabia's book, which had come out about ten years ago. It had a dark red cover with black drawings of megaliths and flint tools, and I took it into the dorm. It was much less pompous than Roland's books, with fewer long words, and she told you where you could see some of the artefacts, in local museums or the British Museum. I wondered what had happened to the finds from Sir Finamore's extravaganza. Gail came to bed quite late, after the others.

"So how did Derek get on with your parents?" asked Donna with a significant look.

"Oh, fine!" said Gail.

"I hope he didn't mind being taken to meet the parents QUITE so soon," said Nadine. "Is that what you did, Anna?"

"Oh, shut up, Nadine, don't you remember?" said Donna.

"Oh, Lord, I'm terribly sorry!" said Nadine.

"I don't mind, really!" I said.

"Gail's looking worried," said Donna. "Sorry we took the spotlight off you and your romance for a moment!"

"I'm sure it must be difficult for you to remember not to take the Lord's name in vain," said Gail. "And I suppose none of you would like to come with me to church on Sunday?"

"Catch me!" said Donna.

"I think we should pray for Fabia, don't you?"

"I can pray just as well in an open field," said Donna.

***

Next day I waited till Pete and I were alone, and then asked him what had happened to the finds from the original Sir Finamore dig.

"I don't think they turned up anything spectacular," he said. "Apart from that ceremonial knife we were looking at the other day, in the book. Where is the book, by the way?"

"I think the police took it, didn't they?" I fudged.

"The knife's not on display anywhere. Well, the dig was officially under the auspices of the Archaeological Society, as well as the BBC, so I expect the boxes would have gone there. The Society was embarrassed by the whole thing. They probably wanted to forget about it. And once the poor old geezer died, that was the end of the Sir Finamore industry. Everybody wanted to be more academic and respectable after that. You could say dull!"

"Roland's not exactly dull."

"Say no more."

"Is it all right if I take a long lunch?"

"Yes, of course. Did you ever check anybody's alibi?"

"Yes – they all live too far away, apart from Colin – his folks live in Tavistock. I suppose he could have been pretending to take the dogs for a walk."

"And turn up here with some dogs hoping nobody would notice him?"

"No, that would be silly, wouldn't it? But I suppose his parents might cover for him."

"We ought to think about winding down and clearing everything away to be taken back to Blackhampton. There'll be plenty for the students to chew over for the next couple of years. Jonathan's up at the trenches taking photos and making plans now."

\*\*\*

At lunch time I made myself a couple of sandwiches on white sliced, and cut the crusts off, put an apple in my pocket and the sanis in a paper bag, and headed for the village. I ate my picnic sitting on the churchyard wall, then I went to the phone box and phoned Mike at work. He said he missed me as usual, and asked how the investigation was going.

"Take care, won't you?" he said. "Don't let anybody know you're on to them. Where are you?"

"I'm in a phone box in the village. I had another idea. The finds from the original dig were all put into boxes and sent to the Archaeological Society. They've probably still got them in their archives in London."

"That's a thought," he said. "It might be worth going through them. I'll suggest it to our Cornish colleagues and see if I can get along there."

"Have you heard anything on the grapevine?"

"Well, they're pretty sure the first body is this Asian girl who 'went home early'."

"I was afraid it might be her. Did they find her parents?"

"Yes. They thought she might have turned up back at home all those years ago, but sadly, no."

"But didn't her parents look for her?"

"I haven't got the full story on that yet. So who are our suspects? Were you all around? Does nobody ever get time off?"

"Roland actually gave some of us a long weekend off – Derek and Gail, Gareth and Bridget, Colin..."

"Hang on, I'm writing it down."

"He was going to let me and Pete go too, but Pete said we had too much to do."

"Shame. Any ideas why he chose those particular people? Almost as if he was getting them out of the way."

"None of them are in the inner circle. I mean, they're not at Blackhampton, and they don't belong to the Pearman Foundation. I think."

"The Pearman Foundation?"

"Yes, it's an archaeological club some of them belong to, some of the tutors too. Roland's its head. There's a branch in Blackhampton, and they've got a club house in London. They do a lot of re-enactment. Colin says it's sort of masonic and you have to be asked to join."

"I'm taking notes," he said. "I'll look into it. See if I can get a list of members."

"Perhaps that's why they bully Colin," I said.

"I hope they don't bully you?"

"No, no, they're fine. Just not terribly friendly."

"I've got to go. Lovely to talk to you. Ring me again soon. I'll talk to the Cornish lot and see what I can do up at this end. But I don't like to think of you down there with a maniac on the loose."

"There are loads of policemen around. I'll make sure I'm not alone with anybody I don't trust."

"That's pretty much all of them, remember. I love you! Goodbye!"

We said goodbye and I hung up. I supposed Jonathan and Roland were both one-third likely to have done the earlier murder, if Sir F was the other suspect. Unless Fabia had done it. Jonathan seemed so meek and mild-mannered, but I'd avoid being alone with him all the same.

I dropped my postcard into the box and walked round the church anticlockwise before going inside and reading some info pasted on a wooden bat. It said that worship had taken place on this spot for thousands of years, and the yew tree (sacred to Hecate) might be older than the earliest church. I followed its directions and found some gargoyles and a Green Man. When I got back they were still having coffee, and I told Gail I'd been inside the church and she got rather excited and said it showed that the Lord was working in my life, or something. Well, at least she has the right attitude about demons.

177

CHAPTER 28

One morning a few days later Bridget came into the barn and said she'd had a call in the office from Mike, and he was coming by to see me at 4pm.

"Does he know where to come?"

"Yes, I told him to drive into the stable yard."

Pete said: "Take all the time you like! Bring him in to meet us."

So at just before four went out to wait in the yard. Gringolet was still guarding my rucksack, so I whispered to him:

I know your name now, Gringolet
And you know mine and who I be
When I speak, hear and obey,
As all beasts must, when they meet me.

A police car drove into the yard, Mike jumped out and I flew into his arms, as they say in romantic novels.

"I've got lots to tell you!" he said. "Where can we go? Is it OK to leave the car here? The Eldritch boys lent it to me. Shame I can't stay long."

"Shall we walk round the gardens? We can get in free."

"Yes, let's."

Mike took my hand, and we went to the little pond. Joan was standing against a rose hedge in her orange and white dress and I waved to her discreetly.

We sat on one of the marble seats and I scattered a few rose petals onto the surface of the water and some goldfish came up, thinking they were food.

"Who was that girl you waved to?" asked Mike.

"Oh – just someone who works here. We got chatting one day. How did you get on?"

"It's a long story. I rang Inspector Forrester and explained who I was and he said you'd been a big help and he supposed it was OK to talk to me about it but could you be trusted to keep your mouth shut?"

"Really!"

"Of course I said yes. I told him what you told me, about the finds from the early dig ending up at the Archaeological Society, and the Pearman Foundation. Tell me again who Prof Blair gave the weekend off to?"

"Out of the tutors, Bridget and Gareth, and he wanted Pete to go too, and me. And Gail and Derek, and Colin."

"Right, that checks with the list of Foundation members. They're not on it. When I told the Inspector about the finds he went quiet. And then he said 'Look into it, Sergeant. I'll square it with the higher-ups at your end. Report back.' So I rang the Society to ask if I could drop in. A nice bloke called Bernard something answered. I gave him a bit of background, and he said he'd been reading about the case in the papers, and to come round. So I did. Bernard took me down to the basement and he said that since my call he'd looked for the Sir Finamore stuff and managed to locate it.

"There were tons of metal shelves down there, all stacked with what looked like shoe boxes only bigger. Bernard said: 'We talk about archaeology in terms of boxes!', and took out the relevant ones. He hung about, but I said I'd better look through them on my own. He said to call him if I needed anything explaining and went upstairs again.

"I got out my penknife and started opening the boxes. They were all sealed, and labelled and dated. Most of them had bits of old pottery and flint tools and bones and things inside. But the human bones looked pretty dried out and were mostly in bits. Some of the tools were still sharp. But about halfway through this process I opened one and inside were some women's clothes. Everything down to the bra and pants, and some jewellery, and a handbag, and shoes. He must have stripped the body to make it less identifiable. And he must have thought she'd be left alone where she was. For a good long time, anyway."

"Yes," I said. "It's taken ages to get another permit to dig here. And most people couldn't get into the cave. He probably thought nobody could."

"Just his bad luck that you turned up."

"Yes, I expect his heart sank. I don't think the dig was ever written up properly and published, so they wouldn't have looked in the boxes. What would he have done if it had been?"

"Probably found some excuse to sneak the box away."

"And the book of the TV programme is just that. The Society were a bit embarrassed by the programme and probably wanted to forget all about it and try and look more serious. Did you look through the other boxes?"

"Yes, but there was nothing but 'finds' in them. I took the box with the clothes upstairs and told Bernard I'd have to take it with me. He was curious, but I said I couldn't discuss it. But I asked him about the Pearman Foundation and he said they were somewhat secretive but there was a book on them in the Society's library and he'd lend it to me, though it only went up to the war. I rang Forrester and we agreed I'd better bring the box in person, so that's what I'm doing here."

"Did they look at it while you were there? Was there anything in the handbag to identify Jeannette?"

"Yes, letters and so on. Some stuff in Chinese. And they've even superimposed a picture of her onto a photo of the skull – they match up."

"Nobody seems to have missed her. I mean, wouldn't you think it was odd that she had just gone?"

"Somebody looked up her university record – she didn't do very well on the course."

"Yes, Fabia said she was worried about breaking her fingernails and anyway they lost a lot of girls. Drop-outs, I mean. But that could have just been Fabia being bitchy."

"Was she like that?"

"She was mean about everybody."

"Bernard lent me a copy of that old book about the TV programmes as well. Fabia was quite dishy."

"Yes, wasn't she? I gave ours to the police. I suppose all Jeannette's things were gone, and everyone thought she'd just got the train. But what about her parents?"

"Forrester's talked to them, via an interpreter. They've grieved for her ever since. They blame themselves for pushing her to go to England and go to college. They said she picked archaeology rather than English or History because she thought it would be easier to get onto the course."

"She must have written home?"

"Yes, and then the letters stopped. But just before she disappeared she wrote to them that she was really happy and she loved England and that she was going to start a new life – unspecified, but it was going to be wonderful. She'd tell them about it later and not to be worried if they didn't hear from her for a bit."

"It really was from her?"

"Who here could fake a letter in Chinese? Eventually her parents sent private detectives to look for her, but time had passed. As a foreign student she didn't have much stuff. And her friends just thought they'd lost touch. There was no trace of her where she'd been living – she'd packed everything into a suitcase and gone off to the dig. Inspector Forrester's boys have been looking for the suitcase in the stables and outbuildings – to no avail. Could it be in the cave?"

"I think I'd have seen it."

"So anyway, before I came down here with the box I went to find the Pearman Foundation. They've got a nice little gaff north of Oxford Street, with a dining room, and a library, and meeting rooms. Members can even stay there. There was a secretary who came out to talk to me – podgy, balding, middle-aged. He revealed that the distinguished Professor Blair was their head, but he didn't want to show me the list of members at first. I put on a bit of pressure and said it could go up to the highest levels and he turfed over the membership book. I've got the list here..."

It read: "Roland, Jonathan, Fabia, Jeannette, Sir Finamore, Gavin, Malcolm, Donna, Nadine."

"Who was the head before Roland?"

"Sir Finamore, would you believe? So then I stayed up all night reading the book Bernard lent me. Seems the outfit was founded by some eccentric in about the year 1800. He invested some money to revive the Druid religion and collected some followers – well, these batty establishments do. And now of course it's pretty rich. The head gets a salary and it's a bit of a sinecure, though apparently these days they do a lot of dressing up and play-acting. I got that from one of the newspapers, which kept a file on them. Kind of antics that get coverage from time to time, like that lot at Stonehenge. They seem to have dropped the Druid aspect. It looked more like a club."

"Yes, they do a lot of spinning and weaving now, and making drinking horns."

"And bows and arrows. Forrester showed me the evidence. But there was one odd thing: the Foundation seems to lose one of its members every 19 years. I made a list of them, with the dates. Of course there was natural wastage – most of them died in their beds. I'd read quite a long way through the book when it began to add up, and I had to start again from the beginning. One of them popped out of his house for some cigarettes and was never seen again. One was found on Hampstead Heath, thought to have been struck by lightning. One was found sitting in the London Library, been there for days, cause of death unknown. One said he was going on holiday and never returned. Another odd thing – it was always on or about Midsummer Eve that they went."

"And the TV programme was filmed around then - midsummer. Did you tell all that to Inspector Forrester?"

"Of course. He told me not to try too hard, and elaborate patterns like that were usually the work of one man, and they were rarer than people think."

"You said 'he' – the earlier murder. It's down to two people, isn't it?"

"Three, with Sir Finamore. But the recent one – almost any of them could have done it."

"Them?"

"The Foundation members. Even the girls. They'd all done archery practice."

"I think Nadine dropped out of archery, and I couldn't even hit the target."

"That lets you out! And it wouldn't be easy – you'd have to strike in just the right place. They're trying it out at the cop shop. On shooting targets and pig carcases. You know I don't like to leave you here. Did I say I miss you loads?"

"The dig will end soon, and the police don't mind us going then."

"They'll keep tabs on you all. It's a shame the others aren't too pally."

"The tutors are OK: Gareth and Pete and Bridget."

"What about Jonathan?"

"He's not very friendly with anyone."

"And Professor Blair?"

"He bosses us all around. He's sarcastic, a bit like Fabia. Perhaps that's who the boys caught it from."

"I'd like to think you had friends to look after you – somebody who couldn't possibly be involved."

"They've left us some constables. And there is somebody at the big house."

"That girl you waved to?"

"Yes, there's her, and a bloke I got talking to."

"One of the staff too?"

"Yes, he belongs here."

"The uniformed are going to search the wood for the suitcase, anyway, and a spare longbow. You couldn't walk about carrying one."

"And how would you sneak it back into the cupboard?"

"Just don't tell anybody what I've told you. Pretend I just wanted to see you. And don't tell anyone you've spoken to the police – apart from me."

"I haven't."

"I've got to go soon and catch my train back. Perhaps I'll get some sleep!"

We got up to go.

"It's romantic here, isn't it?" he said, and kissed me. "Do you remember when we went to Hyde Park? Can't you really come back with me?"

"Well... The police wouldn't like it. And what about the others? They'd think it was unfair. And I've got a job to do." I was thinking about the Object.

"All right – but stay with a crowd."

We'd reached the stable yard by now, and Pete just happened to come out of the barn.

"This is my husband, Mike," I said. "This is Pete – one of the tutors."

"Hello, Mike!" said Pete, and they shook hands.

"Look after her, won't you, sir?" said Mike. "I don't like leaving her behind."

"We keep an eye on her all the time. Is this just a flying visit?"

"Yes, I've got to go now."

"Don't tell me you drove here all the way in that!"

"No, I came by train and borrowed it in Eldritch. Anyway, I must be off."

Pete left us to say goodbye, and Mike drove away. I told Pete that Mike had just come down to see me, and the Eldritch lot had lent him a police car, and they hadn't told him anything about the case. I knew he'd pass it on.

***

While we were having dinner, one of the ladies from the café came to the door with a note for me. I took it but didn't open it.

"Don't you want to know what's in it?" asked Nadine. "Is it from your friend next door?"

"I expect so," I said.

"You are a dark old horse! And on the very day your husband visited! Did he tell you anything about what the police have found?"

"I don't think they told him anything, just lent him a car."

"And you had more important things to talk about. I asked Pete what he looked like and if he was good-looking but he said men couldn't tell about other men."

"And now you're going to sneak out for an assignation!" said Donna.

"He's just a friend."

"Is he interested in archaeology?" asked Malcolm, making it sound like a perversion.

"No, botany," I said, hoping they'd think he was a gardener.

"Very Lady Chatterley's Lover!" said Gavin.

I locked myself in the bathroom to read the note – they weren't above snatching it out of my hand. Gilles said to meet him at the back door at eight, but he'd understand if I didn't turn up. I read a book until Gail and Derek went off into the gardens, and the other four went to the pub as usual. I didn't mind about Colin – he was probably watching telly, and the tutors had gone up to their flat. Once everyone was out of the way I went round to the back door where Gilles was waiting.

"Have there been any fresh developments?" he asked. "I presume that was your husband – you wouldn't be so affectionate with anybody else."

"You were watching!"

"There isn't much to do while I lurk and wait for the police to go. I suppose they will one day – when they've identified the murderer. I thought you waved at me."

"At somebody else."

"Do have a look at these book titles! Imaginary books can be somewhat whimsical, but I'd like to read Practical Lycanthropy, De Vermis Mysteriis, or Clothes: Their Origin and Influence."

"Did you make up some of those yourself?"

"What do you think? After you."

We went up to the turret room. From the front window I could see Joan walking around the Italian garden, and Gail and Derek sitting by the pool.

"There's nobody there – just your two fellow students who haunt the place."

"They're harmless," I said.

"Unless they're in it together – but they seem too involved in each other."

I sat on the sofa again. There was a tea tray with some langues du chat and a little spirit stove.

"I found this samovar arrangement in one of the attics," he said.

"Perhaps you'll find an Old Master," I said.

"Come and help me search! So does your husband know anything about the investigation?" He handed me a cup.

"Yes – I've got lots to tell you."

"Wait – let's have some music for atmosphere." He went over to a modern record-player that looked incongruous among the Arts and Crafts cupboards and Chinese vases, though I expect the original inhabitants mixed up styles and periods without giving it a thought. He put on a record of tinkly piano music and said: "I think Chopin suits the surroundings, don't you? That sense of melancholy decay."

"I don't really know. I'll give it a listen."

He sat down opposite me, saying: "Now tell me all about it." So I began my story.

CHAPTER 29

"You mustn't tell anybody anything I'm about to tell you," I said. "But I thought you might know the answer to some of it, or know how to find it out."

"I have nobody to talk to but Mrs Collingwood, and you."

"Anyway, the police have worked out that the first body, the one that had been in the cave for 19 years, was a Chinese student called Jeannette, who was at the original dig. Fabia and Jonathan thought she'd gone back to London or Hong Kong and they'd just lost touch. They weren't particularly friends."

"At that age – I suppose they were all students then? People just pass out of your life and you forget them."

"Did I tell you that Roland, Fabia, Jonathan and Jeannette were the students on the original Sir Finamore dig? That's why Roland has always been desperate to get permission and funding to come back here. It was all interrupted when the Archaeological Society kicked up a fuss about them uprooting the stones and just shut down the whole project and forgot about it."

"Oh yes, the stones, we'll come back to that. Go on."

"Anyway, I think Jeannette is only in the first programme."

"Have you watched them all? You could watch them again."

"Yes – Roland only showed us some highlights but I think he's got the whole series on film. Anyway, I told Mike about the finds from the original dig being sent to the Archaeological Society. So he liaised with the Cornish police and they told him to go and look for them. And in one of the finds boxes there were her clothes and handbag. Just the ones she must have been wearing."

"So he stripped her naked before disposing of her body. Perhaps even when she was alive."

"How horrible!"

"What about her parents?"

"She wrote to them, it was her last letter, saying she was really happy and she wanted to stay and she was starting a new life and not to worry if they didn't hear from her for a while."

"So they didn't look for her?"

"They did in the end, but the trail had gone cold. They still clung to the hope that she was living a different life somewhere, I expect. Did I tell you about the Pearman Foundation? It's a kind of archaeological club, and some of the people here belong to it. All of the ones who were on the Sir Finamore dig, and Sir Finamore himself was the head then, and Roland is now. So Mike looked them up too, and someone lent him a history, and he read it all night and he said the odd thing was that every 19 years one of their members dies mysteriously or goes missing. On Midsummer Eve."

"And you think Jeannette disappeared on Midsummer Eve, 19 years ago? And Fabia was found on Midsummer Eve. So what do these Pearman people get up to? I must make some notes."

He fetched a notebook and pen and asked me to repeat what I'd said. I went on: "These days they have a club in London. And the Blackhampton students – Donna, Nadine, Gavin and Malcolm are members, and Roland and Jonathan of course. Donna goes out with Malcolm and Nadine goes out with Gavin. Anyway, they do a lot of what they call experimental archaeology, with wattle and daub, and woad. Jonathan runs that side of things, I think."

"Do they actually tattoo themselves with woad?"

"I don't think any of them have got tattoos! Not that I've seen, anyway."

"So who's not in the inner circle? You..."

"And Bridget, Pete, Gareth, they're the tutors, and Gail and Derek – the lovebirds, and Colin. He goes to Keele."

He put down the notebook and turned over the record. "What do you think of Chopin?"

"It's sad. It sounds like a folk song."

"He probably borrowed a few melodies. Do you want to hear about my researches?" He picked up some books from the desk and put them on the coffee table.

"This is an account of the folklore of the area, from the 19th century. The well-known story of stones going down to drink at a river, or bathe, is ascribed to these ones too. The woodcuts are nice, don't you think?" He passed it to me. "And the black human-like shape has been seen from time to time, although a Reverend Greenhalgh was supposed to have laid it in seventeen-something. Sir Finamore must have disturbed it again. Amateur!"

"Does it say what it is?"

"It's known locally as a 'bogle' or 'hellymental', but I think it's a landwight." He flipped back through the notebook. "They dwell in boulders and bodies of water, tors and pools. Giant size, sometimes look like trolls. They can take different shapes, humanish, manlike. The early Icelandic settlers had a few problems with them. They are protectors of places. They guard gold hoards."

"There are lots of stories about those."

"And there's usually a dragon, or an ancient white cobra who tells you to keep off!"

"Or else you take the biggest diamond and it turns out to be fake."

"And all the gold turns into dead leaves. I wish I could do more to help. I'll see if I've got anything on this Pearman Foundation. When was it set up?"

"In the 18th century, I think, by someone who wanted to revive the Druids. Mr Pearman, I suppose. And then it became more of a learned society. Are landwights dangerous?"

"You probably have to keep on the right side of them."

The Chopin record came to an end and he got up again to put it back in its sleeve. "I found this in one of the attics, too. It's an old wind-up gramophone. And a lot of old jazz records." He carried it over to the table – it was quite small – and I opened the lid.

"We've had a few come into the shop. They don't often have records, though. Tiger Rag, Kitten on the Keys, Tea for Two, Happy Feet."

"Shall we play some of them? You wind the handle."

I wound the handle on the side while he looked through the records.

"This is a fox trot." He put it on the turntable and pressed a lever and put the needle on the beginning. "More cheerful than Chopin."

"It's a bit sad too, though," I said after listening for a bit.

"Do you fox trot? I suppose these days you just freak out."

"Actually I learned ballroom dancing at school, and Mike won medals for it. We go to a club in Soho where they play music like this."

"Shall we dance?"

"There isn't much room."

"We could move into the gallery."

"But you're so much taller than I am."

"Perhaps we'd better play Scrabble instead."

"Are you serious?"

"Yes – I found this set in the gallery with the Meccano and Cluedo."

He took the familiar box from a table piled with stuff.

"Why not? You can use your notebook to score in," I said.

"I don't suppose you play chess?"

"No – it's too like maths."

"What do you usually do in the evenings here?"

"Read, or watch telly, or play terrible games of ping pong with Colin. He's almost as bad as I am. Sometimes go to the pub."

We set out the board and picked some tiles, and he turned on a few lamps.

"Can I offer you something stronger?"

"No thanks."

"Perhaps you find it interferes with the vibrations."

"Something like that. Tell me how you met Melusine."

"My partner in crime? She was a friend of someone I met in prison. She sounded interesting, so I tracked her down and found she had some ideas – just needed some capital. So I took over McRobbie's – it was such a respectable firm, the perfect cover."

We played on, listening to more of Joan's records. He turned out to be rather good at Scrabble, and won. I said I'd better go back – it was almost dusk outside, and a gibbous moon was rising, so he led me down the staircase again. He promised he'd look into the Foundation and see what he could find out.

"What do your colleagues think about the notes from next door?"

"They think I'm having an affair with one of the gardeners."

"Do they disapprove?"

"They pretend to – but I think they approve really. It might make them tease me less."

In bed, I flipped through Fabia's book to see if she'd had the idea of Stonehenge having a roof and Silbury Hill being a sculpture of the moon, but she didn't mention it. I wondered if Roland had the full set of TV programmes in the lecture room. What had Jeannette meant about "starting a new life"? And where was her suitcase?

CHAPTER 30

I was kept busy fetching and carrying, and seiving and washing. I was trying not to be left alone with Jonathan, but he just shimmered about greyly as usual. And in the barn I make sure I'm facing him so he can't creep up behind me, and the others are nearly always there. I can always tag along with Pete, he doesn't mind. At lunchtime they all made for the kitchen, but I said to Pete: "Can I just show you something?"

"OK," he said. Gareth and Jonathan went out, and I took the cloth off the Object.

"Look at this metal rim," I said.

"Yes, I noticed it the other day."

"I uncovered another bit on this side – the whole thing must be quite big. Is it safe to leave it here every day?"

"As long as we don't talk about it, and we keep it covered up, nobody will be curious. You're good at that, aren't you?"

"Not bad." I looked round to make sure the others had gone. "Actually I wanted to ask you – has Roland got a whole set of the TV programmes, or just the highlights?"

"He's got the whole set there on film, in cans. Very proud of them. High point of his life."

"Even better than becoming a Prof?"

"I'm surprised he hasn't made us sit through the whole thing."

"Do you know how to play them? How to work the projector?"

"Yes, I do. Do you think they could tell us anything? They're 40 minutes each..."

"I'd like to watch the first one, with Jeannette in it. The Chinese girl who left. She's only in that one."

"Do the police think she might be the body from the cave?"

"It's the obvious conclusion."

"I suppose it is. How terribly sad! Does your husband know anything? Or did he just come down here to see you?"

"If he'd said anything, I wouldn't be able to tell you, would I?"

"All right. I suppose you have to sign the Official Secrets Act, or something. Loose lips sink ships, walls have ears, as they used to say in the war."

"What were you doing then?"

"Oh, I had an inglorious army career."

"I suppose you can't talk about that either."

"It's more that I'd rather not. What about this evening, when everyone's at the pub or otherwise occupied? The keys are in the office and we can lock ourselves in and pull down the blinds. Sounds cosy, doesn't it? Shall we say at about nine?"

"You're on."

And we went in to lunch.

***

At nine we met at the door of the lecture hall. Pete unlocked the door. I was about to turn on the lights when he said: "Better draw the blinds. We'll just use this working light on the desk."

"Has Roland gone back to his B&B?"

"Yes. He doesn't seem to mind being alone there. He's got a policeman of his own, too."

"The usual foursome went to the pub, and Colin's watching telly."

"Gareth and Bridget and Jonathan are doing the same up in the flat – I made sure they were engrossed in Z Cars. And I suppose Gail and Derek are off somewhere fornicating as usual. How does she square that with God?" He was pulling out the cans of film that were on a low shelf.

"She says there's a dearth of nice Christian men and God doesn't mind as long as you're engaged."

"God's changed his tune! I thought it was hellfire and brimstone. Ah, this is it. If you unroll the screen I'll set it up."

"That's what they said at the convent. That we'd all go to hell, I mean." I unrolled the screen.

"Did you take any notice?" He was threading the film through the projector.

"No. But I don't think anybody did."

"How old were you – sorry, that's a personal question."

"Eighteen. That's quite old. And then we got married."

"Did you shack up first?"

"Yes."

"There was no doing that in my day. That's why I got married so often. And marriages didn't last long in the war." He flipped some switches and a light appeared on the screen. "Come up here." The picture came into focus and the titles and title music came on, rather loudly. He turned down the volume and I sat on a bench near the projector.

We laughed at Sir Finamore posing in front of the stone circle and the moors. He took the viewers on a tour of the site, including the barrows at the end of the ceremonial way, which we'd never really looked at. "Who knows what lies beneath these grassy mounds?" he boomed. The students hung about in the background, and handed him plans and books and artefacts, and occasionally had stilted conversations about the history. He'd say "The Cornovii were fascinating, weren't they, Roland?" and Roland would give a prepared speech about the Cornovii probably being part of the Dumnonii.

"Gripping stuff!" said Pete.

Now we got the bit with them looking into the cave mouth that we'd seen before, and I kept my eyes on the students this time. Jonathan looked even more like a romantic poet. He wasn't paired off with Fabia, though. He seemed to hover next to Jeannette. The credits rolled, and as they all stood around the cave entrance registering excitement, Jonathan slipped his hand through Jeannette's arm and held it for a moment. And he'd definitely been holding Fabia's hand in the photograph in the book. I wish I still had it to check. Well, he'd certainly changed, but I didn't see that it got us any further.

"Tell you anything?" asked Pete. "You don't want to watch all the others, do you?"

"Can we just watch the start of the second one?"

He changed the reel and we watched for a bit. We saw the students running a tape measure over the stones, but Jeannette wasn't in the picture. After a bit I said I'd seen enough, and Pete turned the projector off and dismantled it.

"She was pretty, wasn't she?" he said.

"Jeannette, or Fabia?"

"Both of them, actually. I suppose you think the fashions are dragsville, or whatever you say these days, but I thought girls looked nice in them."

"Dragsville has rather gone out! And all that hippy talk. Thank goodness."

"Are you telling me the Permissive Society wasn't any fun?"

"I never noticed it much. I don't really know what other people got up to."

"You disappoint me. We'd better put all this stuff away."

I rolled up the screen again, and he turned everything off. "I don't think we need wipe off our fingerprints – or should we?" I wondered.

"Perhaps we should have worn gloves! Well, I suppose the police will arrest somebody soon, and let us all go home. Or else they'll be baffled, and we'll never know. They'll have to let us go anyway, there's a hiker group coming to replace us."

We sneaked out of the door into the dusk, and Pete looked elaborately right and left, and tiptoed off like a cartoon character.

"See you tomorrow!" I said, and went back to the dorm.

\*\*\*

Next day I went into the gardens at lunchtime. There were quite a few visitors, and children having rides in the Victorian pony carriage, led by one of the stable girls. I saw Joan sitting on one of the stone seats by the pond, so I went and joined her.

"Hello!" she said. "I hoped you'd come again. Who's that you were kissing under the rose arbour?"

"My husband, he came down to visit me."

"Really? You're married? I thought you were young, like me."

"I am young. I'll be 23 soon."

"That's quite ancient enough to be married, I suppose. There's nobody near us, but talk quietly. Pretend to be looking into the pond and reciting poetry or something."

"All right."

"Someone was playing all our old records the other night. I danced in the gallery. I think it was the new owner – he got the gramophone out of the attic and a few other things."

"So you've seen him?"

"Yes, it's just his flat I can't get into. I can see him when he comes out. He's quite odd-looking."

"How odd?"

"Tall and thin, with white hair. He's gone through all our things up there, and left suitcases."

"Isn't the attic full of suitcases?"

"Yes, old trunks. But plastic suitcases are so common! None of us would have had one like that. I wonder what he's looking for?"

"Old books? Antiques? Something nobody knew was valuable?"

She laughed. "He won't find anything. Though he did open up a trunkful of old clothes and costumes, and makes the guides wear them. Some of them were just dressing up clothes. That's where we used to do plays and charades." She indicated the lawn, where several families were sitting and eating picnics. "What meal can they possibly be having?"

"Lunch? Tea?"

"It's a bit late for lunch, isn't it?"

"Is it? I'd better get back to work."

"Do come again. They did archery there too, in Victorian times. There are pictures in old albums. They look such frights!"

"Are the albums in the attics, too?"

"They're in the gallery. I suppose you'll be going soon and new people will come and I'll have to find someone else to talk to. Come and say goodbye!"

"I will!"

A plastic suitcase – but how was I going to "find" it without giving away Joan or Gilles? He'd have to get Mrs Collingwood to find it. We'd have to hope there was something in it to identify the owner. I ran back to the dorm and wrote Gilles a note saying I had some news and I'd be at the back door at nine. I sealed it in an envelope and wrote GD on the front and went in at the visitors' entrance and approached the lady behind the desk, who was dressed like a Victorian servant in a white cap and apron.

"Good afternoon!" she trilled. "You're one of the students, aren't you? You can go right in."

"I wondered if Mrs Collingwood was about."

"I think she's in her office, shall I give her a call?"

# 196

"Oh, would you?"

And she rang Mrs C from a phone on her desk, and the housekeeper soon appeared from a back room.

"Hello," I said. "Can we talk in your office?"

She must have recognised me from when she brought us tea, but she had a completely deadpan expression and just said: "Come this way".

I followed her into her office and she sat down behind her desk and said: "Now, how can I help you?"

"Would you see that Mr Dominus gets this note? It's quite urgent."

"Thank you. I'll see that he gets it immediately. You know he doesn't like to be disturbed, and we think it best to give out that he is away. On the continent."

"Yes, I know all that."

"Of course." She actually smiled then. "Any time." And I went out the way I came, wondering how I was going to explain it to Gilles. How would he feel about being haunted by a real ghost?

CHAPTER 31

I went over at nine. There was a tray of coffee things on the Chinese table and Gilles poured me out some.

"Well?" he said, handing me a tiny coffee cup. "This is real coffee, you've probably missed it."

"Thanks," I said.

"I saw you earlier sitting by the pond."

"You've been spying on everybody again!"

"I was looking at the circle as well. Have a look." The telescope was set up in the window facing towards the moor. I peered through it and saw mist lying over the wood like a cottonwool hat. The stones looked startlingly near.

"I wonder if you could identify which stone hides the treasure?" he said.

"I should have to be doing it for you, and not myself."

"We'll pretend I'm not intending to give you half."

"I don't think the stones would be fooled, do you? And what about the landwight?"

"Yes, we'd have to square him somehow. You could do that. So what did you have to tell me?"

"I think I know where the missing girl's suitcase is – Jeannette, the first body."

"The 19-year-old murder. And she was probably only 19. Do you have clairsentience? Finding hidden things is one of the witch's powers."

"Can we look in the attic? There is an attic, isn't there?"

"Yes, and anyone could have hidden a suitcase there, 19 years ago, and been pretty sure it wouldn't be found. It's filthy in there, though – I'll get some gloves."

He went out, and came back with two pairs of leather gloves. He handed me some beige ones, saying "I found these in the dressing-up box. They look about your size."

They fitted OK – perhaps they were Joan's – and he put on a black pair. We went out of the other door, down some steps, and along a little passageway with rooms off it and a crooked door at the end leading to the attic. It covered several of the rooms downstairs, with odd beams holding the roof up, and chimneys, and stuff stacked everywhere: a rocking horse, chairs, brass bedsteads in bits, old mattresses, tin boxes, and a lot of thick grey dust. A little light came in from dormer windows in the roof.

"Where shall we start?" he asked, lifting the domed lid of a trunk. "There's a lot of old fabric in this one, being eaten by moths."

"It looks too old. He'd have packed her clothes in her own suitcase."

"Which might look quite smart for 19 years ago. I probably missed it because I thought the old ones would be more interesting – I'll go through them all one day. We might find things we can display downstairs. How about over here – I noticed some more modern stuff. Mind where you're walking – we don't want to put our feet through the ceiling."

In some places there weren't boards, but just joists and plaster, so we went carefully as if on stepping-stones.

"I remember," he said, hanging onto a rafter and giving me a hand over a gap in the boards. "It was in this corner by the chimney."

Stacked against the chimney and half covered with an old carpet was a pile of ordinary suitcases. He pulled the carpet away and clouds of dust hit us in the face. He slid the top case off the stack – it was a solid affair in cream. He opened it and pulled out the contents, but it was just old jackets and trousers.

"On to the next one!" he said. It was brown and looked old, and held evening dresses and feather fans and satin shoes. He shut it again and put it to one side. The next one was blue, and had the word "Revelation" in gold on the lid. He clicked open the fasteners and lifted the lid.

"You have a look," he said, so I knelt down and went through the contents. There were several pairs of jeans, and smart plaid trousers with narrow legs, and some gathered skirts in bright patterns, and pastel blouses and cardigans. There was a box with a few brooches and pendants and a chain. I picked up a blue folder and opened it. Inside were photographs of a Chinese couple, smiling. I showed it to Gilles without speaking.

"Her parents," he said.

Underneath some pants and bras and petticoats there was what looked like a diary, with flowers and hearts drawn on the outside. I opened it up, and it was all written in Chinese.

"She didn't have to worry about keeping her thoughts a secret," I said, handing it to Gilles.

"I expect the police have some Chinese speakers." He leafed through the pages. "Have a look at this last entry." He handed the book to me. The entries were dated, and this one was headed "20 June". There was a lot of Chinese writing again, in turquoise biro, and exclamation marks, and a drawing of a rose and some hearts.

"We'd better put it all back," he said. "Good thing we're wearing gloves."

"How are we going to get somebody to find it?" I asked, piling the clothes back inside.

"Yes, not you – what would you be doing up here? And you'd have to explain what gave you the idea."

"That would be difficult."

"I see. Well, I think I'll arrange for Mrs Collingwood to 'stumble across' it and then hand it to the police. She can say she went into the attics to check on things. She was worried about the students wandering about – they really did get out some books and games in the long gallery and leave them lying around. Or was that you?"

"No, not me, but I can guess who it was. But don't forget the murderer is still at large – she'll have to be discreet."

"I pay her to be discreet. Let's leave everything as it is for now. I'd better lend you a clothes brush – and there are cobwebs in your hair. You can borrow my bathroom."

I shut the case again and we picked our way back to the door. He showed me into a primrose and black bedroom and handed me the brush, and left me. I used it on my clothes, and washed my hands and face in the adjoining eau-de-Nil bathroom, then went back to the sitting room and said I'd better go.

"All right. I'll brief Mrs Collingwood tomorrow and leave her to make the 'discovery'."

"What if the police want to come and see the attic?"

"The 'locus in quo'? There are higher turrets I can hide in."

He showed me out the usual way.

***

Back in the dorm the girls greeted me with: "And where have YOU been?"

"Playing Scrabble with my friend next door."

"If that's what you want to call it!" said Donna.

Nadine was laying her makeup out on her bed. She held up a bottle of nail varnish. "I've never even used this yet – no point painting my nails. When I get back home, though..."

"What do you want green nails for?" asked Donna. "And they won't look right for the Last Supper."

She went out to the bathroom, and Nadine stuffed her things back in her sponge bag muttering: "I'm so tired of the whole thing. But don't tell anyone I said that."

"I suppose the police will keep us here until they've made an arrest," said Gail. "And we've got to do the back-filling and tidy up the site."

"And there's loads of labelling and boxing-up to do," I said.

"I suppose if we run out of time we can just box it, and go on with the sorting back at Blackhampton. So that lets you out."

"I suppose it does."

"But we'll have to go some time," said Nadine. "The place must be booked up all summer. They can't keep us after the dig was supposed to end. They know where we'll all be. They'll just say 'Don't leave the country', won't they?"

"I expect they will," I said.

\*\*\*

I didn't see the police taking away the suitcase next day – there was still a constable in the yard, and a few others scattered about. We were kept busy "back-filling" – not me, as it involved spades – putting stuff in boxes and generally packing up. This went on for a couple of days. Gail was right, we did almost throw stuff into boxes in the end. Jonathan had hired a van and packed the boxes in it. The Object still had a hard lump of old mud stuck to the front which I couldn't shift, but they said to keep going and they'd leave it to last. Eventually the activity wound down and Donna and Nadine filled in the time hand-sewing Ancient British costumes.

Soon there were only a few days of the official dig left. Roland came in at dinner-time and we fell silent. "Not long to go now!" he said. "Not much left to do. And then then we assess and write up – but not till next term. I don't think we need everybody to stick around – Gail and Derek, would you like to go early?"

They looked at each other and then said how kind and they'd love to. "Everybody else will need to keep beavering away, however," he went on. "Though, Gareth – you're dying to get home to your wife and family. Pete and Jonathan and Bridget can oversee the rest of the clearing up. I think you've got all your stuff pretty squared away, haven't you?"

"I won't say no," said Gareth, and Malcolm and Gavin laughed. Will they never get tired of laughing at people's accents?

"That's almost it," said Roland. "I'd like to thank you all for your good work, and your help and support."

Everybody murmured rather sheepishly.

"The police will be keeping tabs on us all, of course. And we've got to make way for some hikers, Mrs Collingwood tells me. We'll have a spring clean before we leave. That's your department, Bridget."

"All under control!" she said.

"And I've got in some booze for our last night," he said. "The night of the full moon! And then after dinner there'll be a little entertainment – the kiddies have planned it all themselves."

"Amateur night!" muttered Pete. "Never mind, we can duck out early."

CHAPTER 32

Gareth came in at breakfast and said goodbye to us all.

"It's been great fun – most of the time. I hope the police sort it all out soon. Come on, Gail and Derek, our carriage awaits!" Gail and Derek picked up their rucksacks and coats and went out into yard, and we followed them. "Goodbye!" said Gail to Donna, Nadine and me. "I hope the Lord works in your life. See you next term!" The boys said goodbye to Derek in their own way – hitting him on the arm and laughing. They got into the minibus and Jonathan drove them away.

"I hope He doesn't!" muttered Nadine. "How's Derek going to stand all that stuff about 'my Christianity is very important to me'?"

"Oh, she'll get sick of it now she's discovered sex," said Donna. "Come on, we'll miss our bus." They were going in to Eldritch to get some special food you couldn't get at the Spar in the village.

***

The girls started cooking early, but told the rest of us to keep out, as it was something special. I skulked in the dorm and read, and later on Nadine came in carrying some folded clothes. She dropped them on her bed, and picked up a black dress from the pile.

"Are you going to dress up?" I asked.

"We all are," she said.

Donna came in and picked up a garment. Then she looked at me and said: "Shall we dress her first?"

"But I haven't got anything to wear," I protested.

"We've been sewing in secret," said Donna. "We took your clobber as a guide."

"Take off what you've got on," said Nadine. She held up the black dress, which was a plain T-shape.

"What are you wearing?" I asked, peeling off my T shirt and clean jeans.

"Oh, the same. We brought ours. Everything off – including the underwear. Ancient Britons didn't wear any." She dropped the dress on my bed.

"Oh, OK," I said. "Is the food Ancient British too?"

# 203

"You'll see! They didn't wear makeup, either, but you don't usually, do you?"

I took everything off and pulled the black dress over my head. It came right down to the ground, but Donna handed me a woven girdle, also black, so I tied it on and hitched the dress up.

"Are there any shoes? Or sandals?"

"No – no shoes."

I sat on my bed while they dressed. Their costumes were pale brown, with green and rust embroidery. Nadine took out her hairslide and combed her hair over her shoulders. She'd taken all her makeup off, too. When they were ready we all went into the kitchen.

The table was laid with pottery dishes. There were bottles of beer, and candles stuck into old wine bottles. Bridget and Pete were there, wearing smartish ordinary clothes, but Gavin and Malcolm were wearing tartan trousers and nothing else. Colin was wearing a white dress like the girls' ones, but without embroidery.

"Sit down, everybody," said Nadine. "And I'll explain the food."

"What, no little flags saying 'fish paste'?" said Pete.

There was a whole cod on a bed of grass, veal with raspberries, and some eel chowder with milk, onions, parsley and parsnips. There were "bannocks" – rather hard-looking rolls. Donna handed round plates and bowls saying: "Take a bit of everything". While we were doing this, Roland and Jonathan came in. Jonathan was dressed like the boys, with a bronze knife stuck in his belt. His thin white torso was covered in tattoos: dragons and interlaced patterns.

"Welcome to our feast!" said Roland, sitting in the chair that had been kept for him at the head of the table. He was wearing a robe and a cloak, clasped with a brooch. Jonathan sat beside him in Fabia's usual place. "Now do dig in, everybody. There's wine in the fridge – Gavin, get us some out. Vines grew here in the Little Climactic Optimum. And one thing we know about the Ancient Britons – they drank BEER!"

Laughter at this, and the sound of opening bottles. Bridget opted for wine, Pete for beer. I fetched myself a glass of water.

"Adam's Ale? You must celebrate!" said Roland. "It's our last night, our last supper."

"That's what we used to say at school," I said, pushing away a glass of wine Gavin was trying to give me.

"Relax!" he said. "No more sitting on the hard school bench, no more toiling in the muddy trench!"

"At least for now," said Malcolm.

The food was surprisingly tasty. Bridget asked Donna if her dress was natural brown wool.

"Like a Shetland shawl!" she said, fingering the material.

Everybody drank rather a lot, and Gavin and Malcolm sang some rather rude songs about being married to a mermaid, and "Oh, Sir Jasper!", and most of them joined in. Halfway through the festivities Gavin turned off the electric lights and we sat there by candlelight.

Dessert was apples. "No bananas or oranges in the Bronze Age!" said Roland.

"Just like the war," said Pete. "Well, it's been fun, but I think I must retire before I pass out. Sorry to miss the show, but I can't keep my eyes open."

"I'm sure the play will be marvellous, but I'm going with Pete," said Bridget. "I'm simply dropping with sleep. I suppose we've been working pretty hard, in all this nice fresh air. Delicious food, thank you, cooks!"

They went out together. The boys went on singing, and handing out bottles of beer, then Roland said: "Time for charades! Can I just say how beautiful the ladies look? Don't they, Jonathan? There's just something missing from Anna's costume."

"I've got it," said Donna.

"Shouldn't we tidy the place up first?" I asked.

"It'll all keep till the morning," said Roland. He strode out into the yard, and everybody followed him. I looked round for the usual policeman, but there was nobody there. Gavin and Malcolm dodged into the ping pong room and came out with a long wooden staff that they handed to Roland, bundles of sticks they passed to the girls, and what looked like some fur hearthrugs. They handed one to Jonathan, who swung it over his shoulders – it was a whole wolf's skin, its head and muzzle forming a hood that hid his face. The boys did the same, and one of them lit the sticks, which turned out to be torches.

"You will tell me what to do, won't you?" I asked Nadine. "Are we going into the lecture hall?"

"You'll find out," she said.

Donna handed her torch to Malcolm, and came towards me, holding out a black scarf. She quickly laid it over my eyes and somebody, Jonathan I think, wound it more times round my head and tied it at the back. Colin squeaked "What are you - !" and then went silent. All I could see through the blindfold was the points of light from the torches. I put up my hand to adjust the scarf, but two people grabbed my wrists and elbows on either side.

"No more talking now!" said Roland. "Follow me!"

Whoever was holding my arms, and pinching me hard, swung me round to face the gardens, and we set off in that direction. The gravel paths were painful on the feet, but everybody was quiet. Now we were walking over wet grass. Every so often we stopped, to open a gate, or go up steps. We were going uphill and it was muddy underfoot. It seemed quieter and more stuffy – we must be going through the wood. We came out into the open air, and they led me round to the right, and turned me round to face the other way.

"Hail, Blind Seeress! Welcome, offering to Odin!" declaimed Roland, and the others made howling, growling and stifled whining sounds. There were answering howls from far off on the moor.

"Tell us what you see!" adjured Roland, laying a heavy hand on my shoulder. As before, all I could see were the torches and, when I looked up, the full moon. As the others bayed, I recited quietly:

Queen of outlaws
Queen of broken men
Queen of fleeing slaves and wretched wights
Queen of witches,
Minions of the Moon
Queen of all the creatures of the Night
Remove this darkness and award me Sight.

Like a photo developing in a tray of chemicals, the scene before me appeared. I was standing at the Western end of the stone circle, looking towards the sacrificial stone. The torches were stuck in the ground all around us, and the moonlight struck the central slab. Someone was lying on it, their arms and legs held by men in wolf skins. I thought I'd better play my part and declaim something, so I made it up as I went along:

I see a maiden
Clad in white

206

I see the moon,
A silver boat
I see the children of the night
I see the oak
Of seven limbs
I see the fire
Of evil hearts

Now Roland chanted, from somewhere behind me.

*Those songs I know, unknown to sons of men*
*Unknown to queens and kings*
*A third I know: if need should come*
*of a spell to defeat my foes;*
*when I sing that song, which blunts their swords,*
*neither weapons or staffs can wound.*

*A sixth I know: when one would harm me*
*in runes carved on a tree root,*
*on his head alone shall fall the ills*
*of the curse that he called upon mine.*

He walked into the circle, carrying the staff in his left hand. He
pointed it at the body on the slab, which must be Colin in his
white robe. He went on:

*"Odin is my name.*
*But before they called me Terror,*
*and before that Thunder,*
*and Waker and Killer,*
*and Confuser and Orator,*
*Heat-Maker, Sleep-Maker!*
*All these names were used for me alone."*
Hail Odin!"

"Hail Odin!" the others repeated in chorus.

"Hail Dark One!" They chimed in again.

"Hail Hornéd One! Hail Oak-Splitter! Hail Hooded Ones!"

Roland held something in his other hand, a long, reddish flint
knife with a black handle. Still chanting, he approached the slab
and raised the knife over Colin, who writhed, making muffled
noises behind his gag. He wasn't blindfolded and could see
everything. The others all hit the megaliths with their staffs until
they rang. I began to chant myself:

Veni, veni, genius loci!
Landwight, aid me!
Stones, defend me!

# 207

Hermes, keep me!
Blow, winds and crack your cheeks!
You cataracts and hurricanoes, spout!
Festina, festina, currite noctis equi!


The knife approached Colin's neck, but one of the wolf-men grabbed Roland's arm and the two of them struggled for a moment. Then there was a flash and a crack of thunder and my eyes were dazzled. Somebody ran past me into the circle towards the slab and the figures around Colin fell to right and left. The ground rumbled and heaved as if a tube train was running underneath us. A white figure vanished into the trees, while the other actors lay stunned on the ground. Heavy, cold raindrops hit us. I lurched from side to side, but my captors' fingers only dug further into my arms. I sagged to my knees, but they pulled me up again. The torches fizzled and spat, then dwindled and went out.

I flung myself about, stamping on the feet of the girls holding me. One of them fell over, and I pulled my arm out of her grip. She picked herself up and sped away along the ridge crying out: "I can't take it any more!" It sounded like Nadine. Donna dropped my right arm and went after her, shouting "Come back!" and two of the wolf men got to their feet and followed them.

The stones rocked, working themselves free from the earth, and Roland came towards me brandishing the knife. I turned and ran, pulling off the blindfold, while he followed close behind.

CHAPTER 33

"How dare you counterspeak the sacred rites of Odin!" screamed
Roland. I struggled up the hill, slipping on wet rocks. The ground
levelled out and I flew along, splashing through puddles and
scratching my legs on bog grass. It was still raining, but not so
hard. I stopped and looked back. The moon shone fitfully through
speeding rags of black cloud on Roland in his pale druid robes. He
was quite far off, but still coming on, shouting "The stones
demand a sacrifice!" Behind him loped a grey figure in a wolf
mask. The moon came out and I hoped against hope that Gilles
was watching from the tower.

I turned to run again, but there was a huge black shape blocking
my path. It had slanting yellow eyes, and it moved towards me,
growling. It was a wolf, and behind it a grey, furred pack. I held
out my hands and declaimed.

By Anubis, Fenrir and Cerberus,
I, Inanna, Potnia Theron, command thee!
Do my bidding and do not harm me!
Do my bidding as in days of old.
Thwart those who would steal ancient gold
Thwart those who would desecrate with blood
The ancient guardians of the hoard.
Vargs, lupes, hear my word!

The wolf stood still when I began to chant, and looked at me with
its amber eyes. Inanna is my real name – she was a Babylonian
goddess. It crept closer, lowering its head, showing its teeth and
keeping its eyes on me. I held out my hand to it.

It crouched down and whimpered. Stumbling footsteps
approached from behind me, and the wolf rose. It wreathed itself
round my legs, and I pulled up my black robe and climbed on its
back. It cantered through the pack with me clinging to its mane,
and on over the moor along the lich road.

I glanced over my shoulder. The grey wolves kept up with us, and
further off were Roland and the wolf man. They were followed by
the megaliths proceeding in lurches and hops, and a human-like
figure cut out of pure night. The wolf galloped on. When the
boulders of the Witch's Tor loomed up, it wheeled round, and the
other wolves massed around us.

Roland approached slowly. He was muddy and out of breath, but
still held the knife. The other man was a few paces behind him,
and the stones swayed and thumped as they came on.

"Be reasonable, Anna!" Roland called out, stopping. "I'm not
going to hurt you! Why don't we all go home? I can't leave one of

my students wandering on the moor again, particularly at night. Where did all those dogs come from? They must be strays." I said nothing, but the wolves flung back their heads and howled in a minor key.

Roland took a few steps towards us, and the wolves went to meet him, grinning and snarling. He shouted "Odin demands blood!" and surged forward, but the wolves lolloped towards him and he stopped in his tracks.

"Stop that, Roland." It was Jonathan's quiet, unassuming voice. Roland turned round.

"What are you doing here, Jonathan?"

"I followed you. You were threatening Anna. This is not part of the instructions."

A wolf sniffed Jonathan's pelt and growled. He pulled the mask off his face, and threw the skin to the ground, where the wolf worried it. Quietly the megaliths shuffled closer and took up their usual places around the two of them, and the grey wolves slunk into the circle.

"They're more afraid of us than we are of them!" said Roland, shrinking back towards Jonathan as a wolf snapped at his hand. The wolves howled again, and there was a drumming sound, and a white horse galloped towards us out of the darkness.

"Back, you foul beasts! Back, I say!" Roland made threatening gestures, but the wolves encircled the two men, only feinting away when the knife came near them. The man riding the horse pulled it up and stopped near me and the wolf.

"What do you mean, not in the instructions?" Roland turned to face Jonathan and flourished the knife. "I am the Archdruid! I have the power of life and death."

"You are the leader, but I am the executioner. You know that now."

Gilles dismounted and I slipped off the wolf's back and went to meet him.

"Are you all right? I assume you have these creatures of the night under control," he said. "I was following you and the druids – and the megaliths!"

"Be quiet and listen!" I said. I could still see Roland and Jonathan through the gaps in the stones.

"It's Professor Blair!" whispered Gilles, putting his arm round my shoulders. "Who's the other man?"

"Jonathan."

They were still facing each other, surrounded by wolves.

"I couldn't let you sacrifice Colin – or Anna," said Jonathan.

"You like her, don't you?"

"I don't like anybody any more."

"Where did she go? Anna!" called Roland. "Anna – are you still there?"

"Don't answer!" whispered Gilles.

"Gone home on wolf-back, I expect," said Jonathan. "She's an unusual girl. Knew more about ancient religions than we suspected."

"Sir Finamore made me leader with his dying breath! He said everything had to be authentic!"

Jonathan drew his dagger. "But he didn't make you executioner."

"Why Fabia? Why not pick one of the students? Isn't that why we recruited them, as the date approached?"

"Fabia was mine before you took her from me."

"I thought you'd got off with Jeannette! And so did Fabia!"

"I had to do that."

"You killed her too!"

"I had to. And you have bullied me ever since."

"We were just joking! I thought you took it in good part! It's all forgotten!"

"You used Fabia's sarcasm as a weapon. I never forgot any of it. Not one word. And, yes, you both rose through the ranks while I was left behind. But I had my job, and I bided my time. And Fabia was beginning to crack. She might have given us all away."

"You might have killed ME!"

"The leader must appoint a successor, and an executioner."

"Why wasn't I told? Why didn't Sir Finamore...? I read the history and worked out the cycle – but those other deaths – they could have been accidents! Or the work of the Old Gods! We all thought Jeannette had gone home to Hong Kong..."

"And you hoped that somehow the cycle had ended? Didn't it occur to you that leaders tend to be figureheads? Mr Pearman left instructions, but only the Secretary knew the full strength. And the executioner, of course. You would have received sealed orders when you reached 60."

"Yes, yes, of course," said Roland. "The sacred king, the priests of Nemi... I've been looking over my shoulder for 19 years. Fabia too."

"You must have been expecting something to happen. Why else did you send the non-members away for the weekend?"

"I couldn't be sure. And I wanted to rehearse the ceremony, remember?"

"And then you sent them home early."

"We couldn't get them all out of the way. Remember how hot Sir Finamore was on authenticity? A mimetic display would have been risible."

"Doesn't Frazer talk about bloodthirsty rites that became a mere pantomime of themselves?"

"This is hardly the time and the place for a seminar! And besides, when did you read The Golden Bough? You never open a book! You're just a craftsman, you work with your hands, not your brain."

"Why didn't you keep everybody around? There'd have been so many suspects the police would have been confused."

"I didn't think of that. And I wasn't sure anything would happen. I hope Fabia knew nothing."

"I hid the bow and arrows in the wood early one morning. Nobody ever counted them. They were my province – just a bit of handicraft! Fabia had gone back to finish the mapping. When everybody left the barn I took my chance. I came out of the wood and called to her. She turned round, and I took aim. We didn't speak. She turned away again and faced the sun. I only needed one arrow. The bow is still hidden in a hollow tree."

"And Jeannette?" asked Roland. "It was you – not sir Finamore?"

"I told her I was in love with her and we'd run away and live happily ever after. It was easy to get her to go into the wood with me, and take off her clothes. I aimed at her and she thought it was just a game. She was laughing. And the best bit is that if you tell anyone, you'll implicate yourself. If we get out of here alive!"

He glanced at the wolves, who were wreathing around their legs. Roland took a step towards him, holding out the knife. "You're not going to kill me!" said Jonathan, but Roland came on.

I raised my hand and the black wolf growled. The grey wolves crept between them, and both men stood still.

"They've decided for us," said Jonathan, smiling. "Do you recognise these megaliths? The gold must be lying open to the sky. Shame we can't get at it."

""I'm getting out of here!" said Roland, but the wolves leapt up at him and the megaliths shunted closer together.

"We'll just have to wait until morning, or until someone comes to look for us," said Jonathan.

"I'm tired," said Roland, letting his arm fall to his side. "So tired. And there's nowhere to sit down."

"They'll be safe there until sunrise," said Gilles. "And I think we've heard enough."

"What if they kill each other?" I asked.

"The wolves won't let them."

Gringolet was still standing patiently, with the reins trailing on the ground - but no saddle. Gilles lifted me onto his back and got on behind me, and we headed back to the path.

"Stop!" I said. "I heard something following us."

We halted and looked round, but it was only the black wolf and the landwight.

"The landwight's job is to protect the hoard, and we're going that way," said Gilles.

He urged Gringolet into a canter and we rode back the way we'd come - I clutched the horse's mane. We pulled up at where the stone circle should be - now looking odd and bare, with dark pits in the ground. It was still raining gently. Gilles dismounted and said he'd lead me through the wood. I looked back - the landwight and the wolf were standing on the skyline. Gilles saluted them, and I leaned over the horse's neck to avoid getting caught in the branches. Quickly we went through the gardens and round to the stables.

As we approached I said: "Look out, there's usually a policeman on duty in the yard."

"He wasn't there earlier - what shall we tell him?"

But there was still no sign of the policeman who'd been stationed there since we found Fabia's body. Gilles lifted me down, and opened the stable door and led the horse inside.

"We'd better ring the police," he said quietly. "I'll do it - you don't want them asking you awkward questions."

"I've got quite good at telling elaborate lies," I said. "Won't they think it odd that the stone circle has moved?"

"The stones have to be home by dawn, according to the legend, and it's almost upon us. The wolves and the landwight will guard our prisoners until the police find them."

He took off Gringolet's bridle and hung it up. I unhooked my rucksack from the peg and explained: "It's just some stuff he was guarding for me, that I didn't want the police to find." We went out into the yard.

"Won't you come back with me?" he asked.

"I'll be OK with Donna and Nadine. I don't think the students thought the ceremony would involve a real sacrifice. I knew Roland was obsessed, but I never realised he took it so seriously. Before you got there he was threatening to kill me. And I protected our dorm because the girls were frightened of ghosts."

"Yes, you have powerful protectors." He looked at me thoughtfully. "I'll call the police now and disguise my voice. After all, we heard their confession. I'll try not to involve you. I'll pretend I'm a poacher, or a sheep rustler, or something. Come and see me tomorrow. Isn't it your last day?"

"Yes. Tell me what happens."

"Until then. Goodnight." And he walked out of the yard, and I went into the dorm.

CHAPTER 34

I tiptoed past the sleeping forms of the others, peeled off my
sodden robe, draped it over a chair and got into bed just as I was.
My feet were freezing, and sore from running over stony ground,
but I soon fell asleep.

I opened my eyes, and it was light. Donna was asleep on her back,
and Nadine was hunched under the bedclothes. I reached for my
dressing gown and knocked over a bottle of shampoo which fell on
the floor with a thud. The person in the opposite bed sat up.

"Hello!" said Colin, rubbing his face. "I didn't really fancy sharing
a room with the others. I'm sure I've got bruises from where they
were holding my arms and legs. I mean, re-enactment is all very
well, but…"

"But where's Nadine? That's her bed."

"Oh, is it?" he pretended to look around for her.

Donna sat up. "My head!" she groaned. "Oi, Colin, what are you
doing there? Get out at once! Where's Nadine?" She got out of
bed and stood there in blue viyella pyjamas.

"Perhaps she's in the bathroom," I said, putting my arms in my
dressing gown. "But where did she sleep?"

"Perhaps she swapped with Colin," said Donna.

I got out of bed and tied up my dressing gown and went into the
shower, where Nadine wasn't, brushed my teeth and came back.
"Not there," I said.

"She's got dressed, anyway," said Donna, pointing to a wet robe
lying across a spare bed. "And her handbag's gone. What's this?"
She picked up another wet garment from the floor.

"That's my Druidical nighty," said Colin. "They say you should
never sleep in wet clothes. I'm glad rain stopped play - I didn't
like the way Roland was waving that knife around and calling me
an offering to Odin. So I am completely starkers."

"All our clothes are soaked," said Donna. "I can't really force you
to put that back on." She looked into Nadine's hanging cupboard.
"She's left some of her gear behind - wouldn't her jeans fit you?
And I can lend you some knickers. What size are your feet?"

"Sevens."

"So are mine. You can have my spare boots." She handed him
over some pants and socks, and a T shirt and jeans of Nadine's.
"You can get dressed in the showers."

"Fine, but how do I get there?"

"She's left her dressing gown as well," and she chucked it on the bed.

Colin put it on, took the clothes and went into the showers, saying: "I suppose I *could* go back to my quarters wearing a lilac kimono..."

"I could do with a massive fry-up," said Donna, gathering up the wet dresses. "What happened to you? You weren't here when we got back. There won't really be time to dry these, but I'll put them in the airing cupboard anyway. Don't let me forget them."

"So Nadine came back with you?"

"Yes, she did. She's got her bag, wherever she is, and a jacket and a rucksack. She must have snuck out while we were snoring."

"I came in soon after you – anyway, you were already asleep," I lied, putting on my clothes discreetly under the dressing gown in case Colin came back in. There were bruises on my arms.

"And you didn't notice her go?"

"No, I slept really soundly."

"So did I. We did drink rather a lot I suppose. What was that you were spouting up at the circle? Did Roland give you some lines to say?"

"Just some poetry I remembered from school. I thought I ought to play along."

Colin came back in wearing Nadine's clothes, which were a bit big for him.

"How do I look?"

"Thank heavens for unisex," said Donna. "I wonder if anyone's cooking breakfast?"

"Let's go and see," said Colin, and he and I went into the kitchen so that Donna could get dressed.

Gavin and Malcolm were there, wearing ordinary clothes and throwing empty wine bottles into the bin.

"You might give us a hand, skivers!" said Gavin. "What did you think of the reconstruction? Shame we couldn't go through with the whole programme."

"I'm not sorry at all!" said Colin. "I think I look better with a head."

"You might have become a prophesying head. We'd have kept you in storage, or buried you on Tower Hill," said Malcolm.

"Roland will not be happy," said Gavin.

"So where are the great and the good this morning?" asked Colin, wiping the plastic tablecloth while I put plates into the dishwasher.

"His car's still here," said Malcolm. "Perhaps he's passed out on a sofa somewhere, unless he walked home. It was every man for himself after the lightning struck and it started bucketing down. I was bowled right over."

"We were out for a couple of minutes! And the girls scarpered – we couldn't let them run off into the night by themselves," said Gavin. "Nadine not up yet?"

"She got up early," I said. "I don't know when – we were all asleep."

"Or passed out. So where's she gone? For a walk? To watch the sun rise?"

"Perhaps she's gone down to the village. She took her handbag."

"Probably desperate for a ciggy – but nothing opens till eight."

"It's well past that, and there's a machine on the wall of the pub," said Malcolm. He fried bacon and eggs while Gavin made toast, and when Donna arrived she and Colin laid the table.

"It's about ten," she said. "Should we wake up Pete and Bridget?" But then they came in, looking tired. I wondered what had happened to the sedatives the doctor gave Nadine.

"I hope you've got pots of strong coffee on the go," said Pete. "Did we all oversleep, then? Never mind, last day. Don't forget we've got a bit of tidying to do, Anna."

"I haven't forgotten," I said.

"Did Roland stay here last night?" said Pete. "Perhaps he thought he shouldn't drink and drive. How were the Bronze Age charades?"

"Pretty impressive," said Colin. "Very life-like. But then it all got rained off, up at the stone circle, and I think everybody called it a day."

"We thought we'd lost YOU," said Gavin. "Did you end up in the hayloft?"

"Oh, I slept in Nadine's bed in the end."

"Well, there's a turn-up for the books!"

"She wasn't it. Perhaps she went and caught an early train."

"Hasn't anybody looked for her?" asked Gavin.

"She's taken some of her stuff," said Donna. "I suppose I can take the rest of it back to Blackhampton. It's a bit of a bind, though. Or I could send it to her parents. I'll ring her home and tear her off a strip. Jolly inconsiderate, I call it."

"Didn't she say anything to you?"

"No, she must have gone while I was asleep, and before Colin turned up. Middle of the night."

"Didn't she wake you, Anna?" Gavin asked me.

"It took me longer to get back – I got a bit lost."

"Jonathan's AWOL too," said Pete. "Perhaps they've gone together! He's not in his room, though his clothes from yesterday are still there. He can't be roaming the moors wearing nothing but Celtic trousers. He'll be arrested for exposure."

"Or die of exposure!" said Bridget. "It must have rained like anything in the night, everything's so wet. Perhaps we should look in the TV room – there's a sofa there."

"So where did Roland sleep?" asked Pete. "Is there a spare bed in your dorm?"

"Well, there was," said Malcolm. "But he didn't sleep in it."

"Let's send out search parties after breakfast," said Pete. "We're getting used to that, aren't we? They'll turn up. I'm sure they're scattered about the place somewhere."

"Don't forget the bow-and-arrow murderer is still lurking out there," said Malcolm.

"Perhaps we should call the police again," said Bridget. "What happened to all those constables? Isn't there supposed to be one in the yard? Perhaps one of them saw where Nadine and the others went."

"Here they come now, I think," said Pete, looking out of the door. "Oh, good morning, Inspector. Yes, we're all fine, except that a few of us haven't turned up for breakfast and we're not sure where they are. We were just about to call you, weren't we, gang? We had a bit of a do last night, and I expect the others are just sleeping it off somewhere."

"Is that so?" said the Inspector, coming into the kitchen after Pete. "Good morning. You remember Sergeant Clavering." The sergeant sat down and took out a notebook.

"I thought you'd finished with us," said Pete. "Though I've seen you around hunting for clues and taking away a suitcase."

"There have been a few developments," said the Inspector. "Did one of you ring us last night – or rather this morning, maybe disguising their voice? One of the men? You perhaps?" He turned to Pete.

"Not guilty, officer. I was sleeping the sleep of the just. I thought the kids – the students – would be all right with Roland and Jonathan. We've only just found out that anybody's missing."

"How about you lads?"

"Not me, guv," said Colin.

"What time was this?" asked Gavin.

"If it's not a state secret," said Malcolm.

"Early. Any of them sound anything like it, Sergeant?"

"No, it was a deeper voice."

"What about the accent?" asked Pete.

"Well, it wasn't Scottish. Kind of neutral."

"Like most of us," said Gavin.

"Couldn't have been a woman disguised," said the sergeant.

"So who's not turned up to breakfast?" asked the Inspector.

"Nadine – but she's taken her handbag and a rucksack," said Donna. "Gareth, Gail and Derek went home early. We're not sure where Roland or Jonathan are."

"Mr Leaf – what was he wearing?" The sergeant prepared to write.

"He was still in costume," said Pete.

"What did his outfit comprise of?"

"Just some woollen plaid baggy trousers and a belt," said Donna.

"Roland may have walked back to the village," said Pete. "He changed in your dorm, didn't he, Malcolm?"

"Yes – his clothes are still there. He must be still wearing the robes of an Archdruid."

"And why was he dressed like that?" asked the Inspector.

"We were re-enacting a ceremony up at the stone circle," said Malcolm.

"But then it started tipping it down," said Donna. "I thought the boys had been struck by lightning! They all fell over. The torches went out and it was completely dark and we ran back here. The boys followed us, well, Gavin and Malcolm did."

"I see. And all of you took part?" He looked round at us.

"Not me and Bridget, we were tucked up in our flat," said Pete. "Separately, I might add."

"I see. Now, I've got a bit of an announcement to make." The Inspector got to his feet and looked solemn. "I'm going to ask you to keep this under your hats for the moment," he continued. "There's no need to worry about your colleagues, Professor Blair and Mr Leaf. We received a tipoff early this morning, and we went for a look-see up on the moor. We found them both wandering about, cold and frightened. As the voice on the phone said we would."

"Were they together?" asked Pete.

"No – they seemed to be scared of each other. After all, they were both armed."

"Armed? What with?"

"Mr Leaf had a metal dagger, and Professor Blair had a wicked-looking knife. Stone, like the arrowheads. Now this will probably distress you, and as I said you must keep quiet about it. They both accused each other – the Professor claimed Mr Leaf had killed the two women, and Mr Leaf said he'd stopped the Professor murdering a couple of the students. When we got them back to the station, Mr Leaf was keen to talk. He claimed he'd been told to do the murders by Sir Finamore Whitelock and that Professor Blair knew all about it. The psychiatrists are with them now. Did any of you notice what became of them, after the storm blew up?"

Everybody looked rather stunned, then Malcolm spoke up: "The girls ran off, like I said, and we went after them. Our dorm's on the other side of the kitchen, but Roland was in a B&B in the village and Jonathan slept in the flat. I suppose we assumed they'd just gone home to bed. Colin and Anna as well – we lost sight of them, but here they are."

"Thank you, that's very clear," said the Inspector.

"Could the girl have gone next door?" asked the sergeant. "To the big house?"

"It's possible," said Bridget. "We were going to try the TV room and the hayloft. But Jonathan! He was always so quiet! Perhaps I'd better ring Nadine's parents – she may have called them to say when she was arriving."

"You do that, Ma'am," said the Inspector. "Meanwhile I'll put some constables onto searching these outbuildings."

"Can we help?" asked Gavin, and Malcolm added "Yeah".

"Yes, why don't you give us the tour? And we'll need a fuller picture of what took place up at the circle." He went out, the boys following.

"Let's tidy up, instead of looking at each other in wild surmise," said Donna.

"It's better to keep busy in a crisis," said Bridget, and they both started clearing plates.

"Well, what a thing!" said Pete. "None of it makes sense. Have Roland and Jonathan lost their minds? I can't believe it! But if they did it, Nadine must be all right. I mean, no lurking murderer?" He looked at me.

"She did come back to the dorm, so she was OK," I reassured him. "I think she must have packed up and left as soon as it was light. If anyone had come and taken her things – he wouldn't have known where they were anyway in the dark – and he'd have woken us up."

"It does sound unlikely if you put it like that. Now what? Don't forget we're going to have to box up the Mystery Object. But later, I've got stuff to do in the office. Must concentrate. Funny how they always say somebody told them to do it, don't they?"

I followed him into the yard, where a constable was trying to pat Gringolet. The horse flung up his head and the man flinched.

"She wouldn't have hidden in there," I said.

"Not with this beast – he's not even tied up. We found a lot of odd prints up on the moor, including horse's hooves. But this one's feet look quite clean."

"What about the ponies?"

"I'd better check on them as well. Oh, hullo Sergeant!"

"We haven't found her, yet, I'm afraid," said the Sergeant. "Just Smithers here, asleep on the couch."

"Sorry Sarge, one of the young ladies brought me some cocoa and I just went spark out."

"That wasn't you, was it, Miss?"

"No, not me," I said, and went into the empty barn. So they'd drugged Smithers as well – I hoped he wouldn't get into trouble. I turned on the lamp over the object, and took off the cloth. A crack had appeared in the dried mud. I poked a toothpick into the gap and a whole chunk fell off. Then I just touched the remaining mud and it fell off in several bits. A metal disc remained.

I swept it with a big paintbrush, and it lay revealed as a brooch about three inches across, with entwined animals around a central stone. I gathered all the mud, now dust, into a plastic box. I couldn't just leave the brooch there, so I wrapped it in a teatowel and put it in the pocket of my windcheater – the new one I'd bought in Woolies. While I was draping the cloth over the stand again, one of the stable girls came in and said: "Are you Anna? I've got a note for you." I thanked her and took it.

CHAPTER 35

It was from Gilles: "Have you the police talked to you? Can you meet me straight away?"

I went round to the back door. Gilles was waiting for me, but instead of inviting me in, he said: "Let's go up to the stone circle. It should be back now."

"There are police all over the shop."

"They won't be looking for me."

"You'll be able to come out properly once they've gone."

"I shall stage my return from abroad in a flashy limousine. Come on, we can cut through here to the wood. Shall I open the circle to the public – what do you think?"

"Would they have to come this way?"

"Perhaps I'll let them walk along the ridge and view the stones from afar, like at Stonehenge. I don't want them damaging the wood. And besides, there's the cave, though it's inaccessible now."

"You heard about that?"

"I heard the explosion, and sent Mrs Collingwood to find out."

In the circle, the sun was glowing through mist. The ground was trampled and muddy and the grass was torn where the stones slotted into the earth.

"Have the stones all gone back into their proper places?" he asked.

"I think this one was further to the east." It was the one Sir Finamore had tried to uproot. "If anybody surveys them again they'll think our observations were all wrong."

"It was quite a sight. Pretty rare. Such a pity we didn't notice which one hid the treasure," said Gilles, laying a hand on the nearest megalith.

"The landwight would never have let you take it."

"Amiable though he is. Remember what happened to Sir Finamore, poor fellow!"

"You don't think he just had a heart attack?"

"Who knows? But if any interfering parson tries to exorcise our friend I shall protest in no uncertain terms. And I don't think I'll allow any more excavation. Too much publicity – and he won't like that. But I feel we should leave something for him. And the stones."

I took the brooch out of my pocket, unwrapped it, and laid it on the sacrificial slab.

"What a very lovely thing!" he said after a pause. "Did the students find it? So the stories were true. There must be more out there."

"Yes, they did. It'll end up in a museum. I just wanted you to see it."

"It's incredibly fine. But it's my land – don't I get half the proceeds?"

"I'm not sure if finds are a 'trove'."

"They should be!"

"I must take it away now." I wrapped it up again and put it in my pocket. "I hoped you were watching from the tower last night."

"I saw lights moving up through the wood, and then you all came out into the circle, so I had a look through the telescope. I assumed the archaeologists were playing at being Ancient Britons, but then it got a bit wild. I'd spotted you, and after the lights went out, I saw you on the skyline, running towards the moor. I thought it was time I took a hand, so I fetched Gringolet and we came up through the field and followed Roland's screams. And the howling. Did the police find the professors?"

"Yes, they've got them back at the station. What did you say on the phone?"

"I told them I'd overheard a confession, and they'd find the murderer near the Witch's Tor. They started asking who I was and what was I doing on the moor, so I hung up. I didn't mention you, of course."

"It would all be hard to explain."

"And you solved the mystery by magic after all!"

"I had to stop Roland sacrificing Colin."

"Yes – he took authenticity too far." He sat down on the slab.

"Jonathan needn't have confessed – he might have got away with it," I said, sitting down too.

"He thought he was about to be torn to pieces by wolves – and he wanted Roland to understand."

"I didn't quite follow who knew what, and why. Did your books say anything about the Foundation?"

"Quite a lot. One of the writers commented that they unfortunately lost a member in mysterious circumstances every so often. He put it down to the dangers of exploration, but hinted that it might be something like the Curse of Tutankhamun - he was writing about then. I took note of the dates, and it was every 19 years."

"Yes, that's what Mike told me."

"Sometimes they just disappeared, or were found dead in mysterious circumstances in locked rooms. I remembered that the Druids had followed an astronomical cycle, and I looked it up. It turns out to be something called the Metonic cycle, when the moon comes back into synch with the sun. It takes 19 years, and the Druids used to sacrifice a human at that time."

"And if you studied the Druids, you'd know about that."

"Yes, some of them must have worked it out - even though the Pearmanites thought it was a secret."

"Even Roland didn't really know."

"Though he said he'd been looking over his shoulder all the time."

"Any of the Pearmanites could have been the executioner."

"You mean the old buffers in their London headquarters? There was a lot about it in the book, fine historic building and so on. And they might have picked on an academic of retirement age. They might even have drawn lots!"

"Perhaps that's what Roland thought. But then we found Jeannette. I'm sure Fabia worked it out - that the executioner must be Roland or Jonathan. And she might have been living with a murderer for 20 years. Or it could have been Sir Finamore. Though can you be the leader and the executioner?"

"It sounds like the Tarot pack."

"Doesn't it? And Nadine suspected something would happen at midsummer, or the full moon."

"So last night Roland took on the role of Archdruid?"

"He must have been planning it for ages."

"And you thought you'd better step in?"

"I called for help. Perhaps you heard me. What would have happened if...? But the Druids didn't worship Odin, did they?"

"No, they had many gods."

"Roland did go on about Odin a lot."

"Perhaps his approach was syncretic. And what better cover for a genuine revivalist than a Druidic society?"

"That's rather clever. But Colin wondered – what was the point of it all?"

"They always hoped for something back from the pantheon. Those stories of pots of gold at the end of the rainbow – they're not all fairytales. And the Foundation seems to be pretty well-off. Their scholarly researches may have led them to many hoards. I wonder where their treasure is now?"

"Jonathan could have just gone on murdering people."

"I wonder what happened to the other executioners? Probably pillars of Victorian society. And what will happen to the Foundation now?"

"Perhaps it'll be wound up."

"The police are bound to investigate."

"Gavin and Malcolm will be disappointed. I'm sure they wanted to take over one day."

"Somehow I don't feel sorry for them. And which one of their number would they decide to sacrifice, 19 years from now?"

"They'd have to recruit some more people. They must have kept on doing that."

"I wonder how much of all this will be made public. Will your husband tell you all about it? You'll have to pretend to know nothing!"

"I expect he will, and yes."

"And now what about you?" he asked, getting up. "What are you doing for the rest of the summer? And the rest of your life?"

"I'm going to quit college and go back to Junk and Disorderly – the antique shop. One year of archaeology was enough. And we want to adopt a baby eventually."

"I see. Leaving a husband is one thing, but leaving a child – you'd never do that. And of course any natural child of yours would be a witch too. May Brigid and Cernunnos watch over you – Celtic deities seem appropriate."

We walked towards the votive causeway.

"I wanted to thank you," I said. "I always wanted to be rescued by someone mounted on a milkwhite steed."

"You hardly needed help. And you've rescued me before now."

"But Roland was threatening to kill me."

"He wanted to dig up the hoard, too."

"And I couldn't have rung the police. What could I have said?"

"Did you know there were wolves on the moor?"

"Some 'escaped' from the zoo a few years ago, remember? They never found them all. Or so Mike says."

"How could I forget? And since you are their mistress, perhaps they won't harm me. You might tell them."

"I forgot to thank them, too."

He stopped and looked at me. "This is au revoir, not farewell. Must you really go?"

"I must."

"I shall watch you into the distance."

I held out my hand. He took it for a moment and then I turned and walked towards the sleeping places of the ancient dead, a procession of one. I wondered if we would meet again.

As I walked, I recited:

Faced with foes both fierce and hateful
For your protection I am grateful
Wolves, until my chapter ends
Follow me, touch not my friends


\*\*\*


"There you are at last!" said Pete. "I was beginning to fret. Did you put the Mystery Object in a box? You should have labelled it."

"I thought it would be safer in my pocket," I said, putting the brooch back on the stand. I turned on the Anglepoise. "Have a look under the lens."

"Oh my stars!" he said. "Is this it? It's exquisite. What metalworkers they were! Interlaced beasts... The Museum will love this. We might even get into the papers, if we aren't already."

"Has Nadine turned up?

"No. The police searched all the stables and haylofts, and she hasn't phoned home."

"Perhaps she's gone to start a new life."

"I suppose people really do that sometimes, even if it is a cliché. Perhaps the cliché gives them the idea. By the way, don't say anything about this find to anybody. I'll have to consult... I suppose the Archaeological Society will be in charge of publicity." He was wrapping the brooch in wadding and tissue paper. "I'll talk to Bridget and give Gareth a ring. I suppose I can't check in with Roland!"

While he was writing a label for the brooch, Sergeant Clavering came in.

"No sign yet of the girl Nadine," he said, taking out a notebook. "But she probably took a train, and someone must have seen her en route. She'll turn up at home sooner or later I expect. Now, it's Anna Savage, isn't it? I've talked to the other students about the party at the stone circle and we'd just like to get your angle."

"I wasn't involved in the planning," I said. "I didn't know anything about it, just that the other students were cooking up something."

"And I wasn't there," said Pete. "Slept through the whole thing."

"Right, sir. So you all went up to the stone circle when?"

"After dinner – it must have been about ten. It took us a bit of time to get there – we were all bare-footed."

"Really. Which way did you go?"

"I don't know – I was blindfolded. Through the wood, I think."

"Blindfolded." He drew in his chin and looked dubious.

"Yes, it was the part I was playing, the Blind Seeress."

"I see. And how long did the... charades last?"

"About half an hour before the storm broke."

"And you were still blindfolded?"

"Yes. I could just see the torches, but then they went out, and there was a lot of shouting and running around. Then I took the scarf off."

"The other girls and boys made a run for it back here – why didn't you follow them?"

"Well, Roland shouted at me. He was angry that the re-enactment had been interrupted."

"That was hardly your doing – unless you can control the weather! What kind of a man is he: easy to get on with, or somewhat abrasive?"

"Short-tempered."

"And you'd come up against this aspect before?"

"Yes. We all had."

"Which way did you go?"

"Towards the moor. I got a bit lost, but then I found my way back down again."

"And you'd all been up there earlier. And you didn't see Professor Blair again – or Mr Leaf?"

"It was dark and raining."

"You didn't call out?"

"I didn't think anybody would hear. I couldn't see anybody – I thought they'd all gone home."

"And you didn't want another wigging from the Professor. Did you see any stray dogs?"

"I heard some barking and howling, but we always hear that."

"And you saw nothing else untoward? Any moor ponies?"

"Not this time."

He put the top on his pen. "Well, that explains the child-sized footprints. We were a bit worried that they went up to the moor and didn't come back."

"It was more grassy on the way down."

"We've got your details, and if there's anything else we'll give you a ring."

He went out, and I turned back to Pete, who was holding up the plastic box.

"What's this?"

"It's the mud off the brooch. Take care of it! It might have fragments of gold in it. But I don't think there are any bits missing."

"No, it looks intact."

"So where's the rest of the treasure? Hidden under one of the stones after all?"

"Completely the wrong date... This is Saxon. The circle is thousands of years older. We found the brooch near the causeway, not the kind of place you'd cache a hoard. Somebody probably dropped it – or deposited it. Hang on, though, I'd better take a photograph before I box it up." He lifted down Jonathan's camera from a coat hook.

"The Saxons worshipped Odin, didn't they?" I unwrapped the tissue paper and wadding and put the brooch back on the stand under the light.

"Under the name of Woden, yes." He took a few photos, and put the brooch back in its wrappings, and the box. He put the plastic box of mud in as well, and some packing, and stuck on the label. "I'll hang on to this one until I can hand it over to someone with a safe."

"I suppose the police will pack up Jonathan and Roland's things. They'll need some clothes in their cells. We all got soaked. I hope they gave them some blankets."

"Bridget's packed them a bag."

"Oh, of course, she would've. I just don't like the idea of anybody being in prison – particularly not people I know."

"Do you know many jailbirds? I still can't think of them as murderers. But surely they should be shut up as a danger to themselves and others?"

"I suppose so."

"I'd better keep the camera and get the film developed. We weren't much good as sleuths, were we?"

"But we did work out that one of them must have done the first murder, unless it was Sir Finamore."

"Did we? I suppose we did. But anyone could have murdered Fabia. And I can't see why..."

"I think she was Jonathan's girlfriend before she was Roland's."

"Woman's intuition?"

"Have a look at the book of the dig, there are clues – except the police have still got it. Or the TV programmes."

"Sir Finamore seems to have blighted all of their lives. It's sad."

"Jonathan must have been wondering all the time if he'd got away with it. He knew what I'd find in the cave."

"Perhaps that's why he was so quiet. Or fatalistic. Let's hope Nadine doesn't turn up as a corpse!"

"Things got a bit wild up at the circle, but she came back with Donna."

"Wild? Orgies, do you mean?"

"No, but I think Roland took it all a bit literally. He had that flint knife – that one that disappeared from the first dig."

"He took it as loot?"

"He must have done, and made it a handle."

"So that's why the police said he was armed."

"And I think Nadine wanted to get away from Gavin. He got her to join the Foundation in the first place."

"So it's all about relationships? I'm going to miss you, you know."

"I'll miss you."

"And soon there'll be all the excitement of a new term."

"Not for me."

"Had enough of archaeology?"

"Yes. I'm going back to antiques." I unclasped the chain round my neck, slipped my rings off it, and put them back on my finger.

"Not such dirty work. But archaeology in a way all the same! Thanks for your efforts on this thing, though."

"Are you going back to any of your wives?"

"No – none of them are speaking to me. I'll catch up with the kids, though. Can I give you a hug now? There won't be a chance later."

So he gave me a bear hug, which I didn't mind.

"I'd better go and pack."

"You've been packing all morning."

"Actually there's someone from next door I should say goodbye to."

"I'm glad you found a friend your own age over there."

So I went into the gardens, where visitors were strolling about and taking photos of each other against the herbaceous borders. I walked along the flagged path to the little pond, and picked some more roses for Hermes to thank him for giving me winged feet when I needed them.

"Hello!" said somebody. It was Joan, striking a pose between two pillars. "We used to do this a lot, and Cyril took pictures. He filmed the plays we did, too. He got rather famous after that." She jumped down and sat on the bench.

"I suppose you're going. There was a lot of to-ing and fro-ing down by the stables."

"Yes, we're all packing up, and some hikers are coming."

"And you were all wandering about in the night. Was it a party?"

"Kind of, up at the circle."

"I should have come!"

"You wouldn't have liked it much. And it poured with rain in the end."

"Just like a church fête! But I saw one of the girls go down the avenue early in the morning, carrying a bag."

"Yes, she left early. I don't suppose you saw where she went?"

"Towards the village."

"Good, she probably caught the first bus."

"Hikers won't be half so much fun. Though I like being here with all these visitors and children. It was pretty lonely and dull before they came."

"It must have been. Do you have to stay?"

"Only if I want to."

"Where would you go next?"

She just smiled.

"I'll find out, I suppose?"

"Not for a long time. It was OK when the American soldiers were here, though!"

"Could any of them...?"

"There was one who thought I was cute. He thought I worked in the kitchens. But then he went abroad. Do you think you'll come back?" she asked.

"To Malison Grove? I might." I stood up. "Goodbye. I must go now or I'll miss the bus."

"It's been lovely," she said, lightly touching my hand. I went up to the terrace and into the house, and looked at my parents for the last time, and the portrait of my grandmother. I wondered what had happened to the American soldier, and if they'd meet again one day, and how all that was arranged. Better not to know, perhaps. More visitors trooped in and I left quickly.

While I was getting my washing things, Donna came in and swept her toothbrush and sponge into a bag.

"I look awful!" she said, peering at her reflection. "And you look pale. Why don't you nick Nadine's blusher – she's left it behind. I'll ring her parents again before we go."

"Don't worry, I'm sure she's OK," I said. "She did keep saying she was sick of archaeology and wished she was anywhere else. Or perhaps she just said it to me."

"Probably afraid her parents will make her stick at it. Shaming to have a dropout daughter, and she's an only child." We went into the dorm and zipped up our bags.

"Farewell, a long farewell!" said Donna, looking round the room. We went out to get the minibus. Pete was driving, but he wasn't getting the train with us – he was going to take all the finds back to London in the van later. Nobody talked much on the way to the station.

CHAPTER 36

When our train arrived, Pete said farewell to us all. I found a seat with Bridget and Colin, and the others sat in a different carriage.

"Not very friendly of them!" said Colin. "Thank goodness." He was wearing his own clothes again.

Bridget read a Woman's Own, then fell asleep.

"So where did you go last night?" asked Colin. "I hid in a hayloft till the boys came back. I suppose I could have stayed there, but I was freezing, clad only in a wet Druid robe. I waited until everybody would be asleep and then sneaked into your dorm. Were you there? I just felt around till I found an empty bed and got into it."

"I got home eventually, I got a bit lost – it was quite rainy and dark. I'm not sure when."

"Nor me. I think I fell asleep in the loft for a bit. I should have pneumonia now! Good thing you didn't bump into Roland or Jonathan. They seem to have taken leave of their senses! So Jonathan confessed – but what are they holding Roland for? Unless they just think he's bonkers."

"Attempting to murder you?" And me, I thought, though I didn't say so.

"Yes, I'm sure flourishing an ancient flint knife in a manner likely to terrify is mentioned in some statute or other. I thought they were joking to start with, or just re-enacting. But they began to look horribly serious. And perhaps he threatened Jonathan with it as well. After all, if Jonathan killed Fabia..."

"That would look like a motive."

"I predict that the police will hush it up. Or else the tabloids will get hold of it. And someone will turn it into a horror film. I think I'll direct it. Shame there was no nudity or sex involved."

"They can always pretend there was."

"They usually do. Anyway, what are your plans? Going anywhere nice?"

"I seem to have told everyone – but I'm not going back to college. I'd rather restore old pictures and paint Welsh dressers. And I might go back to modelling, if I'm not too old."

"You don't look old!"

"I'm about to be 23."

234

"Ancient! Have you got anything to write on?"

I took a paperback out of my bag and handed it over.

"Strong Poison! Any good? You don't mind if I scribble on it?"

"Carry on. The detective gets the murderer to confess by – but you might want to read it."

"I just might." He neatly wrote his address and phone number in the book, and handed it back. "Let's stay in touch. As the sane members of the party."

I wrote my address and phone number for him on the flyleaf of Strong Poison and tore it out. "What are you going to do next?"

"Going to France with my parents for two weeks," he said, taking the flyleaf. "They like museums and cathedrals. And then my final year."

"Will you get a job in archaeology?"

"Oh, definitely! I shall prove my theories and build a lifesize model of Stonehenge with a roof. I shall do an MA, and then a PhD."

"Will you get planning permission?"

"I shall say it's a house and live in it. And I shall reconstruct Silbury Hill. I may even get my own TV series!"

Bridget opened her eyes and said, "How long have I been asleep?"

"About half an hour. We're in Dorset."

"I change trains soon," said Colin. "And you too, Bridget, you're not mad. And Pete and Gareth are OK. I thought Jonathan was sane too, but it seems I was wrong."

"Well, I'm glad to hear it!" said Bridget.

We chatted some more, then Colin had to change trains. Bridget lent me her Woman's Own, hugged me goodbye at Paddington, and said she was really looking forward to seeing her dogs again and she'd let us all know about Fabia's funeral. I spotted the others going into a burger bar, but I hung back so they didn't see me, and got the tube to Kentish Town.

CHAPTER 37

There isn't much more to tell. Mike told me never to go away again, and to stay out of trouble in future. He got all the papers the next morning to see if there was anything about the dig. They just said that two men were being detained in connection with Fabia's murder, having being found wandering on the moor partially clothed after the police acted on a tip-off.

"Did Inspector Forrester tell you anything?" I asked. "After all, you were quite helpful."

"Yes, he rang to say you were all coming home and you were fine, and they seemed to have caught the perp or perps. They were about to pick up those two anyway, for more questioning. You did stay close to the others, didn't you?"

"I was only alone with Pete, and my friends from the big house. I couldn't see Pete murdering anybody, and besides, we were together most of the afternoon when Fabia was shot."

"And what would the Malison Grove staff have to do with it? It had to be an inside job."

"And they weren't into Stone Age archery. Did they compare the arrowheads?"

"They said they were leaf-shaped, whatever that means."

"Like the ones Jonathan made, and kept. When he was showing us how to do it."

"We're going to look into the Foundation some more – I'll have to bring Fred this time and get a warrant. What are you going to do? Why don't you take a few days off? And we might go away for the weekend."

"Lovely! I thought I'd phone Lawrence, and Pauly in the shop."

"Haven't you got reading to do? Or do you get a holiday now?"

"I've made up my mind," I said. "Yes, I know I keep changing it. But I'm too small to lift a spade, and I don't really fancy spending the rest of my life kneeling in the mud with people who talk about real ale. And the studying we've done was pretty dull."

"Finding a skeleton in a cave must have been pretty scary."

"Yes, that put the lid on it, really."

"I don't know what they were thinking, letting you go down there."

"Roland must have planned to investigate – or why would he have brought all those ropes and hard hats?"

"Did he know the cave was a pot-hole?"

"He said they never investigated, back then."

"Will you go full-time at the shop?"

"That's what I was thinking. Perhaps there's something I can study part-time. What will happen to the flint knife – the one Roland had? He'd kept it from the original dig. That should go in a museum."

"It will – Scotland Yard's Black Museum! Almost a pity he didn't stab anybody with it – though it looks like he was about to. Where do you want to go for your birthday?"

"Oh, I don't know, you find somewhere. Somewhere sophisticated."

"As usual!"

"I'm so tired of 'rice medley'!" And I described the horrible food cooked by the students.

\*\*\*

I rang the college to say I wouldn't be coming back, and they said to come in for an exit interview. I rang Lawrence, and he said "Brilliant!" and booked me in to come and model their spring line for the petite figure. "We're expanding into outsize," he said. "No, we can't call them that. Tall girls! We've got a tall model, and I'll get your average friend Christine in again."

Pauly at Junk and Disorderly seemed pleased to hear from me too. "Come along!" he said. "We can do with someone sitting in the shop. And there's that lace and embroidery needs washing and sorting. Do you fancy cleaning an oriental carpet? It's been kept in someone's garage and it's not colour-fast. How much time can you give us?"

"Lots. I'm giving up university."

"So the dig was too much hard work?"

"It certainly was. And the students were unfriendly. But I wanted to ask you – what could I learn up that would be useful in the trade?"

"There's always gemmology."

"Isn't that all folklore?"

"Yes, you could do the folklore, the punters love it, but it's the science and the geology and how to tell a Ceylon sapphire from a topaz that matters. And gets you a qualification."

"That sounds like fun."

"I've got a brochure somewhere, I'll dig it out. You know, you're a bit of a divvy. You just know when something's right."

"It's just luck."

"Do you hear the tinkle of silver bells? Does it work for archaeology?"

"I never found anything very exciting. An Anglo-Saxon brooch, but somebody else dug that up, I only cleaned it. Oh, and a skeleton."

"Charming! But I expect it was pretty old."

"Didn't you read about it in the papers?"

"I never read the papers - full of lies and adverts and politics!"

\*\*\*

I brushed the rug, and stuck silver paper onto old theatrical prints, and sent off to the gemmology society for a brochure. It can't possibly be as boring as the spread of agriculture.

Out of the blue, I got a call from the lawyers who look after the money my parents left in an account for me. They said a parcel had arrived, and would I like to come and collect it. So I went that day, and the lawyer handed me a small square packet.

"Can I open it here?" I asked.

"Whatever you like," he said, handing me some scissors. The writing on the brown paper was my mother's. I cut the string and took off the paper and opened the box. I'd hoped there was a letter, but there was only a brooch lying on some cotton wool - the ruby and enamel brooch she was wearing in the painting.

"Beautiful!" said the lawyer. "Almost looks Elizabethan. Do you want to take it away with you, or shall we put it in the bank?"

If I kept it, I could take it down to Malison Grove and compare it to the paintings and make absolutely sure - the reproduction in the postcard is too small. And I'd never got a postcard of my grandmother.

"Let's put it in the bank for now," I said, putting the lid on the box and handing it to him.

"Meanwhile shall we keep it in our safe?" So we did that.

239

CHAPTER 38

I had a card from Bridget saying when and where Fabia's funeral was - at a crematorium out by the North Circular. Mike hired a car, and wore a suit, and I wore one of my old temping outfits. It was a do-it-yourself kind of ceremony. Someone from the university talked about Fabia's distinguished career, and Malcolm got up and read a Norse poem:

'Lo, there do I see my father
Lo, there do I see my mother and
my brothers and my sisters
Lo, there do I see the line of my people
back to the beginning.
Lo, do they call to me,
They bid me take my place amongst the halls of Valhalla
Where thine enemies have been vanquished
Where the brave shall live forever
Nor shall we mourn but rejoice for those who have died a glorious death."

Donna and Bridget cried. Nadine didn't show up. There wasn't a do or anything afterwards, we just drifted out of the chapel into a garden. It was nice to see Pete and Bridget and Gareth. We all hugged each other which I suppose is allowed at funerals, and Mike shook hands firmly with everybody. I said hello to Colin, and Donna took me by the arm and muttered, "Don't worry about Nadine. Don't say anything to the others."

Gail was wearing an engagement ring and said she'd been praying all through the ceremony.

"Who to, though?" said Gavin.

Malcolm said: "We should really have burned her on a pyre, but I suppose this will do."

We hung about in the garden for a bit, and then gave Bridget a lift to the tube.

***

I went along to Lawrence's firm for the fashion show - he has premises above some shops. His colleagues were all there in stripy three-piece suits and even longer hair than usual. Not like the hippies, but cut into a kind of shape.

"Wonderful to vous voir, heartface!" he said. "Christine's here already, and Danielle. And Geraldine's going to be your dresser."

I went into the room where all the clothes were organised on rails and Christine bounced up to me and said, "Guess what, Benny's mother has come round to the idea, and we're going to have lots of beautiful children and they'll all be models! And how are you?"

I told her my news, and she started to ask about our old friends, but Geraldine called us to order and talked us through the clothes we'd got to wear and showed us the rota.

"And this is our tall girl range," she said, leading us across the room. Danielle was over by her own rail, putting on a tall outfit in front of the mirror. She turned round and said: "Oh my God, Anna! You won't give me away, will you?"

"No, of course not, 'Danielle'," I said. "But you don't have anything to worry about now. You must have seen from the papers."

We didn't have any more time to talk, as we had to climb into our outfits and get going. My first ensemble was some Oxford bags and a yellow jersey and butcher boy cap. Nadine was dressed in the same style, with a tweed waistcoat.

"Well, this is more fun, isn't it?" she said, as we waited in the "wings" for Christine. "And I've met someone new."

"This season, the word is Unisex!" said Lawrence, and we swanned out onto the catwalk between rows of buyers sitting on collapsible chairs. Nadine looked good, and they'd taught her how to do the model walk – pause, drop the hip, smile and turn.

When we'd shown all the clobber, we got back into our own gear and came out for the drinks and nibbles. Christine got chatted up by one of the men in suits, and Nadine and I stood by the window eating little sandwiches and drinking sparkling wine (her) and Coke (me).

"Did you ever call your mother?" I asked.

"I've talked to her, so she knows I'm OK, but..." She dropped her voice. "She doesn't know where I'm living, and I told her not to talk to the police. I just don't want her to try and persuade me to go back to Blackhampton. Archaeology's terribly macho, don't you think? It's all right for people like Donna – she's one of the lads. And I don't want Gavin to find me."

"But you'd better tell the police – otherwise they'll go on looking for you."

"Don't YOU tell them!"

"I won't. Where are you living?"

"My new man, Josh, has a flat in Acton. You shacked up before you married, didn't you?"

"Yes, nobody cares these days."

"Don't they? You didn't have parents to disapprove. Sorry, that sounds callous. I'm not really that thick-skinned."

"But surely you've only just met him?"

"How long did you wait?"

"I can't remember – not long! There were circumstances..." Like being kidnapped, I didn't say. We moved in together soon after that.

"Actually we met in the Easter holidays. You saw it in the Tarot cards. It cheered me up, I can tell you. I kept telling Gavin we were over, but he said nobody left the Foundation and I'd been given to him by Odin. There was even a ceremony about that, would you believe? We had to jump over bonfires. What happened to the Foundation – the papers didn't say."

"It's been shut it down."

"You see I read up on its history, and something weird happened every 19 years at midsummer. Somebody died mysteriously or disappeared. I was terrified. What if it was a curse? What if I was next? Was that why Gavin didn't want me to leave? And then you found the skeleton and it turned out to be the last victim. I think poor Fabia had worked it out too and that was why she was so snappy all the time."

"Yes, I thought that too. Somebody told me about the history."

"But I don't want to talk to the police again. Sorry if I pinched your arm. You were about the only decent human being there, apart from the tutors. Old Pete and Bridget and Gareth were good sorts. Even Colin! What's he doing?"

"He's going to rebuild Stonehenge and become famous."

"He probably will!"

"Did you go straight to Josh?"

She nodded. "I rang him from the village and he said to come straight away. I'd been telling him I'd broken up with Gavin. I didn't like having to lie. I'm glad that's all over."

"What are you going to do now?"

"I suppose I'd better get a proper job! I just fell into this through a friend of a friend. I didn't know you did it, though."

"I started off modelling children's clothes. I got talent-spotted in the street."

"That sounds a bit dodgy!"

"It was, as it turned out."

"I want a job where I can wear nice clothes. I suppose I'll just have to learn to type. Is it hard?"

I said it wasn't, and Christine came and joined us and I told them I was loving working in the shop. We gossiped some more about old friends and explained to Nadine who they were, and she pretended to be interested.

CHAPTER 39

On my birthday we went out to dinner and had Steak Diane set on fire at our table, with French beans and mashed potato nests, followed by fruit salad with kirsch. Mike gave me a diamond pendant to go with my engagement ring, and had a bunch of red roses delivered to the table. Then we got talking about the case - the papers aren't saying anything because I suppose they're not allowed to before someone goes on trial.

"Where did they find Roland and Jonathan?" I asked.

"Roaming around the moor. Professor Blair seemed very out of it, rambling that the stones let them out when the sun rose, but the wolves led them off separately. Delusional, poor chap. So everybody else went home when the storm broke? What happened to you?"

"I wandered around in the rain for a bit till the moon came out again and I found my way home."

"Didn't you call out to the others?"

"They'd all scarpered. And I wanted to keep out of Roland's way."

"He didn't threaten you, did he?"

"He was waving that knife around. He shouted a lot of things. He was cross the ceremony got interrupted."

"Well, that was hardly your fault. Mr Leaf claims he stopped the Prof. slaughtering the student, and followed him in case he decided to stick the knife into anybody else. I suppose you knew them quite well?"

"I never really knew Jonathan, but Roland talked about human sacrifice the whole time."

"Quite good cover, if that's what he really wanted to do."

"What will happen to them?"

"They may not come to trial. I mean, they claimed they were trapped in a stone circle by a pack of wolves. There's no sign of a wandering Stonehenge, and anyway those things are too heavy to move, but there were loads of animal footprints. The Cornish force say there's a feral dog problem, and they've gone out with rifles."

"I hope they don't hit anything."

"Not likely! You know we went back to the Institute with a warrant and made the Secretary open the safe and hand over the papers. It was all there in a book in spidery writing, property of the original Mr Pearman. Fred made me read the whole thing. There was a lot about procedure covering every eventuality. The Secretary was the one with the knowledge, him and the executioner. The leader was more of a public face. I wonder if they always chose an exhibitionist?"

"Were any of them women?"

"Yes, there was a Miss Gertrude Somebody in the 20s – a formidable old bat. Anyway, the Secretary knew the full strength, so we arrested him as an accessory. We'll be reopening a lot of cold cases going back decades. I wonder if anybody else took the opportunity to work off a grudge? Except Mr Pearman left instructions that the executioner must avoid being caught. Forensic science wasn't up to much in those days."

"What if he did get caught?"

"The secretary would turn to Secret Annexe No. 9, paragraph Q, and it would tell him what to do. But they never did get caught. They must have used some bizarre methods. Of course you mustn't tell anybody all this. It may never come out."

"Who would I tell?"

"We appealed for the man who gave the tipoff to come forward. He'd be a valuable witness, but we never heard from him again, and nobody around there would admit it was them."

"So the other members were in the dark about the 19-year cycle, unless they looked at the history and put two and two together?"

"Yes. Mr Pearman wanted to revive the Druids warts and all."

"What did they do with the gold?"

"What gold?"

"I thought they might have dug some up."

"Good guess. There were some bits in glass cases, and more in the safe, and a ledger detailing what they'd sold and how much they got for it. But they drew everything first and described it."

"Did Donna ever say what Fabia told her at the pizzeria?"

"At the pizzeria? No, what happened?"

"Fabia stomped out, and Donna went after her and they talked for ages on the pavement."

"Perhaps she'd worked out that the first murder might have been done by her boyfriend."

"Or former boyfriend. Did they find any fingerprints on the bows and arrows? Or work out how many there'd been in the first place?"

"They were a jumble of everybody's. And some people had worn gloves and smudged them."

"What about the other bone fragments?"

"All ancient – they've gone back to the Archaeological Society."

"Did they say anything about the skeleton? I mean, how was it skeletonised? And how come the arrow shaft rotted away?"

"They said it was the chemicals in the water, though they couldn't get back in and check once they'd caused that rock fall."

"Will they keep it as evidence?"

"For a while – then they'll send her home to Hong Kong."

"I wonder how much Roland had worked out?"

"He seems pretty confused, apparently."

"I mean, it was just possible Sir Finamore or even Fabia killed Jeannette, and one of the boys killed Fabia... No, that wouldn't work."

"The psychiatrists say Professor Blair's "in denial". And even if he fingered the other bloke – they weren't supposed to get found out, were they? So that had to mean the others couldn't give them away. There's an oath somewhere in the archives about not giving away the secrets – it must be in there. For most of them it was like a long game of Murder in the Dark. Once you'd puzzled it out, you knew someone was for it, but you didn't know who or how. Let's forget about it!"

Mike led me onto the tiny dance floor and we fox-trotted while a bloke played the keyboard, and I decided not to think about it any more. But I hoped Jeannette would find somewhere peaceful to rest.

\*\*\*

When Mike was at work, I wrote Gilles a long letter with the bits that never got into the paper. Of course I didn't put my address.

The Regent College exit interview was with the same tutor who'd urged me to do A Levels and a degree.

"Well, I gather you want to leave us, Anna," she said. "Isn't it a waste of all your hard work?"

"I didn't really take to digging." I didn't like to tell her the studying had been as dull as ditchwater.

"Not all digs are like that, you know! Though of course it was simply terrible what happened to Fabia Thompson. Very dangerous to play about with Stone Age weapons. What were they thinking? Of course, it must have been quite frightening for you."

"I wasn't really scared. And anyway, we want to adopt a baby some time."

"Well, you'd have to give up your studies in that case!"

"Actually my friend Ginevra had a baby in the middle of studying. She came back and did history."

"You can always do that – come back, you know."

"That's nice of you, but I don't think I will."

I explained about my plans, we said goodbye, and I went out into the familiar hall. I checked my books back in to the library, and found the one about Sir Finamore's dig. There they all were in the past, in the sunshine, looking young and happy - even Roland. I looked for the picture of Fabia and Jonathan holding hands, but I couldn't find it.

***

When I got home Mike was lying on the sofa reading a thriller – he was working the night shift. He jumped up when I came in and threw the book over his shoulder.

"Guess what?" he said.

"I don't know, what?"

"The adoption people rang this afternoon and said would we consider fostering a baby who needed a temporary home. He's called Lee and would we like to go and see him? We might get to keep him if we're lucky."

"What did you say?"

"I said yes and made a date. It's somewhere out Egham way. An orphanage. What do you say?"

I said nothing. We hugged each other for a long time, and went out to Soho to dance while we still could.

247

THE END

Printed in Great Britain
by Amazon

36633561R00142